Dead Flesh
(Kiera Hudson Series Two)
Book 1

Tim O'Rourke

ISBN: 10:1478375957
ISBN-13:978-1478375951

Story Editor
Lynda O'Rourke
Book cover designed by:
Carles Barrios
Copyright: Carles Barrios 2011
Carlesbarrios.blogspot.com
Edited by:
Carolyn M. Pinard
carolynpinardconsults@gmail.com
www.thesupernaturalbookeditor.com

Dedicated To
Kimberly Costa

More books by Tim O'Rourke

Vampire Shift (Kiera Hudson Series 1) Book 1
Vampire Wake (Kiera Hudson Series 1) Book 2
Vampire Hunt (Kiera Hudson Series 1) Book 3
Vampire Breed (Kiera Hudson Series 1) Book 4
Wolf House (Kiera Hudson Series 1) Book 4.5
Vampire Hollows (Kiera Hudson Series 1) Book 5
Dead Flesh (Kiera Hudson Series 2) Book 1
Dead Night (Kiera Hudson Series 2) Book 1.5
Dead Angels (Kiera Hudson Series 2) Book 2
Dead Statues (Kiera Hudson Series 2) Book 3
Dead Seth (Kiera Hudson Series 2) Book 4
Dead Wolf (Kiera Hudson Series 2) Book 5
Dead Water (Kiera Hudson Series 2) Book 6
Witch (A Sydney Hart Novel)
Black Hill Farm (Book 1)
Black Hill Farm: Andy's Diary (Book 2)
Doorways (Doorways Trilogy Book 1)
The League of Doorways (Doorways Trilogy Book 2)
Moonlight (Moon Trilogy) Book 1
Moonbeam (Moon Trilogy) Book 2
Vampire Seeker (Samantha Carter Series) Book 1

Prologue

She thought it would hurt, but in fact, dying was agony. It felt as if her entire being had been stretched, pulled and twisted out of shape and then sucked in on itself. There was blackness and it rushed at her like a wall. Solid and unbreakable. She looked into the darkness and it was as if she were standing at the very edge of the universe and staring down into nothingness. The silence was deafening and it made her want to scream.

There was a crashing sound. The noise cut through the darkness. Her lungs emptied as the air was forced from them like a balloon being strangled. Branches clawed at her like hands trying to break her fall as she appeared in the night sky above the trees. Dropping like a stone, she cut a jagged path through the leaves and branches as she tumbled to the woodland floor below.

The young girl hit the ground, her head bouncing off the leaf-covered floor with a gut-wrenching thud. She cried out, throwing her hands to her face and rolling over onto her back. Opening her eyes, she noticed something had gone wrong. Her hands didn't feel right against her face. The young girl counted the fingers on her right hand. One, two, three....

Three!

Turning, she looked at her left hand – it was worse.

Two! What's happened to my fingers?

She staggered to her knees like a drunk and touched her face with her three-fingered hand.

"NO!" she screamed, and this time it wasn't inside her head; her voice had forced its way out of her throat. Patting her face with her hands, she knew that she was in trouble. The lower half of her face had slipped. Her face, once beautiful and perfect was now grotesque; nose and mouth were now imbedded into her left cheek. Her face looked distorted, like a child's painting that had been hung upside down while wet and the colours and shapes had bled across the paper.

Her blond fringe swung in front of her eyes like a curtain and she knocked it away. Moonlight shone through the canopy of trees above her head in milky shafts. Then she was startled by the sound of a dog barking in the distance.

Or was that the sound of a bigger creature? A wolf perhaps?

The noise came again, which was followed by another and another. Cocking her head to one side, the young girl listened. The barking came again and it was followed by the sound of snapping jaws and woofing. She knew there was more than just one of these creatures, there were several of them, and they were getting closer.

Spinning round, the young girl peered into the darkness. In the distance and weaving towards her amongst the trees, she could see torchlight. The beams of light sliced through the night and splashed against the tree trunks.

"This way!" A voice barked. "This way!"

The barking and howling grew louder and keener as the creatures raced towards the area of the wood where the girl had appeared. She looked back one last time, then ran deeper into the woods.

The sound of woofing and snarling came from the throats of the young girl's pursuers. They had reached the area where she had appeared, but she had gone.

"I want this entire area locked down!" one of them ordered.

Then wheeling around, he hissed at the others, "Don't just stand there! Get after her!"

Without question, the others in the pack set off after the young girl, ferocious-looking, whining, and slobbering.

She raced amongst the trees with the agility and speed of a wild horse. Her long hair billowed out behind her like a mane, and her brilliant green eyes glinted in the moonlight. In the distance she could hear the sound of howling as they raced after her. Her legs propelled her forward as she stumbled and staggered through the woods. Her arms whispered by her side, working like pistons.

She broke into a clearing, and ahead in the distance she could see turrets spiralling up towards the moon like giant ogres. The building sat on a hill and was surrounded by trees and a stone wall.

With sweat streaming into her eyes, the young girl raced across the field towards it, leaving her would-be captors deep in the woods. Reaching the wall, she looked up at it towering above her. The wall was at least twenty foot tall and she wondered if it had been built to keep something out or to keep something locked in. With her three-fingered hands, she gripped hold of the wall and began to climb. And as she went, the young girl stifled the urge to scream out in agony as her hands bled. Once at the top, she held on with hands that looked like bloody claws.

What she had believed to be turrets, she could now see were search towers. There were four, and each was manned by a hooded figure. Their faces were hidden by the robes draped over their heads and shoulders. The search towers cast beams of light across the grounds like giant lighthouses.

The sound of barking and woofing echoed in the distance. Glancing over her shoulder, she could see her pursuers run free of the woods and start across the field towards her. Turning her back on them, the young girl leapt from the wall and into the grounds of the strange-looking building.

Pressing her back against the wall, she inched her way around the circumference of the building. She watched the hooded figures high up in their towers as they covered the grounds with their searchlights. Small plumes of breath leaked from her cheek and disappeared into the darkness like small clouds. The building itself was in total darkness, not one light burnt from inside. Apart from the odd rustle high in the trees above her, the building and its grounds were silent.

What could this place be?

She reached a set of black iron gates in the wall, which were padlocked. They stretched up into the night sky like bony black fingers. To the right of the gates stood a wooden sign, and engraved upon it were the words:

Welcome to Ravenwood School

Before she had the chance to even ask herself what sort of school would be surrounded by twenty foot high walls and searchlights, an alarm had started to sound. Covering her ears *with her deformed hands, the girl winced at the sound of the alarm that wailed across the grounds like a World War Two siren. The hooded figures swung the searchlights, picking out a figure that was running away from the far side of the school. It headed towards the trees which lent against the wall like drunks propping up a bar.*

Screwing up her eyes to get a better look at the figure, she could see it was a man. His face was panic-stricken and his eyes bulged from their sockets in fear. But he looked overweight, and with several chins wobbling like whale blubber, he was no match for the four hooded figures that raced across the grounds behind him.

The figures howled, leaping through the air and snatching hold of the escapee. The noise which came from the figures was nothing like she had ever heard before. It sounded as if they were choking on their own tongues.

"Pleeeaaassee," the male screeched, his voice sounding as if his throat had been cut. "I just want my son!" Then he fell silent.

The young girl couldn't see how they had silenced him, but she watched as they carried him like a stretcher, making their way back into the school. The searchlights followed them, then swung away, leaving the building in darkness.

Standing amongst the shadows, with the sounds of those dogs now yakking and slobbering on the other side of the wall, she crouched onto all fours and crawled away into the undergrowth, then...

Chapter One

Kiera

...I sat up in bed. I rubbed my eyes, covering the backs of my hands in the blood that dripped from them. The last broken fragments of my nightmare jabbed into my brain like broken pieces of glass. I'd dreamt the same dream for over a week now. It always started and ended in the same place. I didn't know the girl's name or what she had been running from. We were connected, though. The fingers, the shift of her facial features knocked out of place – but that wasn't all that had been knocked off balance. But the more I thought about her after waking, the foggier the dream became, and faded away like an early morning mist.

I swung my legs over the side of the bed. The room was in semi-darkness, the first rays of morning light creeping around the edges of the heavy curtains. Wrapping my blanket about me like a shroud, I crossed my room to the adjoining bathroom. After leaving the mortuary, Potter had raced us through the night. We only had one place to go, and that was back to Hallowed Manor. The manor had belonged to Doctor Hunt, it had been where Kayla had grown up, it was her home and she had wanted to return.

Hallowed Manor was ideal. It was remote, laying miles from the nearest town on the Welsh Moors. Surrounded by a moat, walls, and a gate house, it was somewhere we could hide in safety – be apart from the rest of the world, the rest of the living. At first, being together had been wonderful. To have my friends back had seemed like the Elders had blessed me, but now I wasn't so sure. Now I wondered if their blessing wasn't in fact a curse, like they said it would be. We were all dead. Yes, we still inhabited the Earth, but not really. Not like the living. We were freaks and not just because we were dead. The Elders had called Potter, Isidor, and Kayla angels – but what sort of angels were they? Potter was a chain-smoking Vampyrus with attitude, and the rest of us were half-breeds – half and half's as the Elders had called us – half Human and half Vampyrus. Not only didn't we belong amongst the living, we were a completely different species. And I was cracking up – not mentally, although I had questioned my sanity since waking up in that mortuary six weeks ago. I was physically cracking up.

I turned on the taps and splashed cold water across my cheeks, washing away the blood-red tears that had dried on them. Once they had gone, I began to fill the bath with cold water. Not hot and no bubbles like I'd enjoyed so much before...before dying...but the colder, the better. I liked the water to be ice cold now. To feel it lap against my pale skin made it tingle, it made my flesh feel alive and it numbed my cravings for the red stuff. Death hadn't silenced them – it had made them worse – added another layer to my torment. There were supplies of Lot 13 left behind by Doctor Ravenwood in the makeshift hospital hidden in the attic. But there wasn't much. I knew that Kayla, more than Potter and Isidor, had been drinking it. I couldn't stop her and part of me didn't want to. She had been through enough – she had been murdered, her life taken away from her – so at night, I lay awake and listened to her sob herself to sleep from down the hall. How could I add to her suffering?

With the bathroom in near darkness, I brought my face close to the mirror fixed to the wall above the sink and stared into it. My face now looked just as it had before dying, not deformed and misshapen like it had when waking in the mortuary. To look at me, I appeared normal, my bright hazel eyes losing none of their sparkle, my skin pale as always, but without blemish. I dropped the blanket from around my shoulders, letting it flutter to the tiled floor. I rolled back my shoulders and my wings unfolded from my back. They were as black as ever, those bony fingers folded into fists at the tip of each wing. I looked at my fingers and my claws appeared like a set of knives, and my mouth filled with blood as my fangs drew down from my gums. I looked at my naked reflection, at the *half-breed* staring back at me, and there were cracks. Not on the surface of the mirror, but on me. I'd first noticed them on the morning after fleeing the mortuary. All of us had slept in, and I had woken to find Potter lying next to me, his head resting against my chest.

I had gently eased myself away, not wanting to wake him. Once in the bathroom, I had looked at myself in the mirror. I'd wanted to know if being dead had changed me. Did I still have my wings, my claws, my fangs? And yes I did, but there was something else. When in my true half-breed form, there were now cracks. With my fingertips, I touched the skin covering my left cheekbone. The cracks were very faint, barely visible, but they were there. Like the tiny cracks you get at the bottom of a very old china teacup. There were others, too. A network of cracks like a very faint spider's web, covered my neck, shoulders, and down between my breasts, over the flat of my stomach and down across my thighs. I rubbed at them, then snapped my hand away. I looked at the dust-like powder that now covered my fingers. I rubbed my fingertips together in a circular motion and it felt as if they were covered in ash.

Potter had stirred in the other room, and I swung the bathroom door closed. I didn't want him to see me like this. What was happening to me? Like I said, it was as if I were cracking up.

That had been six weeks ago, and now as I looked in the mirror, the cracks were still there, more visible, as if deeper somehow, giving me an ancient-looking appearance. From a distance they looked like wrinkles, the kind that I shouldn't be finding until my late fifties – but I was never going to reach my late fifties, right? Now that I was dead, was I going to age? Was I going to stay at the age of twenty for the rest of eternity? Every young girl's dream – but not mine. I knew deep inside of me I wouldn't last another fifty years alive or dead. Whatever curse or blessing the Elders had cast upon me wasn't for eternity – it was for now. How long was now? Weeks, months, years, before I cracked up totally and turned into a pile of ash – just like the palace where I had died?

I just had this feeling, like a knot in my stomach, that I was back from the dead for a limited period of time. But why bring me back at all? Why bring any of us back? Couldn't we have been left to rest in peace? I mean, isn't that the whole point of dying – that we finally find peace? Was bringing me back just a punishment for failing to make my choice? No. I didn't believe that. Why punish Potter, Isidor, and Kayla too? I had been brought back for a reason – we all had.

I turned off the taps and changing back, I took my iPod from the shelf and slipped into the water. Turning it on, I thumbed through the tracks, and closing my eyes, I lay back and listened to Leona Lewis sing *Happy*.

Chapter Two

Kayla

Lot 13 tasted bitter, as usual, but I screwed up my nose as it slowly rolled down the back of my throat. It was disgusting and nothing like real blood. The real stuff - *the red stuff* - was lovely. Lot 13 was like Diet Coke - the red stuff was like the full-fat version. There was no comparison. But it was better than nothing and it dulled that constant itch that wouldn't go away. But that itch, the one that drove me half-crazy at times, seemed like a mild irritation today - like a wasp hovering around your ice cream, compared to the noise.

I could hear Kiera going to her bathroom, even from my room all the way down the hall. The sound of the water rushing from the taps and filling the bath was almost deafening and I wanted to scream at her to turn them off. But there had been a lot that I had wanted to scream about lately, so taking one of my pillows, I buried my head beneath it. With the pillow smothering my face and ears, I could still hear the sound of Kiera's blanket flutter to the floor. She stopped and I knew that she was looking at herself in the mirror again. Not out of vanity - Kiera wasn't like that - she was looking at something else. I didn't know what, but I knew that she was staring at herself again. I could see it in her eyes. Kiera hadn't been the same since coming back - but then again, I don't think any of us had been the same.

I heard Kiera climb into the bath and at last, the sound of running water stopped. My hearing wasn't usually this intense - but whenever I got upset - angry or frightened, the sounds around me became louder - oh yeah - loud wasn't the word. Sometimes I felt like stuffing my fingers into my ears and screaming. There had always been a *soundtrack*, as I had called it, since the age of six - a faint background noise, like someone whispering at me from behind a wall. But sometimes it intensified and was worse than deafening. And it was like that today and had been since I'd come back from The Hollows - the dead.

Listening to music helped and I was forever swiping Kiera's iPod - the music helped to drown out the *soundtrack.* But Kiera had it now - she was listening to it in the bath. I could hear the music hissing from beneath my pillow. I had my own but it was busted. Dropped it throwing a hissy-fit at my mum and cracked the screen - the thing was screwed after that.

And I knew it was because of my mother, my father and...I didn't want to think of the other one's name, that the soundtrack had been cranked up to full. Since being back from The Hollows, I'd had time to think - reflect about everything that had happened there. I'd wanted to come back here, it had been my idea, it was my home. But to walk the quiet corridors and passageways, to sit alone in the vast kitchen, and walk the grounds had made me think of the ones I had loved and lost...because of *him.*

I was angry - no - I was fucking raging inside. Even though I was dead I could still feel things – pain. I still hurt. But even though he humiliated me, cut my ears off and then murdered me, I knew that I was angrier at myself than him. How had I been so dumb? Why had I been so flattered by the words that he had whispered? And I knew the answer to those questions - I had been desperate. I had been desperate for the red stuff that he had supplied me. But even more desperate to be loved. I had lost my mother and father but I had found a brother - Isidor. Why hadn't I turned to him? Even when he tried to warn me, I didn't listen. For someone who can sometimes hear too much - I had failed to hear my brother's warnings and that's why I was freaking angry with myself.

But hey, Kayla, you're alive, girl - you came back from the dead - you got another shot. But not really. I'm still dead, right? The Elders told me I was a Dark Angel - a *dead* angel more like. And what exactly was a dark angel? What was I brought back for? To help protect Kiera, they had told me. Protect her from what? I mean, Kiera didn't need looking after - I'd seen her kick more Vampyrus butt than I cared to remember; she looked after Kiera and I wished that I could be more like her. Kiera was my protector - she was my friend, my sister.

Maybe Kiera didn't need that kind of protection - the fang-ripping and clawing, tearing kind. Maybe she just needed a friend? Someone to be there for her - to be there for each other. Like I said, I knew she was troubled by something - the walls of her room were covered from floor to ceiling in those newspaper cuttings. It was like she was looking for something. I knew she didn't know what, exactly, but I knew that she would *see* it eventually.

The *soundtrack* had started to fade a little, so pulling the pillow from over my head, I climbed from my bed and padded across my bedroom to the large bay windows leading to the balcony. I pulled back the curtains a fraction and peered outside. The day looked miserable again and I had forgotten how bleak this place could be in the winter...spring...oh, who was I trying to kid? The place was freaking bleak all year round.

From my window, I spied Isidor coming back through the woods carrying an armful of branches. His dark hair was swept off his brow and his Shaggy-Doo beard jutted from his chin. He hated it when I called it that. That's what Potter called it and was always taking the piss. And that was another thing - being dead hadn't stopped those two from bitching at one another. They were constantly at each other's throats. But Isidor hit back just as hard as Potter now, or should I say Gabriel! I couldn't help but snigger aloud every time Isidor taunted him. Seeing Potter get wound up had been my happiest moments since coming back.

I watched Isidor drop the pile of branches onto the drive at the foot of the steps that led to the front door. He took a flick-knife from the pocket of his jeans and sat down where he began to sharpen them. Pulling on a pair of jogging bottoms, trainers, and a sweatshirt, I left my room to join him.

"What are you doing, Isidor?" I asked, sitting beside him on the step.

"Making stakes," he said back, as he carved away at the tips of the branches.

"Why?" I asked.

"Why not?" he smiled at me, then went back to the sharpening. "What else is there to do around here?"

"Don't tell me you're missing The Hollows and what happened there?" I half-smiled, placing my arm about his shoulder.

"It's because of what happened there that I'm making these stakes," Isidor said, not looking at me.

"I don't understand?" I said. "That's all finished with now, we're safe here. Besides, we're dead already - how can we die twice?"

Then, stopping what he was doing, Isidor turned to face me. "You've noticed the changes, right?"

"I guess," I said, looking straight at him.

"Then I don't think we're safe - dead or alive," and he went back to his cutting.

Chapter Three

Kiera

Isidor had said something bad had happened. I remembered him saying those words to me as we raced from the mortuary. And something bad *had* happened – people had gone missing. Not just one or two, but thousands. I had come back to find that in an instant, people had just disappeared. And as I looked at the hundreds of newspaper cuttings that covered the walls of my room at Hallowed Manor, I knew that they had been the Vampyrus, snatched back by the Elders as The Hollows had been sealed. But the Elders had said that the humans wouldn't remember and they didn't – it was as if the Vampyrus hadn't ever existed. And that wasn't the only bad thing to have happened. It seemed that the Elders had either failed to understand the consequences of their actions, or they knew exactly what would happen and this was just another part of their curse, because the world had changed. Not drastically. But it was different, as if it had been nudged off-kilter, shoved to the left a bit. There were subtle changes and as I trawled through the Internet during the hours that I sat awake unable to sleep – I noticed these changes. And it was as if by taking the Vampyrus back, the Elders had erased any subtle influence that the Vampyrus had had on human civilisation. It was my iPod that first drew my attention to these differences. Although it was still called an iPod, the Apple logo had been replaced with the shape of a crescent moon. And when I thumbed through the tracks, I noticed that some of the songs had changed slightly – sung by someone else. For example all of the *Rihanna* songs had been replaced by a singer named *Robyn*, the *U2* tracks had been replaced by a group called *Feedback*. The band looked vaguely familiar and the songs similar in tone and music style to *U2* – but like I said, just different – as if knocked off-kilter. When I tried to search for *U2* on the Internet, there was no trace of them on any search engine – not even the biggest, Toogle, which seemed to have replaced Google. But other songs had stayed just the same. Bruno Mars, Leona Lewis, and many others were as they were before. But it wasn't just the tracks on my iPod which had altered; the car manufacturer *Ford* didn't exist – but there was Nord. The number one fast-food chain was *McDonnell's* started back in the 1940's by the McDonnell brothers.

As I sat alone in the darkness of my room, the only light coming from my *Moon* laptop, the one that had the same crescent-shaped moon logo as my iPod, I tried to make sense of these little differences to what I had known before. Where had the company Apple gone? Ford? McDonalds? The singers and songs that had disappeared from my iPod?

And what about the newspaper cuttings that covered my walls, which told the stories of people waking up six weeks ago to feel that everything wasn't quite right? I knew that humans, on a subconscious level, knew that something was wrong – that something was missing – something had been knocked slightly off balance.

I read and reread the stories of how men had woken to find their closets were full of women's clothes, shoes, and hats. Where had these things come from? Who did they belong to? After all, they hadn't girlfriends or wives, but why had they woken to find silver and gold coloured bands around their wedding fingers?

What about the passenger trains that had stopped suddenly, en route to their destinations because the drivers had suddenly vanished? The co-pilots, who suddenly looked up to find that they had taken off without a pilot, and were now thirty thousand feet above ground. And the patients who bled to death on operating tables, the medical team gone.

My walls were covered in a thousand similar stories, and even though I knew what had happened to all of those missing people, I still found it hard to comprehend that so many Vampyrus had infiltrated human civilisation and made lives for themselves. Those who had been left behind were now left to stare, dazed and confused. It must have been similar to being halfway through a conversation only to suddenly forget what you were talking about. That awful searching, scrambling of the mind as you tried desperately to remember but just couldn't.

Sitting in one of the dusty armchairs that I had taken from the attic, I looked at the walls, which were a collage of black and white lines of print and faces. Why had I collected them? I didn't really know the answer to that. Potter said that I had lost my freaking mind. He either failed to see the changes that had taken place since coming back from The Hollows – coming back from the dead – or he just refused to notice them. But I think Isidor and Kayla understood why I had collected all of those news cuttings and trawled for hours on the Internet.

Each day, Kayla and Isidor would make the long drive into the nearest town and a buy a copy of each available newspaper. They would bring them to me, and sometimes in silence, but more often than not while listening to music Kayla selected on my iPod, we would cut the articles from the newspapers and tack them to my bedroom walls.

Glancing at them, I could see that they both looked lost, a perpetual look of confusion engraved across their faces. Isidor was eighteen, Kayla sixteen, and neither would grow any older. But like me, the euphoria of being alive again had worn off and the reality of being dead but alive weighed heavily upon them. Coming back to life where *things* had changed, however slight, had changed them too.

"What do we do?" Isidor had asked me as the three of us had sat and cut articles from the newspapers.

"How do you mean?" I asked, cutting carefully around an article about how no one could understand how a Chief of Police had never been appointed in London. And if there ever had been one, what had been their name and where were they now?

"What do we do for the rest of eternity?" Kayla asked, stopping what she was doing and looking at me. "We didn't come back to sit on the floor of your room cutting up newspapers. I mean I love spending time with you Kiera, but..."

"What did the Elders tell you?" I asked, peering over the corner of the newspaper at them.

"They said we were angels – dark angels – whatever that's s'posed to mean," Isidor said, scratching the tiny beard that jutted from his chin. "They told me I was to be called *Malachi*, Kayla, *Uriel* and…" with a smile on his face, he added, "And Potter was to be called *Gabriel*."

I smiled back and said, "I wouldn't let him hear you call him that."

"I know – it's great," Isidor grinned. "It really pisses him off."

"Did they say anything else?" I asked them.

"Only that you would need us to help you," Kayla explained, going back to her cutting. "But they didn't say how or with what."

"They said I'd been 'cursed to walk in the shadow of death', as they described it," I told them, laying the scissors on the floor beside me. "They said I was one of the Dead Flesh – cursed."

"But a curse can be lifted, right?" Isidor said.

"The Elders said that it could be, but they didn't say how," I told him.

"So how will you know?" Kayla pushed. "What are you going to do?"

"I'm going to wait," I told her, taking the newspaper article I had cut out and tacking it onto the wall along with the others. "I'm just going to sit in my chair over by the window and wait."

"But what about the changes?" Kayla asked me as she knocked her auburn fringe from her brow. "Why do you think some things are different now?"

"I don't know," I told her, looking straight into her green eyes.

"It's like kinda freaky," Isidor said. "I noticed it as we raced to the mortuary to get you. We passed a motorway sign which gave directions to London. Except the sign didn't say London. It said, *Linden*. I had to look twice because at first, I thought I had misread the sign."

"How can London be called *Linden*?" Kayla asked, sounding spooked.

"I don't know the answer to that either," I told her, picking up another newspaper from the pile on the floor. "Like I don't know why people are all raving about a book called *Harvey Trotter* who happens to be a twelve-year-old dragon slayer." Then, holding up the paper, I pointed out an advertisement for the movie of the book. "It appears that *Harvey Trotter & the Dragon's Throne* was written by someone called K.J. Dowling."

"K.J. who?" Isidor said, staring at the newspaper advert. "I mean couldn't J.K sue this K.J dude? She's been ripped off."

"But that's the thing that scares me the most," I said, looking at both Kayla and Isidor. "I don't think *Harry Potter* exists here – a version of those books, yes, but not the ones we know. Wherever *here* is, they have their own version of the *Harry Potter* books, like they have *Moon* instead of *Apple*, *McDonnell's* instead of *McDonald's* and a whole other bunch of stuff."

"Linden instead of *London*?" Isidor said.

"That's right," I nodded.

"So *where* are we then?" Isidor asked.

"Are we like in a different time or something?" Kayla added.

"No – not a different time," I said looking down at the newspaper in my hands. "Look at the date – its twenty-twelve all right – but just a different version of it."

"But how has that happened?" Kayla pushed, as if I knew all the answers. "I mean, I know I died and all, but those Elders had brought me back within hours. How come so much has changed?"

"I wish I knew the answer to that," I told her softly.

"So what do we do?" Isidor asked me again.

"We wait," I said looking at him. "We just wait."

"For what?" Kayla asked, looking at me as if I'd lost my mind.

"The answer."

"And how do you know it will come?" Isidor asked, shooting a glance at me, then back at his sister, as if he too couldn't believe what he was hearing.

"I don't know where the answer will come from," I told them, getting up and crossing my room to the chair I had positioned by the large window with the balcony. Then, sitting and looking out the window, I added thoughtfully, "The answers will come – I've been brought back for a reason – we all have."

Chapter Four

Kiera

All I'd been doing for the last six weeks had been waiting. But I didn't know for how much longer I could bear it. It wasn't only the waiting – it was the cracks. How long did I have before those cracks became splits, fractures, and then complete breaks? Either way – if I sat and did nothing, I would fall apart.

So, as I sat alone in my room, staring out of the window at the leafless trees that surrounded the grounds of Hallowed Manor, I knew that I had to do something – anything that would break the monotony of being dead. It wasn't like being in a book or a movie. There was no glamour to being immortal. It was a curse. And I had to do something until I was told what I needed to do to lift it.

My thoughts were broken by the sight of Potter below. Even though it was mid-January, and the temperature was close to zero outside, I could see him stripped to the waist as he raked the leaves, which had fallen onto the wide gravel drive, into a mushy pile. Potter was restless, just like the rest of us. I watched him as he worked. His face was ashen and hard-looking, a cigarette dangling from the corner of his mouth. I could see that although he was keeping himself busy, his mind wasn't on the job at hand, but on something else. His eyes were dark, and he seemed to stare down at the copper and gold coloured leaves as if they weren't even there.

On returning to the manor, I wondered if Potter and I would at last be together – just like other couples. Share the same bed, the same likes and dislikes - but that hadn't happened. Any daydreams I might have had of us curled up together on the sofa watching movies, strolling hand-in-hand on long meandering walks had failed to materialise. At first we shared the same room – the same bed – but as the cracks started to appear in me and on me – so they started in our relationship. It wasn't that I found myself loving Potter less, in fact, now free of The Hollows and the nightmare that I had journeyed over the last year, I felt as if I could breathe again – for a short time at least.

But the nightmares came – the girl forever being chased – her desperate escape – the school named Ravenwood – and deep inside of me, I knew there was trouble coming for me again. Just like how you know that a storm is brewing on a warm summer's evening. The sky starts to darken, almost thicken. The atmosphere feels almost electric. That's how I had started to feel, as if a storm were coming and I didn't know when, from what direction, and if I could find shelter from it.

So gradually, Potter and I had stopped holding each other during the night. I would lay on my side, watching the gentle rise and fall of his chest as he slept, his strong arms enveloping me. But gradually we had started to sleep apart, back to back, until eventually Potter moved out of my room and then from the manor, taking up residence again in the Gate House. Somewhere inside of me, where my cravings for the red stuff kept me from sleeping, I was grateful for that. If I were to be honest with myself, I didn't know how long I could fight the urge – need – or was it pure desire, to sink my fangs into him and feed again.

But I missed him and my heart ached to think of him alone in the Gate House, so I often went to see him there, only to find him sitting quietly, deep in thought, and I would remember how we had shared our first kiss in that rickety shack. I would sit opposite him on the flea-bitten sofa and talk was light. But you know, I needed to be with him and I knew that he needed to be with me. Sometimes we lay before the fire that he had roaring in the hearth, and I would lie in his arms and fight the tears that stood in my eyes. But before the talk turned to anything meaningful between us, I would slip away, back to the manor, leaving him to his private thoughts.

It was as if just being together was enough, during those intimate moments we were showing how much we loved each other; but for whatever reason, words were more difficult to find when trying to express how we felt.

I knew in my heart that Potter was hurting and I suspected

now that he was away from The Hollows, he had found time to reflect on what had happened there. The betrayal by his best friend, Luke and the death of Murphy, I figured, were weighing heavily upon his soul. And like Potter, now away from The Hollows, I too was able to look back on everything that had happened. I too had been betrayed by Luke – we all had. I'd lost my mother and Murphy had been like a father to me.

Sometimes, I would stand alone in the quiet of the night before the mirror in my room and look at the maze of hairline cracks that covered me. I would stare at those little black fingers that wriggled at the tips of my wings, my claws, and fangs and knew that I truly had been cursed. So many times, as I'd lain in Potter's arms before the fire in the Gate House, I had fought the crippling urge to tell him about the cracks that covered my body when in my half-breed form. But I just couldn't tell him. I could *see* he was consumed by his own worries, doubts, and grief, and being back from the dead wasn't easy to deal with – like I said – it isn't like being in the movies.

So I sat at my window and watched him rake the leaves away, both of us lost to our thoughts. For how long I sat there, I don't know – that is another thing about being dead – time kind of just stands still. Nights could seem to last fifty or sixty hours and days only moments. Like I've already said, the world had been shoved to the left a bit.

Eventually, Potter propped the rake against a nearby tree, and turning his back on the manor, he walked into the woods and disappeared from view, his head down. I wanted to go after him, so jumping from my chair, I left my room and the manor.

Chapter Five

Kayla

While Isidor kept himself busy with his stake-making, I decided to explore what was once my home. For years Mrs. Payne had stopped me from going into the West Wing of the manor, and as I placed my foot on the bottom stair and looked up into the darkness, I could hear her voice again as if being blended into my constant *soundtrack* by an invisible DJ.

"It is the forbidden wing, young lady," her voice seemed to whisper in my ear. *"You are not to go up there - not now - not ever!"* That last word of warning seemed to stretch out forever inside my head as if the DJ were playing the track at the wrong speed.

But Mrs. Payne wasn't here now - not *ever* - I smiled to myself and lit the candle that I held before me. Potter had promised to fix the lighting but still hadn't gotten around to it. He'd spent loads of time on his own, shut away in that creepy Gate House. Why he wanted to shut himself away in there was way beyond me. And when he did come out, he just scowled at everyone and looked pissed off. I'd asked him to lend me the money so I could buy a new iPod. But he just flipped his middle finger, told me to fuck-off and lit another cigarette. He could be a real freak at times.

Forgetting that arsehole, I began to climb the stairs. Although it was still light outside, this part of the manor had always seemed gloomier than the rest. There weren't any windows leading from the staircase, for starters, and the rooms on either side of the hallway, as far as I could remember, had always been shut. With nothing else to do, maybe now was as good a time as any to find out what was hidden inside them.

With the light from the candle stretching my shadow up the walls like smudged lines of mascara, I made my way down the hallway, set between the row of doors. The candlelight was weak, and I couldn't see what lay ahead of me. I was kinda grateful for that, because I knew what lay at the end of the hallway - that rickety old staircase that led up to the attic and the hospital. That was the place where the half-breeds had been nursed by my father and Doctor Ravenwood. I had never been allowed up there, but Isidor had told me enough. He had described what he, Potter, and Kiera had discovered up there. The bodies of all those poor children, murdered by Sparky and...

Still unable to even think of his name, let alone say it, I came to the first door set into the wall on my right. The patterned wallpaper hung in torn strips and it smelt weird. The wall peered out from behind the paper, which looked scarred with black mildew and damp. Then I remembered how my father had insisted that the walls be coated with queets, the stuff that killed vampires.

The manor was very much how I had remembered it to be. I pushed against the door which swung open and then I changed my mind.

"Where has that statue come from?" I whispered. I couldn't ever remember there being any statues in the manor - not in the grounds and definitely not inside. But then again, I couldn't actually recall ever being in this room, so perhaps it had been here all the while. With the flame flickering before me, I cupped my hand around it, fearing that it might go out and leave me in total darkness. I could just make out that the windows had been boarded over with planks of wood so no one could see in and no one could see out. But that's what made the statue so odd. It was kneeling down. At first I thought that it had been made to look as if it was in prayer, but as I stepped through the darkness, I could see that the figure had been shaped to look as if it were peering through a gap in the boards that covered the window. It looked as if the statue were trying to see outside.

I held the candle to the figure and could see that whoever had made it had failed to give the statue, eyes, ears, nose, and a mouth. Even so, I could tell that the figure was a young man. It had short hair and its body was carved with muscle. Not like one of those freaky bodybuilders you see on T.V., but just nice, like a well-toned guy. His upper body was naked and his lower half had been sculpted to look as if he was wearing a set of baggy jeans. As I peered through the orange glow of my light, I was mesmerised by the web of cracks and breaks that covered it. There were so many, I feared that should I touch it, it would fall apart before me in a pile of grey ash.

Apart from the statue, the room was empty. There wasn't a bed, wardrobe, not one stitch of furniture, just the statue, which looked as if it were secretly trying to look out of the window. Then from behind me, the door suddenly slammed shut, snuffing out my light. The room went black and I screamed. With my free hand, I fumbled in my pockets for the book of matches I had found in the kitchen drawers. Placing the candle on the ground, I struck one of the matches, and a brilliant glow of orange light flared up before me and I screamed again. In my panic, I dropped the match and it went out. But in that split second of light, I had seen that statue again. He had no longer been looking out of the boarded-up window, but had now been standing before me, its blank, featureless face just inches from mine.

I stumbled back into the darkness, desperately trying to free another match from the book. But my hands were trembling so much, that it seemed impossible. Drawing a deep breath and backing away towards the closed door, I managed to free a match and strike it. At once there was a flare of orange light. With the flame jerking to and fro between my shaking fingers, I could see the statue knelt before the window.

"Get a grip, Kayla Hunt," I spoke aloud, and even though it was my own voice in the darkness it gave me some comfort. I picked up the candle from the rough wooden floor and lit it. Snuffing out the match before it burnt my fingers, I reached out behind me and fumbled for the door handle. Unable to take my eyes from the statue, I could see that it was in exactly the same place and position it had been before the door had slammed shut and blown out my candle.

The statue hadn't moved – it couldn't have. I would have heard it, right? Feeling kinda dumb for spooking myself, I yanked open the door and stepped back into the hallway, closing the door behind me. I looked into the direction of the rickety staircase and, convincing myself that I had probably done enough exploring for the day, I headed back down the stairs and left the forbidden wing behind me. Maybe that old cow Mrs. Payne had done me a favour by forbidding me to go up there.

I reached the bottom landing and once back in daylight, I blew out the candle. How had I been so easily spooked after everything I had seen and been through in the last year? After all, I was the dead one around here. I was the ghost stalking the stairwells and passageways. What did I have to be scared of? So, feeling embarrassed at myself, I decided not to tell the others what I had found up in the forbidden wing - especially not Potter - he really would take the piss and he didn't need too much encouragement to do that.

So pushing the thoughts of that dumb statue from my head, I went in search of Kiera's iPod. I needed to drown out my *soundtrack* - I needed to drown everything out.

Chapter Six

Kiera

As I crossed the lawn in front of the manor, my boots left footprints in the frost that covered the grass. Before I had died, I would have expected to see plumes of breath escaping from my mouth and disappearing up into the cold morning air, but that didn't happen now. Not since I had come back. It was like I was colder on the inside than the icy cold wind that blew about me.

Before entering the woods, I looked back at the manor. It sat like a giant grey shell, its walls ancient-looking and covered in ivory like greedy, green-coloured hands. But as I looked back I noticed for the first time that all of the tarpaulin had been removed. The last time I had been at Hallowed Manor, the Forbidden Wing had been undergoing extensive repairs. The windows were still boarded up but there had been several skips surrounding that part of the manor, all of them filled with rubble. As I turned away, I wondered if Potter had removed them in an attempt to keep himself busy.

Although most of the trees had shed their leaves, there were still enough Fir and Conifers to cast the woods into a gloomy darkness. I passed amongst them, heading away from the manor in the direction that I had seen Potter head in. I came across the group of weeping willows that stood before me like a cluster of elderly people with curved backs. From within them I could hear the sound of wood breaking. Gently, I parted the branches of one of the willow trees and peered into the tiny graveyard where the half-breeds had been buried over the years when the Vampyrus had lived above ground. I hadn't been back here since watching Murphy carry the bodies of his two dead daughters to this secluded place. With his back to me, I spied on Potter as he broke two thick branches over his knee. Then, with a piece of twine, he tied the two pieces of wood together to make a large cross. Silently, he made his way towards the other graves. I watched him as he skewered the bottom of the cross into the ground. When he had fixed it securely, he stepped back from it and looked at the cross. I knew who he was remembering and it filled me with sadness.

I pushed the branches of the weeping willows aside and made my way quietly towards him. As if hearing my approach, he looked over his shoulder at me then back at the cross he had made. Without saying anything, I stood next to him. Then taking Murphy's crucifix and chain from around my neck, I hung it over the cross that he had fixed into the ground.

"Murphy would have wanted you to keep it," Potter said without looking at me. "He would have wanted you to be safe."

"Do I have to worry about vampires now?" I asked him, my voice low as if I were in a church.

"Who knows what dangers lay ahead," he said, turning to look at me. His eyes were dark and looked troubled.

"What's wrong, Potter?" I asked him, reaching out and brushing his thick forearm with my hand.

"I could ask you the same question," he shot back, but his voice wasn't angry – just confused sounding. "What's happened to us?"

"I don't know," I whispered and took my hand away.

"I wasn't expecting to spend the rest of eternity sniffing red roses or dancing in the hills singing, *The Hills Are Alive With the Sound of Music* like Julie-freaking-Andrews, but I did think that perhaps we could…"

"Play happy families?" I cut in.

"Not that either," he said. "Just you and me…together."

"We are together," I said, but I knew exactly what he meant, so I added, "Look, we've been through so much. None of us are finding this easy. At first I was so happy to wake and find that I had you, Isidor, and Kayla back again, but that happiness soon faded. And I know you feel the same. We all feel it. I lay awake at night listening to the sound of Kayla crying – it can't be easy for her to know that she was murdered by Luke. He betrayed her."

"He betrayed all of us," Potter spat and stuck a cigarette in the corner of his mouth. "He was my friend too. To know that he was behind everything that we went through – to know that he set Murphy up like that – that's hard to deal with."

"Exactly," I said, looking at him as he lit the cigarette. "We all lost one way or another and then to wake to find that we are the walking dead and..." I cut off before I said anything more.

"And what?" he asked, streams of blue smoke jetting from his nostrils.

"Nothing," I said back, thinking of the cracks.

"Why don't we just go away?" he suggested, coming closer to me.

"We are *away*," I said and I let him take me into his arms. "Or perhaps you were thinking of some kind of holiday? Disneyland perhaps?" and I half-smiled.

"Grizzel's," he said, looking into my eyes.

"Sorry?" I asked sounding confused.

"There is no such place as Disneyland here, not anymore at least," he said. "There is no Walt Disney or Mickey Mouse. There is Cornelius Grizzel and a maggot called Frogskin – but no mouse called Mickey. It's like good old Disney never existed." Then looking at me he added, "You're not the only one who has noticed the world has been pushed."

"*Pushed?*" I asked him, sensing he knew more about this than I had first thought.

"It's like the world has been *pushed* off course," he said, dropping the cigarette to the ground and grinding it out with his boot. "The world that we have come back to is different from the one we left behind when we went down into The Hollows. Something has changed – something happened."

"Like what?"

"I don't know," he shrugged. "Not everything has changed."

"Isidor told me about London now being called *Linden*," I told him.

"It gets better than that," he half-smirked, but I could see that look of concern again behind his eyes. "Houston, Texas? Or *Euston*, Texas as it's now known. '*Euston,* we have a problem.' Sounds the same, but not quite."

"So what do you think happened while we were away?" I asked.

"Perhaps nothing changed while we were away," he said, fixing me with a stare. "Perhaps we've come back to a different world, one that has been *pushed* sideways a little."

"But how come no one else has noticed the changes?" I asked him. "I mean, people would notice if Disneyland just vanished, wouldn't they?"

"Not if it was never here in the first place," he said, cocking an eyebrow at me. "Not if it had always been this Drizzle dude."

"You said Grizzel before," I reminded him.

"Whatever! Grizzel or Drizzle – it all amounts to the same thing," he said. "I don't think the humans have ever known any different."

"But why aren't the changes bigger?"

"I think the capital of England suddenly having a new name is a pretty big deal," he said, looking at me.

"No, I don't mean like that," I sighed. "I mean things could be completely different instead of changing a few place names, songs, books, and movies. Whole continents could have changed, Kings and Queens could be different, and landscapes could have changed."

"Perhaps they have," he said thoughtfully. "We haven't been the most sociable of people since coming back from the dead. We haven't even stuck our noses beyond the front gate. There could be a whole new world waiting on the other side of those giant walls."

"I don't think so," I told him. "Isidor and Kayla have been bringing me newspapers and I've been on the net. I would have noticed any big changes like that – they would have noticed, too. The changes that we're talking about are subtle. It's like coming back from holiday and finding that the furniture has been moved slightly and a few new pots and pans have been added to the cupboards. It's the same house, in the same street, but stuff has been *pushed* from where you left it."

Then, taking me by the hand, Potter said, "let me show you something. I've got a subtle change to show you," and he set off through the trees.

Chapter Seven

Kiera

Potter led me by the hand through the woods. Pale shards of wintry sun cut through the leafy overhead canopy and the smell of the pine needles smelt fresh and sweet. Our walk through the woods was quiet, the only sound was the odd squawk from a crow as we startled it by our progress.

We walked hand in hand and for the first time since returning from the dead and back to the manor, it felt as if we were a real couple taking a stroll on a winter's afternoon. But to think of this only made me long for what we could have had if we had met someplace else other than the Ragged Cove – in another time surrounded by a different set of circumstances.

The treeline ahead began to thin, the gaps between them growing bigger. Potter led me out into the clearing where the summerhouse stood.

"Notice anything different?" Potter almost seemed to whisper. "Can you see anything that has been *pushed*?"

Just as I had remembered it, the summerhouse was a small, squat building, painted white, which stood on a raised wooden platform with a small set of steps leading up to its wooden front door. But there was something different – something had been pushed into place that hadn't been there before. There was a statue. Letting go of Potter's hand, I stepped into the clearing and walked slowly towards it. To see the statue just standing there made me feel uneasy – on edge – and if I still had a heart, I knew that it would be quickening in my chest.

I came to rest before it. It was made of grey coloured stone and even though its face was featureless, I knew that it was a statue of a girl. She was bent forward slightly and had her fingers laced together as if in prayer. To look at her reminded me of the many statues of St. Bernadette I had seen. Whoever had sculpted this life-sized statue of the girl had gone to tremendous detail. Her hair looked so real that at any moment,

I thought it might just flutter back from her shoulders. She was dressed in what looked like a shroud, which came to rest against her marble-looking toes. I say marble as her face, hands, and feet were covered in the faintest of cracks. To look at her was, in some freaky way, like looking back at my own reflection as I stood alone before the mirror in my room, studying the cracks and lines in my naked flesh.

"Freaky, don't you think?" Potter asked.

I gasped and spun around, unaware that he had joined me by the statue.

"Where did it come from?" I breathed. "Who put it here?"

"That's the million-dollar question," he said, staring at the statue. "It wasn't here before. I should know – I spent long enough hobbling around these grounds like the bleeding Hunchback of Notre Dame when I was disguised as Marshall. Remember that?"

"How could I forget," I half-smiled, unable to take my eyes from the statue of the girl. "Why do you think it's here?"

"Haven't a clue," Potter said. "You're the Miss Marple around here, I was hoping you might be able to do your *thing* – you know – look for bent-over blades of grass and God knows what else it is that you can see."

Ignoring his sarcasm, which believe it or not was quite refreshing as it was more like the Potter I had fallen in love with, I turned to him and said, "Although the statue looks ancient, it hasn't been here long, which is a curious thing."

"How curious?" he asked me and smiled, as if he too were enjoying seeing that glimmer of my old self reappearing.

"Because we've been here six weeks, okay," I started, feeling that buzz I got when I had a problem to solve. "The grass is about four inches long, but none of it has grown up and over the toes of the statue, indicating that it was placed here recently. But how could that have happened? I mean this is made of solid stone, it's not something that one person could have thrown over the wall, then carried so deep into the woods and placed here."

"Maybe more than just one person brought it here," he said. "What makes you think that it was carried here by just one person?"

I knelt down, and brushing my fingertips over the grass, I said, "can't you see the faint impressions of where the grass has been disturbed? They are almost gone, but they are still just visible if you look for them. There are only one set of footprints."

"Maybe this person worked out a lot," he half-joked.

"No one carried it here," I told him, standing up again as I had *seen* enough. "The footprints would have been deeper if someone had carried it here from the sheer weight of it in their arms.

"So what are you saying?" Potter asked, looking at me like I had all the answers written down somewhere.

I pointed down at the faint footprints that led up to the statue and said, "The tracks only lead up to the statue, they don't lead away. Whoever it was never left this spot."

"So where is this person now?" Potter asked me, searching my eyes with his.

"She's still here," I whispered.

Potter looked back over his shoulder as if checking out the treeline, then the summerhouse. Turning to face me again, he said, "What makes you so sure that this person was a *she*?"

"The footprints are too small to be that of a man, and I'd put her height at about..." Glancing at the statue, I added, "Five-foot-four."

"You've done that measurement thing again haven't you?" he said. "The distance between each stride gives you their height, right?"

"Wrong," I smiled, and slapped my forehead with the flat of my head. "You just don't see it, do you?"

"See what, Sherlock?" Potter snapped, starting to sound pissed off with me.

"Just think about it for a moment," I said back. "There's a set of girl's footprints leading to a statue that wasn't here before. The statue is way too heavy to be carried and we know that it hasn't been here for very long. There are no tracks leading away from the statue – they stop where the statue now stands."

"So what you saying?"

"Oh come on, Potter!" I gasped. "Do you need me to spell it out for you?"

"Now listen here, sweet-cheeks, don't take that tone with me," Potter barked gruffly and inside I smiled.

"Tone?" I snapped back. "What tone? I don't have a tone. "It's not my fault you just don't *see* it!"

"See what?" he growled at me.

"No one brought the statue out here!" I yelled, secretly enjoying this fiery moment between us. It reminded me of how we used to be before coming back from the dead. "Those footprints belong to the statue!"

As if I had just punched him in the guts, Potter's mouth fell open. "Have you finally lost your freaking mind? Jeez, I've heard you come up with some shit in the past, but this takes the piss! So what you're suggesting is that this statue came to life, and for some unknown reason decided to take a stroll out to the summerhouse? Is that what you're trying to tell me?"

"Whoever she is, I don't think she was a statue when she came to the summerhouse," I said, looking back at the faceless girl. "I think she suddenly turned to stone."

"That is the craziest bunch of bullshit I've ever heard," Potter said, shaking his head and fumbling his pack of cigarettes from his trouser pocket.

Then looking him straight in the eye, I said, "Any crazier than coming back from the dead? Any crazier than waking to discover London isn't called *London* anymore and U2 are now called Feedback and my iPod has a crescent-shaped moon on the..."

"What do you mean U2 aren't called *U2* anymore?" Potter suddenly cut in. "This is worse than I thought. You mean I can't listen to their songs anymore?"

I shook my head and said, "No – I don't think so."

"What about, *Where The Streets Have No Name*?"

"Look can we just stop discussing U2 – *Feedback* – for a moment and focus on the statue," I snapped.

"But there's a world of difference between a few names changing and a young girl turning to stone," he argued.

Then, thinking of me standing naked before the mirror, my body covered in those cracks, which wept that white, powdery ash, I said, "Is there a difference? Maybe when everything got *pushed*, as you call it, this young girl turned to stone."

"Okay let's just say I'm prepared to take a stroll down insanity beach with you for a moment or two," Potter said, "There are still a couple of unanswered questions."

"Okay?" I said. "Like what?"

"One, what was this girl doing out here?" Potter asked me. "And secondly, who is she?"

I looked at the statue, and slowly shaking my head, I whispered, "I don't know."

Potter came towards me, and placing his hands on my hips, he looked into my eyes and said, "See, Kiera, I told you we need to get away from here."

"And go where?" I asked, knocking his hands from me. "We have nowhere else to go. And besides, I've been doing some thinking."

"About what?" he asked, lighting another cigarette.

"It's not good for Isidor and Kayla to have nothing to do; they need something to take their minds off what has happened to them."

"Perhaps we can find a game of Scrabble tucked away in the manor somewhere..." Potter started.

"I'm not joking," I said. "We all need something to take our minds off what has become of us. I don't know about you, but I can't just sit and stare at the walls any longer. Whether you believe it or not, everything that has happened – been *pushed* – while we were away, has happened for a reason and I believe that's why we're back."

"So what you're saying is that we've got to push it all back into place," Potter seemed to scoff at me. "Good luck, sweet-cheeks."

"Why do you have to be so impossible at times?" I asked him.

"What you're suggesting is *impossible*," he said back, chewing the end of his cigarette.

"I thought at first that maybe we should wait for the Elders to give us some sign," I said. "But look around you, there are plenty of signs that things aren't right."

"So what are you gonna do?" he smiled at me with that smug grin of his and I remembered how often I'd wanted to knock it clean off his face. "Investigate?"

With my fist clenched and knowing that he was trying to bait me, I said smiling back at him, "That's exactly what I'm going to do."

"How?"

"I'm going to advertise – I did it once before," I told him.

"What, like a private detective?" he chuckled to himself. "You are taking this whole Miss Marple thing way too seriously."

"Well anything has got to be better than just moping around this place and sweeping leaves up off the drive," I snipped back at him. "I haven't been raised from the dead to do nothing. While I'm about it, perhaps I should advertise your gardening services?"

"I ain't no gardener!" Potter growled at me.

"No?" I smiled smugly at him. "Where has your fire gone, Potter? Where's the fight gone? These days you're as wet as those leaves you stand and rake into a pile. I need more than that. I might be dead but I need a life. I miss my old life. I don't have any of my belongings, they're all back at my flat in Havensfield – along with my old life where I was once a cop, but that's hundreds of miles away from here. I don't even have my badge anymore. I just want a little bit of that life back – I want to feel like Kiera Hudson again. Can't you understand that?"

Potter threw away his cigarette end and looking at me, he said, "Kiera, you can't have that life back – it's gone. Can't you *see* that? You ain't a cop no more and neither am I. We're nothing more than ghosts. We shouldn't even be here – we're dead."

"But we are here in this fucked up world that we've come back to!" I yelled at him, my fists clenched. "And I think us coming back has changed things and only we can put them right again."

Potter looked back at me, then rolling back his shoulders, his wings unfolded from his back. "You stay and do the whole Murder-She-Wrote thing, but I need to get away from here."

I reached out, but before I'd had the chance to touch him, Potter had rocketed away, up into the clouds, which covered the sky like a dark blanket. I looked at the statue again and knew that I was right, however odd my theory was. Whoever the girl had once been – she had now turned to stone. What she had been doing in the grounds of Hallowed Manor, I didn't know. But something told me that finding her out by the summerhouse was a sign. A sign of what? I didn't know that, either. Until I found out, I decided that I would keep this to myself. I didn't want to alarm Isidor or Kayla any more than I had to. Whoever the girl had been, she was now just a harmless piece of stone, and it wasn't as if she was going anywhere.

Chapter Eight

Kiera

After Potter had flown away, I headed back to the manor to find Isidor slumped on the sofa reading a book, and Kayla folded up in an armchair, listening to my iPod. She had it up so loud that I could hear that she was listening to *The Wanted* sing *Lightning*.

As I entered, Kayla yanked the earphones out and looked at me. "You look upset."

"Potter's gone," I told them and Isidor glanced over the top of his book at me.

"Gone where?" he asked.

"Don't know," I said and flopped into one of the armchairs.

"When is he gonna be back?" Kayla asked, turning off the iPod.

"Don't know that either," I shrugged.

"Why did he go?" Kayla shot back, and I could see the glint of intrigue in her eyes. I couldn't blame her; Potter deciding to take off was probably the most exciting thing that had happened to her since coming back.

"I think, like all of us, he's having problems adjusting," I said.

"I'd have problems adjusting too if I came back from the dead to discover that my name was *Gabriel*," Isidor smirked from around the edge of his book.

Ignoring his comment, I said, "What are you reading?"

"The Adventures of Sherlock Holmes," he said, holding the book in the air so I could see the front cover.

"Good," I smiled.

"Good?" Isidor said, cocking the eyebrow with the piercing.

"It might come in handy," I said back.

"How come?" Kayla asked, shooting a quizzical look in my direction.

"I don't know about you guys," I said, "but I'm getting fed

42

up with sitting around here every day, twiddling my thumbs. I need something more than that - I need to get the old brain matter working again."

"So what have you got in mind, Kiera?" Isidor asked, placing the book to one side.

"I'm going to write an advert offering to help people with their problems," I explained to them.

"What sort of problems?" Kayla asked me, screwing up her face.

"I don't know – anything I guess," I said.

"You know you're just gonna attract a whole bunch of pervs," Kayla grimaced.

"We don't have to respond to their emails," I said. "We pick the cases that sound most interesting - unusual!"

"When you say 'cases'," Isidor asked, his interest now picking up, "Do you mean like investigations?"

"I guess," I answered. "We'll just have to see what comes up."

So over dinner that evening, we decided what our advert should say. We sat bunched together at the end of the vast kitchen table, our voices echoing off the huge stone walls. It was more like a banqueting hall than a kitchen. We didn't eat much, which was another thing about being dead – we had all lost our appetites. It wasn't as if we needed food to stay alive. Everything had the same bland taste to it - like toast without butter and jam - just dull and boring. Food just got pushed to the edges of our plates, as if we were trying to kid ourselves that we had eaten. Maybe we only bothered to cook a meal each night to try and keep some normality to our newfound existence; after all, the only thing that any of us truly enjoyed was the taste of human blood.

Isidor pushed his plate to one side and said, "I know what the advert could say. What about something like this: 'Got a problem? Need some help? Who you gonna call – Kiera Hudson!' "

Kayla almost choked on her food as she started to laugh. "Isidor, Kiera is meant to be an investigator – not a freaking *Ghostbuster*!"

"Okay, smart arse," he said, looking a little hurt at his sister's teasing. "You think of something."

"Okay," Kayla said thoughtfully. "How about, 'Got a problem that needs to be shared? Got a secret you can't tell anyone else? Then contact Kiera Hudson. Complete discretion assured!' "

"If you write something like that," Isidor grimaced, "You will get a bunch of pervs come knocking at the door. There'll be a queue of them in dirty raincoats from here to God knows where!"

With a smile tugging at the corners of my mouth, I looked at them across the table and said, "We need to keep it simple. You're quite right, we don't want any perverts or ghost hunters..."

"*Busters*," Kayla cut in.

"Them too," I nodded, "but we don't want to be investigating a string of missing pets, either. We all know that we've come back to a slightly different world than the one we left. Maybe there is someone out there who hasn't forgotten everything – someone who remembers what the world used to be like."

"So what have you got in mind?" Isidor asked me.

"How about this: 'Has your world been pushed?' " I suggested, thinking of how Potter had described the changes.

"What's that s'posed to mean?" Kayla asked glancing at Isidor, then back at me.

"I don't know," I said, looking at her. "But someone out there might."

So the following morning, with a dozen copies of the advert in their hands, Isidor and Kayla stood in the great hall beneath the chandelier, their wings out.

"Don't you think you should go by car?" I asked them.

"Are you crazy?" Kayla asked back. "You want us to reach as many towns as possible, don't you?"

"I guess," I said, "but it's just that you might be seen by someone. We shouldn't be drawing attention to ourselves."

"Have you seen outside this morning?" Isidor asked, his wings rippling beneath his arms. "The sky is full of clouds – no one will see us. And besides, the nearest town is over ten miles away – we should know, we've driven it enough over the last few weeks collecting those newspapers for you."

"Why don't you come with us?" Kayla asked me. "You haven't left the grounds of the manor since we got here. It would be good for you to get out a bit."

The offer was a kind one, but I knew that if I were to go with them, I would have to fly and that would mean having to get my wings out and if I did that, those cracks would appear. I still wasn't ready for them to see me like that.

"No, you're okay," I told her. "I think I'll just bum around here for a while."

"And do what?" Isidor asked me, his fangs shining as brightly as the chandelier above us.

"I'm going to sync my iPod to my old email address, make sure that it's still working okay, just in case we do get a response to those adverts."

"That isn't going to take all day," Kayla pushed. "Go on, Kiera, come with us – it could be fun."

I did want to go with them, not really relishing the thought of spending the day mooching about the empty manor on my own. But I just couldn't. "I've got plenty to do – like setting up a room for consulting. We need to look the part should we get any clients."

"Your choice," Kayla smiled weakly at me, but I could tell she knew that there was something up with me.

I followed them to the giant front door, and Isidor had been right, the day was overcast and miserable-looking. A fine rain was coming down, and the leaves that Potter had raked into a neat pile now swirled up and down the drive in the wind.

They both looked back at me one last time, then without a word, they both soared up into the dismal-looking sky. Within seconds, I had lost sight of them amongst the clouds.

"See you in a while, crocodile," I whispered, closing the front door of the manor, and leaving me all alone.

Chapter Nine

Kayla

It felt cool to be flying again. The rain that struck my face was cold but refreshing, as if waking me up. I hadn't flown since The Hollows. For pretty much my whole life, I had resented being different from those girls who had called me 'stickleback' at boarding school. But I had learnt that my wings were just another part of me, like my arms and legs. Those girls back at school would never know the freedom my wings gave me.

Isidor flew beside me, his arms outstretched on either side of him, his wings rippling beneath them. He glanced at me and winked, and I knew that he was enjoying the freedom again as much as I was. The wind roared past us, and the sound of it was wonderful, it deafened the other noises – my soundtrack.

The clouds broke beneath us, and I could see the town of Wood Hill, the one that we had been visiting daily for Kiera. We swooped over it, circled, and spying a small wooded area on its outskirts, we raced towards them. We landed, and rolling back my shoulders, I put on the sweatshirt that I'd tied about my waist, covering my back and the crop-top that I was wearing. Unlike me, Isidor couldn't fold his wings away, he had to hide them, and so he zipped up the front of his jacket.

"Ready?" he asked me.

"You bet," I nodded and followed him out of the small wooded area and up the hill to the town. As we walked together, I wondered if we stood out. Did we look freaky? We were definitely very pale, looking like we had been ill or something. Maybe it was my imagination, but as we headed into town and passed some of the people on the road, they seemed to look away from us, casting their heads down, and some even crossed the road as if to avoid us.

I wondered why I hadn't noticed this before on our trips to Wood Hill, but we had always come by car. I had waited inside, parked at the curb, while Isidor had taken the papers from the newspaper stand outside the store and left the money for them in the honesty tin outside. We had never actually spoken to anyone in the town. Driving through a place was always different than walking through it. You saw more when you walked, noticed things that you wouldn't have while in a car.

Well, I was definitely noticing stuff now. Like how the streets didn't seem that busy at all, and those people who were on them seemed to be in a hurry. It was as if they were all late for a meeting or something. But what was freaking me out more than that, was it wasn't just me and Isidor that they were ignoring, they were ignoring each other. For such a small town, not one of them looked at each other as they passed by. There were no 'good mornings', or 'Hey, how you doing today?' It was like they didn't really see each other – but they did. It was weird to watch how they almost seemed to shy away from one another. I stared in amazement as they crisscrossed back and forth in an almost desperate attempt not to come in contact. One guy, elderly with a stick, stepped off the curb to avoid a scrawny-looking woman who was coming down the street towards him. But then another guy, mid-forties with a belly that hung over the top of his trousers, stepped into the road from the other side of the street as he tried to avoid someone else. On seeing this, the old guy turned, then turned again as if trapped. He shuffled around in a full circle as if trying to figure out which way to go – how to escape.

The thin, homemade cigarette that hung from the corner of his wrinkled old mouth fell out and he swore. Then looking up, he saw me watching him and he cried out. He turned away and covered his face with his arm, as if he didn't want us to see him - or was it that he didn't want to see us? The old guy saw a gap and shuffled away, flinching as someone else came too close to him.

"Are you seeing what I'm seeing?" I whispered, as we made our way through the town. "This place is fucked up."

"What day is it today?" Isidor asked, not looking at me, but watching the crazy people on the street all around us.

"Saturday, I think," I said back. "Why?"

"So it's not a school day then," he whispered, as one of the people toppled from the edge of the curb in a desperate attempt to avoid us.

"I guess," I breathed. "Why?"

"Where are all the kids?" he said, and this time he did look at me. "Shouldn't they be hanging about on street corners with their mates, out shopping, stuff like that?"

"It is cold and it's raining," I reminded him.

"Didn't bother that old guy," Isidor said, his voice still low, just above a whisper.

Then looking across the street, I said, "Over there! That woman, see her? She's pushing a pram and there's a baby in it."

We watched her hurry down the street, her head down as she tried to avoid everyone else. But a man with an umbrella was heading towards her, and she crossed the street to avoid him.

Isidor yanked me by the arm into a nearby shop doorway, and said, "Let's hide in here – keep out of her way."

"Why?" I hushed.

"Because you know that smell that babies always have?"

"No, not really," I told him, watching from the shadows of the shop doorway as the woman with the pram headed towards us.

"Believe me, babies do have a certain odour," he said, "And I can't smell it."

"So?" I asked.

"So look!" he whispered as the woman passed us as we hid in the shop doorway.

I followed Isidor's stare and looked into the pram and gasped.

Clamping his hand over my mouth, he put his lips to my ear and very quietly said, "Shhh, Kayla."

Chapter Ten

Kiera

With the manor to myself, I could hear every creak and groan it made as the wind outside began to blow harder about the eaves. It wasn't that this spooked me in any way, but just intensified my feelings of loneliness. I wandered from one room to another on the ground floor, each one of them dustier than the next. The furniture was covered in white sheets. Cobwebs hung from the corners of the rooms and swung down from the light fixtures overhead. Just off the main hallway, there was a narrow passageway and its walls were lined with mahogany, which gave it a dark and oppressive feeling. At the end of it there was a door. I pushed it open and was pleasantly surprised by what I found behind it, and the sight lifted my spirits.

I had found a small study, which could have easily been mistaken for a library by the amount of leather-bound books that covered the walls. There was a desk and in the centre of this was a large ink blotter. There were several silver-coloured pens lined neatly next to one another, and a photo frame. I picked it up and turned it over. The picture inside the frame was of Doctor Hunt, Lady Hunt, and Kayla. Kayla was sitting on her father's knee and looked happy, her red hair spilling over her shoulders and down the front of the pretty dress she was wearing. Kayla looked to be about six-years-old. I looked at Doctor Hunt as he stared back at me from the picture and I remembered how I had buried his body beneath the tree on the outskirts of the town of Wasp Water.

Was his body still there? I wondered. *Had it been discovered like mine had on the side of that Cumbria Mountain?* In real time, that had only been about six weeks ago. Now that the world had been *pushed*, was his body still there? How much had the world changed on the other side of the manor walls?

Placing the picture back where I had found it, I looked

about the room and with a bit of dusting, I knew that I had found my consulting room – that's if anyone actually came to be consulted with. My brain was beginning to ache with restlessness. I needed something – a puzzle – to awaken it again. But what frustrated me the most was that I knew there was a puzzle to be solved and I was a piece of that puzzle. As was the girl in my dreams, falling out of the sky – only to wake and find herself like I had in that mortuary. Then, there was the statue by the summerhouse – the girl who had been turned to stone.

Until I had more pieces of that puzzle, I knew there was little I could do, so going to the giant kitchen, I found some old dusters and polish and went back to the study. I polished the desk, the bookshelves, and the mahogany walls. I shook the dust from the curtains and opened the large windows to let in some fresh air. When my back had started to ache and my throat and nose were full of dust, I stood back and admired my handiwork. I positioned the chair slightly behind the desk, then sat in it. I wondered if anyone would come – I wondered if anyone else realised that they had been *pushed*.

I closed the door to the study, put the dusters and polish back where I had found them, then left the manor to walk the grounds, needing to clear the dust that was stuck in the back of my throat. The rain had eased and looked more like a fine mist than a drizzle. The only sound was the regular squawk of the crows that flapped their giant wings overhead. I looked up at them and wondered where Potter was and what he was doing. I missed him, but I understood why he had needed to get away.

The trees towered on either side of me as I made my way through the wood and my feet crunched over the fallen branches and twigs. I hadn't intended to head for the graveyard hidden by the weeping willows, or so I told myself, but it wasn't long before I found myself parting their stooped branches with my hands and stepping into that secret place. Although the area surrounded by the forlorn trees held so much death, it was tranquil. It had that feeling of stepping off a busy street into a church. The silence, the mystery of the place – I was drawn to it.

I made my way through the headstones of all those half-breeds that, unlike me and Isidor, hadn't lived past the age of sixteen. And as I looked down at some of the graves, I could see that some of them hadn't even lived as long as that. Snuffed out too early, like a candle before dawn that hadn't had a chance to break and shower the world with light.

There were several graves that didn't have headstones like the rest, but makeshift crosses made from the branches of the nearby trees, like the one I had seen Potter make for Murphy. Passing amongst them, I noticed that one had been inscribed with the name Nessa and the other Meren and I knew that these were the graves of Murphy's daughters. I could remember him saying their names as Potter had argued with Murphy before going to the Fountain of Souls in search of the Lycanthrope.

I bent over and peered at their names.

"Your father was a good man," I whispered, "and I know he loved you so very much. He loved you so much that it blinded him. He wanted revenge for your murders so greatly that he put his own life in danger and took us on a journey where he was tricked and betrayed, where he ended up losing his own life." Then straightening up, and with tears standing in my eyes, I added, "But I guess he has told you everything himself by now. I hope you are all happy together. And one last thing before I go, can you tell your Dad that although Potter would never admit this, he really misses him? We all do."

Then, turning my back on the makeshift crosses, I headed back through the graveyard, passing Murphy's cross as I went. And it was then that I saw it, or rather I didn't. I had hung Murphy's crucifix on the cross that Potter had made, but now it was gone. I searched the earth and grass that surrounded the foot of the cross, wondering if perhaps the crucifix had fallen off, but it wasn't there. I stood up and wondered if perhaps Potter had taken it before we had left the graveyard that day. I made my way back through the woods.

The wind had started to pick up again, and the rain became heavier. With my hair beginning to look like a series of black-coloured rat tails as it clung to my face, I sped up as I headed back towards the manor. Following the route that Potter had previously led me, I headed towards the summerhouse, knowing that to avoid the downpour that the swollen clouds were threatening, I could always shelter in there.

I ran from beneath the trees and into the circular area where the summerhouse stood. Just before it stood the statue that I had seen the day before. But there was something different about it. And as I ran towards it, I was sure that before it had been facing the summerhouse, but now had its back turned towards it, as if the stone girl had turned around somehow. As I drew nearer, I could see that it wasn't just the position of the girl that had changed, there was something different about her hands.

I reached the statue, and with rain running down my face, I looked at Murphy's crucifix as it hung from the statue's cold, stone fist. The crucifix glistened wetly, and I reached out for it. I pulled on it, but it was like the statue of the girl didn't want to give it up. The crucifix wouldn't come free of her grasp, so I left her to hold onto it. Then, looking into her featureless stone face, I whispered, "What are you? Who are you? I know you can hear me."

And as I stood in the driving rain and secretly hoped for a reply, it was me who screeched as a hand suddenly gripped my shoulder.

Chapter Eleven

Kayla

"That wasn't a baby in that pram," I gasped. "It was a doll! Why would she be pushing that thing around?"

"Freaky, huh?" Isidor said, stepping from the doorway and watching the woman with the pram retreat up the road. "And did you notice how the doll's eyes had been removed?"

"Isidor, I don't want to state the freaking obvious, but this place is like, really screwed up," I said, standing in the rain next to him. "Maybe we should just head back to the manor."

"Not before putting some of these adverts around town," he said, taking them from within his coat.

"You're not serious!" I said to him.

"If anyone has been pushed, as Kiera describes it," Isidor replied thoughtfully, "the people of this town must have. Someone has got to respond to these adverts."

I followed Isidor up the rain-drenched streets, as water raced along the gutter and sloshed into the storm drains. We hadn't gone far when we came to a small newsagent, the shop where Isidor had bought the papers from on previous visits to Wood Hill.

With his hand pressed against the door, he looked back at me and said, "Ready?"

"Ready for what?" I asked him, my eyes wide.

"Anything, I guess," he said, pushing open the door and stepping inside.

A bell chimed above our heads as the door swung shut behind us. The shop was dimly lit and dust motes hovered in the air. Two narrow racks ran the length of the shop, and these were filled with groceries, which looked to be covered with as much dust as the air about us. Some of the shelves were littered with magazines, which looked dog-eared, their covers yellowed with age. The shop smelt of sweat, stale cigar smoke, and beer. At the end of one of the aisles was one of those tall displays that turned. It was full of postcards, and just like the magazines had, they looked creased up and old. I turned the display round, and as I did, it made a creaking sound and toppled over. I tried to grab hold of it, but it slipped through my fingers and toppled over onto the floor. The postcards scattered, some of them disappearing beneath the shelves and racks.

"What's going on back there?" a deep voice boomed, and it almost seemed to shake the whole shop.

Together, Isidor and I peered around the edge of the nearest shelf and could see a counter at the back of the shop. Someone was sitting behind it, but I couldn't see who as that part of the shop was covered in shadows. The voice spoke again and said, "What do you want?"

Isidor glanced at me, then, with the adverts in his hand, he made his way towards the counter. I followed him, and as we drew near, I could hear heavy breathing. It sounded out of breath. And as I drew nearer still, I could hear the heartbeat. It was weak sounding as it struggled to push the blood around this person's body. As we stepped towards the counter and through the shadows, I understood why the breathing had sounded like a clapped-out old engine and the heart like a weak drum beat.

The man who sat behind the counter was huge – a giant. His head was the size of a basketball, round with cheeks that glowed red as if it had just been pulled from a fire. Sweat rolled from his brow and down the side of his face and he mopped it away with one of his meaty hands. The fingers looked like overstuffed sausages, and the fingernails were yellow with a black rind of dirt under each one. He wore a vest which was stained yellow with sweat and old food, his belly sat on his lap like a stuffed cushion.

"What do you want?' he asked again, his eyes looking bloodshot. A fat cigar hung from the corner of his mouth, and the end of it was black with spit.

"I was wondering if you could display one of these pictures in your shop window?" Isidor smiled.

"What is it?" the man asked, snatching the advert from Isidor's hand. But before Isidor had a chance to say anything, the man screwed up his flabby face and said, "'Have you been pushed?' What's that s'posed to mean?"

"That's what we wondered," I whispered to myself, checking out the tuffs of thick, black hair that covered the man's arms and shoulders.

"No can do," the man grunted and pushed the advert back across the counter. "Is it some kinda joke?"

"No joke," I said.

"Please," Isidor said.

"But what does it mean?" the man asked again, chewing on the end of his cigar, not taking his eyes from us. "It seems weird to me and weird means trouble as far as I'm concerned."

"No weirder than this town," Isidor frowned.

The man didn't say anything at first, he just stared straight back at Isidor. Then, he took back the advert, looked down at it and said, "The wolves came and they changed everything."

"The wolves?" Isidor asked, shooting a glance at me.

"You musta heard of the wolves?'" the man huffed, sounding out of breath.

"I guess," I breathed, thinking of the Lycanthrope – the wolves that I had known from my past life. "What about them?"

"They took our children," he whispered. "They took all of them."

"Why?" Isidor asked him.

"Because that's what the wolves do isn't it?" the man suddenly snapped. "That's what they've always done – that's just the way it is."

"The way what is?" I asked him, shaking my head.

"Did you not do history at school?" he came back at me, mopping sweat from his cheeks, or were they tears?

"It wasn't my strongest subject," I told him.

"But still, you must know about the wolves?" the man pushed, dumbfounded that we seemed not to know what he was talking about.

I looked at Isidor and he looked blankly back at me. As if seeing that neither of us had the faintest idea what he was talking about, the man said, "The Treaty of Wasp Water. You must have heard of the Wasp Water Treaty? You know, the great battle that took place there two hundred years ago between us and the wolves?"

"No, remind me," I told the man, my heart racing. "I must have missed that history lesson."

"Well go look it up," the man snapped, tired now of our ignorance.

"We know a town called Wasp Water," Isidor cut in. "We've been there."

Then, taking the cigar from the corner of his mouth, the sweaty-looking man said, "You've been to Wasp Water, you say?"

We both nodded at him.

"You lie," the man gasped.

"Why do you say that?" Isidor asked him.

"Because he would have never let you leave," the man whispered and peered about the shop just in case someone we hadn't seen might be listening.

"Who?" I asked him, my mouth turning dry.

"The one and only human the wolves have welcomed into their pack," the man explained.

"What's his name?" Isidor pushed.

With his jowls wobbling from side to side, the man shook his head and said, "No one knows his name – not his real name. Where have you two been for the whole of your lives? I can't believe you've never heard of the Wolf Man – the only human to live amongst the wolves. Now get out before I change my mind."

"About what?" Isidor asked him.

"Putting your advert up in my window," he barked.

"But I thought you said it was weird," I said.

The man glanced up from the words written on the advert and said, "Maybe it's time I pushed back?"

Chapter Twelve

Kiera

"Potter!" I gasped. "You scared the hell out of me!" and although he had scared me, I was so glad to see him again. I threw my arms around his neck and kissed him. He kissed me back, but there was something wrong, it was like he was holding something back somehow.

"What's wrong?" I asked him, looking into his dead, black eyes. Rain dripped from his chin and ran over his naked chest and down his stomach.

"Let's get out of the rain," he said, leading me towards the summerhouse. We climbed the steps. Potter pushed against the white wooden door and it squealed on rusty hinges as it opened. He closed it behind us and for a moment, I stood in the centre of the small, wooden building and listened to the sound of the rain drum against the roof. Potter came towards me, and with the flat of my hand, I brushed the raindrops from his face, shoulders, and chest. His skin seemed to tighten and mine tingled as I touched him. He took my hands in his and bringing them up to his mouth, he kissed them. It had been a while since I had sensed such emotional sentiment from him.

"Potter, what's wrong?" I breathed.

"The world really has changed since we left it, or came back to it," he said. "I don't really know which it is."

"What's happened?" I asked. "Apart from the name changes and the logo on my iPod…"

"That's nothing," he cut in. "I mean, the world has really changed."

"How?" I asked, my heart now beginning to race.

Potter let go of my hands and ran his fingers through his hair. Then staring at me, he said, "It's my worst nightmare."

"What is?" I almost screamed at him, just wanting to know what he had seen on the other side of the manor walls.

"Wolves are living amongst the humans," he whispered.

"But they always have," I reminded him. "Just like the Vampyrus lived amongst the humans."

"Those Vampyrus and Lycanthrope that lived amongst the humans before, lived in secret," Potter said. "The humans never knew of their existence. The humans never knew that the people who were murdering them and their children were Lycanthrope who were living in secret amongst them. Only the Vampyrus knew that, and it was my job to track them down and punish them for their crimes. But there aren't any Vampyrus anymore and it's like there never was."

"How do you mean?" I asked him, the sound of the rain beating off the roof of the summerhouse now growing louder.

"It's like the Elders changed history somehow when they snatched all the Vampyrus back and sealed The Hollows forever," Potter started to explain. "With no Vampyrus to keep the Lycanthrope in check, they've left their hiding place beneath the Fountain of Souls and now live openly amongst the humans as their equals somehow. Where the Vampyrus had once worked as doctors, police officers, formed bands like U2, and helped design the iPod, this world, or this version of it, everything that the Vampyrus achieved, every little influence that they had, is now down to the Lycanthrope."

"So what does that exactly mean?" I asked him, sensing his concern – or was it fear?

"It means we're in deep shit!" he snapped. "The Lycanthrope are killers..." he started.

"But maybe they're different now," I said, but not really believing it myself. "Maybe they're not a race of serial killers..."

"Yeah and perhaps the tooth fairy really exists," Potter growled. "They can't help themselves, you should know that – you were murdered by one of them – Jack Seth killed you, remember?"

"He had no choice," I said, pulling Potter close.

"And that's what I'm trying to tell you, Kiera. They have no choice. They kill, that's what they do. Even though Seth must have known that by killing you he would die beneath The Hollows, he still couldn't resist you. He couldn't stop the urge

58

of ripping you to pieces," he said, taking my face gently in his strong hands.

"But you can't be sure that they are still killing," I said. "The humans wouldn't put up with it."

"What if they didn't have a choice?" he asked me. "What if the humans had struck some kind of deal with the Lycanthrope?"

"Why would they do that?" I asked him.

"Perhaps the Lycanthrope didn't give them a choice," he said, his eyes growing dark. "And we all know how they keep to their word. Remember the deal that they struck with Murphy? Look what happened to him. They killed him."

I looked at Potter and I could see that anger, frustration, and hurt in his eyes again as he remembered how Murphy had been betrayed. "What would Murphy say if he were standing here right now?" I asked him.

With a wry smile tugging at the corners of his mouth, Potter said, "Let's go and catch us some wolf." Then the smile faded and he added, "But Murphy isn't here any longer. There are no Vampyrus left – it's like they never existed. I am all that is left of them."

"So what are you going to do?" I asked him, hoping that some of his fight was coming back – that spark which had drawn me to him in the first place.

"I'm going to stop them," he said. "That's what I did before, with Murphy and Lu...that's all I know – it's what I do best."

"But there is only you left." I pushed him. "How are you going to do it all on your own?"

Then, turning his back to me, he went to the corner of the summerhouse and reappeared with a holdall in his hands. He threw it at me. I snatched it from the air.

"What's this?" I asked him.

"You said that you missed your old life, that you wanted to be Kiera Hudson again," he half-smiled and his jet-black eyes twinkled. "So I went and got you some of your stuff from your flat."

"It's still there?" I asked him, wondering if parts of my old life had been pushed too.

"Kind of," he said, lighting a cigarette, watching me unzip the bag.

"What's that mean?" I asked him.

"Your flat is four streets along now," he said. "At first I couldn't understand why your underwear drawer was full of thick, old woolly knickers and bras that the SAS would have been happy to use as parachutes. Then the old woman started whacking me with her walking stick."

"Old lady?" I laughed. "What old lady?"

"The old lady who lives in your flat, the flat that you used to live in before everything got pushed," he explained. "She caught me rifling through her knickers – I thought they were yours. Anyway she whacks me over the head and calls me kinky. I tried to tell her that I wasn't kinky and she said she was going to call the cops."

"So what did you do?" I said, my hand over my mouth as I tried to stifle a fit of the giggles.

"I ran, that's what I did," he snapped, unable to see the funny side of the story. "And don't you dare breathe a word of this to Isidor. I'm fed up already with him calling me Gabriel every five minutes."

"I promise," I said, unable to hide my laughter anymore.

"It's not funny," he barked. "I didn't have to go and get that stuff for you."

I looked in the bag and could see that it was full of my own clothes, underwear, perfumes, make-up. Just beneath a pile of T-shirts, I found a photograph of my father. I brushed the tips of my fingers over his face.

"I thought you might like that," Potter said softly, coming to kneel next to me on the floor. "There was a picture of your mother, but I didn't bring it. Apart from her ripping my heart out, I didn't think you would want…"

"The picture of my dad is enough," I whispered. "Thank you."

As if sensing the picture of my dad was upsetting me, Potter reached inside the bag and said, "And look what else I found."

"What?" I whispered unable to take my eyes from the picture of my dad.

"Your police badge," he said, waving it before me.

I placed the picture gently back into the bag and took my badge from Potter. *Constable Hudson* it read in silver letters on the front. "Why did you bring this back with you?" I asked him.

"You said that you missed being a copper," he said. "And besides, if you're going to start investigating stuff again, I thought it might come in handy. You never know."

"But I thought you said the whole Miss Marple thing was a waste of time," I said, looking at him.

"That's before I realised the Lycanthrope were back," he said. Then, taking my hands in his, he said, "Kiera we've got to find out what they are up to. And if they are still killing, somehow we've got to find a way of stopping them."

"Just like the old days, huh?" I said, staring down at my badge again.

"Me and you, Kiera," he whispered. "The old team back together."

"Kayla?" I asked him.

"Of course," Potter smiled. "It wouldn't be the same without her whingeing."

"Isidor?"

"Don't push your luck," he groaned. "He can stay here and look after the manor – you know, a bit like Alfred from the Batman comics."

"No Isidor, no team," I said, staring straight at him.

"Okay," he said, throwing his hands up into the air as if in surrender. "But I promise you, one more wisecrack from him about my name and…"

"Why did you go and get my stuff for me?" I cut over him.

"Why not?" he shrugged.

"Tell me the truth," I asked him.

"Because you wanted it and I couldn't bear to see you so unhappy, Kiera," he said. "You haven't been the same since you came back."

"Neither have you," I said.

"I know I haven't."

"Why not?"

"Because I didn't have a reason for being here – I didn't have a fight," he explained.

"And now that you've got the Lycanthrope to hunt, you feel happy?" I asked him.

"Isn't a fight just what you've been looking for, too?" he came back at me. "Isn't that what this whole setting yourself up as an investigator thing is all about? You're looking for trouble. Kiera, me and you are the same. We need a fight in our lives."

"Is that all you need?" I asked him.

"No," he whispered, bringing his face within inches of mine.

"What else then?"

"This," he said, ripping my shirt open with one quick swipe of his claws, and pushing me down onto the floor.

Chapter Thirteen

Kiera

For the first time since returning from the dead, we made love together. We took our time. It wasn't rushed or frantic like it had been in the caves, below the Fountain of Souls. And for the first time, there weren't those guilty thoughts which had plagued me for so long about Luke. He was now gone from my life and forgotten. Even my fears about those cracks that had appeared on my skin slipped to the back of my mind as I lay back on the floor of the summerhouse. Potter was unusually gentle, covering my face, neck, shoulders, breasts, and stomach with soft kisses. There was no music either, just the sound of the rain drumming against the summerhouse roof and the gentle rise and fall of our breathing.

"I love you, Kiera," he whispered against my cheek as he lowered himself onto me.

"I love you too," I smiled, running my hands through his untidy hair. I dug my fingernails into the small of his back and there was a sudden urge to completely let go, but I couldn't, just in case those cracks in my dead flesh appeared. So, closing my eyes, I arched my back slightly, as he gripped my wrists and pinned me to the floor. He pressed his mouth over mine and I could feel his fangs with the tip of my tongue. They felt sharp, and I gasped slightly as I felt the warm sensation of my own blood spill over my tongue. The coppery taste of it in the back of my throat felt sweet and my whole body shivered beneath him.

He felt me tremor and whispered, "You want the red stuff, don't you?"

With my arms and legs entwined around him, I murmured the word, "Yes."

Then, positioning his neck so it brushed over my lips, Potter said, "Well drink then, it's not as if you can kill me, Kiera."

I could smell him against me, but more than that, I could smell the blood beneath his skin. It made my head spin, and even though I didn't have a heart, I could feel a beating starting to build throughout my body. It started in my head, then to my chest, fingertips, and toes. As the beating grew faster and more intense, so did my desire to pierce his skin with my own fangs. But if I did, would those cracks in my flesh appear? Did it matter if they did? Did I really care anymore? All I wanted was to bite him - sink my teeth into him as he made love to me.

And as he moved gently over me, I could feel my claws growing from the tips of my fingers and I dragged them down the length of his back. He sighed and moved faster. I could feel the warm sensation of his blood beneath my claws and the smell was intoxicating. It filled the air like the sweetest of scents. The beating inside me got faster and I pulled him down on top of me, never wanting to let him go. It was like I wanted to be a part of him somehow. It was like our lovemaking wasn't enough – it didn't bring us close enough.

With my head spinning and feeling more alive than I'd had when I was living, and my skin feeling as if it was on fire, I lunged forwards and sank my teeth into his neck. His blood gushed into my mouth. I'd only ever been drunk once before and the sensation I now felt was similar to that. It was like feeling tipsy – the initial happy, giddy feeling you get before you have too much and start to feel ill.

As I sucked away at his neck, I could feel my wings spreading open beneath me and for one awful moment those pictures of me standing in front of the mirror in my room, cracked and broken-looking, swam before me. I opened my eyes and looked at my arms which were wrapped about Potter's shoulders. But instead of the cracks, my skin almost seemed to shine – glow. It was as if taking his blood was somehow revitalising me, like rubbing moisturiser into dry skin.

I closed my eyes again, the soft feel of my wings beneath me making it feel as if we were making love on a soft bed of feathers. Entwining his fingers with mine, Potter raised my arms above my head, and kissed my breasts, never stopping moving above me. A thin trickle of his blood ran from the corner of my mouth; seeing this, Potter licked it away with the tip of his tongue. Then, without warning, he buried his face into my neck and I felt his fangs pierce my flesh.

I cried out. It didn't hurt, not really. If it did, I doubted that I would have felt it anyway. My body felt as if it was on the brink of bursting with ecstasy and there was nothing that could have drowned out that feeling. It was like a madness had overtaken me and I would let him take as much of my blood as he wanted – needed. And when I started to feel lightheaded and that spinning feeling came back, I sank my teeth back into his neck and let his blood gush into my mouth.

It was then, as we made love on the floor, drinking from each other, I realised that we had become one and the feeling of pleasure was almost unbearable. Our lovemaking then took on an eagerness that was like a ravenous hunger until we both collapsed in each other's arms.

I rested my head against Potter's chest as he drew in breath. Just as my body had seemed to thump, so did his. I could hear the blood gushing through his veins. But I didn't want it now. The thirst for it – the lust for it – had gone. It was like I had been thirsty but now my thirst had been quenched.

"That was wrong," I whispered against him.

"Was it?" he said back. "I thought it was…"

"I don't mean it like that," I told him.

"What did you mean?" he asked, rolling onto his side and staring into my eyes. His eyes were black and I could read nothing in them.

"Making love with you is like nothing else," I said, breaking his gaze and running my fingertips across his hard, flat stomach. "But the blood thing – I promised myself that I wouldn't take the red stuff…that I would try and beat it."

"I don't think it's there to be broken," Potter said.

"What do you mean?"

"It's what we are…it's what you are," he whispered. "Taking blood now is as natural as breathing air. But I guess it's more important to us, as technically we're dead and we don't need air to survive. But we do need blood…"

"I don't need it," I cut over him, the fear of becoming addicted to the red stuff scaring me.

"Are you so sure?" Potter asked, cocking an eyebrow at me.

"What's that s'posed to mean?"

"The cracks, Kiera," he whispered, looking away from me.

I pushed away from him, and all of a sudden I felt angry and confused. How did he know about the cracks? Had he been spying on me? I didn't want anyone to see me like that. I looked like a monster – a freak. "How do you know?"

"I saw you..." he started.

"You've been spying on me," I hissed, feeling defensive. Nothing made me angrier than the thought of my privacy being invaded and I couldn't help but think of the time in the shower block back at the Police Station in Wasp Water. The thought of Jack Seth watching me had driven me half insane.

"Take it easy, tiger, I've shared a room with you, remember?" Potter said. "That was until you kicked me out."

"I didn't kick you out," I told him, looking away. "It was just..."

"You didn't want me to see the cracks," he said and moved closer towards me. "I saw you one morning. You had got up early but hadn't shut the bathroom door properly. I could hear you running a bath and I came to the door hoping that perhaps we could share the water, if you know what I mean?" and he half-smiled at me. "Anyway, I pushed the door open just a fraction and saw you standing in front of the mirror. Your wings were out and they looked beautiful, just like now," he said and brushed them with his fingers. "But it was as I stood and watched you that I saw the cracks in your flesh."

To know that he had seen them made me feel uncomfortable and I wrapped my arms around my chest; I felt less vulnerable like that. Sensing this, Potter pulled my arms free and wrapped his muscular arms around me. "What do you think those cracks are?" I asked him. "I look like an ancient statue. Grey and cold, cracked and weather-beaten. I look ugly."

"No one could ever accuse you of being ugly," he half-smiled again and kissed me gently on the forehead. "But I know that's why you've been distancing yourself from me."

"I was scared," I told him. "Scared of what those cracks might be and what might happen to me."

"So have you got it all figured out yet, Sherlock?"

"I think the red stuff, helps," I whispered, not wanting to admit that the stuff that I feared the most was going to be my saviour.

"How do you figure that?"

"I'd been scared of being with you," I started to explain. "Scared of making love to you. I know that when we do, it's hard not to change – you know, the Vampyrus side of me comes out and it's when that happens that the cracks appear."

"But it was different this time?" he asked me.

"Right," I told him. "But only because I drank your blood. It was like the cracks absorbed your blood somehow. Like a dried out sponge being held under a tap. I opened my eyes, and instead of my skin looking old and split, it was glowing - radiant."

"So this can be stopped?" he asked me, sounding more hopeful than I.

"But at what cost?" I asked him. "I don't want to spend the rest of eternity needing the red stuff. I don't want to hurt anyone."

"Who says that you have to hurt anyone?" He asked me.

"Something tells me that your blood won't always be enough," I told him. "Like any addiction, it grows and grows and you just need more and more."

"How do you mean?" he frowned.

"Take your cigarette habit," I started to explain. "Have you always smoked so much? You didn't start smoking sixty or seventy cigarettes a day like you do now. You started with just one or two, I bet. But soon that wasn't enough to satisfy your need. Soon you needed more and more. That's what an addiction is – you just want it – even when you know it's killing you – you just want more. Well I don't want to live my life like that, because there is only so much of your blood that I can have - and what then? I turn to humans and we all know what happens then..."

"Vampires," Potter said.

"Vampires," I nodded and looked away. "We can't ever go back to that or our deaths would have meant nothing."

"There's got to be an answer to everything that has happened, not only to us but the world since we came back," Potter said.

"And I intend to find it," I told him. "It feels like I'm being punished by the Elders for not making that decision back in The Hollows. It's like they are making me suffer."

"But all suffering has to end," Potter said. "It can't go on forever."

"But I guess it's *how* it ends that matters," I told him.

"So what's the plan?" he asked me, running his fingers through my hair.

"I don't believe we are the only ones who have been pushed, as you call it," I said, leaning in close to him again. "Kayla and Isidor have gone to place some adverts around the nearby towns to see if anyone comes forward."

Then, there was a crack of lightning from outside and the rain began to fall heavier against the roof and the side of the summerhouse. "We should get back to the manor, Kayla and Isidor might be back by now."

"Let's wait until the rain eases up," he said, pulling me close. The temperature inside the summerhouse had grown cold, and gooseflesh had covered my naked body. Potter wrapped his arms about me, his body felt warm as he held me against him.

Then, placing his face next to mine, he said, "Whatever happens, Kiera, we'll find a way through this."

I closed my eyes and kissed him, those intense feelings that I had for him started to wash over me. "We should be getting back," I whispered, half of me knowing that Kayla and Isidor would be waiting for me but the other half wanting Potter again.

"Let's just stay a while longer," he smiled, easing me back onto the floor of the summerhouse.

"Until the rain stops," I whispered, hearing it lash against the window to my right. And as Potter ran his hand up the inside of my leg, I turned my head slightly to look at the rain streaking down the window pane. It was then that I screamed.

Chapter Fourteen

Kiera

The statue stared through the window. Even though it had no facial features, I knew that it was watching us. Lightning split the night sky open in a blue shock of light, illuminating the blank face that peered in through the window at us.

"What's wrong?" Potter asked me.

"Look at the window," I gasped, gathering up my clothes and covering myself with them.

"What's wrong with the window?" Potter asked getting up and striding to the window buck naked.

"That statue is watching us," I told him, throwing on my shirt and pulling on my jeans.

"What statue?"

"The one from outside," I said, wedging my feet into my boots and going to the window.

"There isn't any statue at the window," he said, cupping his hands around his eyes and peering out into the dark.

"It was there, I'm telling you," I breathed, standing next to him.

"Well it's not there now," he sighed, stepping back from the window and staring at me. He stood before me naked, his chest and muscles looking taught beneath his pale flesh.

I glanced back at the window as another streak of lightning cut the night in two. The sky lit up in a flash of blue and white and I could see that the statue was no longer at the window.

"It was there," I insisted.

"Are you sure it wasn't your imagination?" he asked, snaking his arm around my waist.

"Give me a break," I groaned. "I know what I saw. Put your clothes on, we should be heading back to the manor."

Without saying another word, Potter picked up his trousers and boots from where they lay strewn across the floor. As he put them on, I went to the door. I opened it a fraction and peered into the dark. The rain came down hard and beat off the wooden steps that led away from the summerhouse. The sky fizzed with electricity again, washing the area in light. Then, I saw it. The statue wasn't at the window, but I knew that it had been. Although it was back on the grass, it was no longer facing the summerhouse. It had turned, as if running away. I ran down the wooden steps and out into the rain. The rain was so heavy that within seconds I was soaked through and it ran done my hair and face. I knocked the water from my eyes and stood before the statue.

"Why were you watching us?" I demanded.

The statue didn't say anything. It didn't move. It just stood solid and heavy-looking in the rain. But it had just turned its back to the summerhouse. The way its arms and legs were now positioned, it looked as it had been in the act of running away at great speed when it had become frozen again.

"What's going on here?" Potter suddenly asked from beside me.

"I don't know," I whispered, unable to take my eyes from the statue of the girl. Then, in another bolt of lightning, something glistened around the statue's neck. It was Murphy's crucifix. It was no longer fastened in the girl's hand.

"Do you see it?" I whispered, reaching for the cross.

"See what?" Potter hissed.

"Murphy's cross," I said back, taking it from over the girl's head.

"Maybe you should leave it," Potter said.

"Why?" I asked him, but then I saw something that told me that perhaps he was right. It could have been just the rain, or just my imagination, but as I lifted the cross away, tears seemed to roll from the part of the statue's face where its eyes should have been.

With the tip of one finger, Potter wiped away what looked like tears and held his finger up. "Put the cross back," he whispered over the distant rumble of thunder. "They ain't tears – they're drops of blood."

"The statue's bleeding?" I asked him, quickly replacing the crucifix. "But that's impossible, right?"

Then looking at me, Potter said, "Yeah and we're dead. Like I keep trying to tell you, Kiera, this isn't the world that we left – everything has been pushed."

We made our way back to the manor in silence. The only sound was the rain slicing through the treetops overhead. Potter carried the holdall with my belongings. I had tucked my police badge into the back pocket of my jeans. I didn't know if it would be of any use in the future, but I was glad I had it back all the same.

Before we had left the summerhouse, I had asked Potter not to say anything to Kayla or Isidor about the statue. He had asked me why not, and I told him that things were already complicated enough without throwing the wandering statue into the mix. But at the sight of the blood weeping from the statue, I couldn't help but make a connection from somewhere deep inside of me. I had seen myself almost turned to stone as I had stood before my mirror, my body covered in cracks, just like the statue that now had Murphy's cross. Whoever that girl was – had been – perhaps she had once been like me? Maybe that girl had started to see cracks in her flesh. Maybe she had been stronger than me and resisted the red stuff and she had completely turned to stone. But not completely, because it was like when she wasn't being watched, she moved somehow.

As we stepped from between the trees and onto the rain-soaked lawn that lay before the manor, I could see by the lights burning dimly in the windows that Kayla and Isidor had returned. The electricity worked in the part of the huge house that we occupied, but there was still no light in the 'forbidden wing' as Mrs. Payne had liked to call it.

Potter pushed open the giant front door and we had barely had the chance to shake the rain from our wet clothes when Kayla rushed into the hallway. She was excited and skipped from foot to foot as she told us about what she and Isidor had seen and heard in the little town of Wood Hill.

Isidor joined her, and passing Potter and me a fresh towel each, I rubbed my damp hair with it. While Potter dried his chest and forearms, Isidor told us about the owner of the shop.

"He said that they had taken their children," Isidor explained.

"Taken them where?" I asked him.

"They've killed them already," Potter cut in. "I told you they wouldn't change. The Lycanthrope are murdering scum."

"They're not called Lycanthrope any longer," Isidor said, looking at the both of us.

"What are they called then?" Potter growled. "You're not the only one who has left the grounds of the manor. I've seen the wolves too."

"They look like wolves," Kayla said, "and just like the Lycanthrope did, they can look like humans and then change into wolves. But this time around, they are different."

"Different?" I quizzed. "How?"

"Come and have a look at what Isidor has found on the Web," Kayla said, leading us into the large kitchen.

We followed her, and sitting before the laptop that was on the table, Isidor started bringing up pages of information. With Potter beside me, we peered over his shoulder and looked at the screen.

"See," Isidor said, pointing at the laptop, "the werewolves aren't called Lycanthrope in this version of reality. They're called 'Skin-walkers.'"

"Skin-walkers?" Potter spat, lighting a cigarette. "What the fuck are Skin-walkers?"

"Shape-shifters," Kayla cut in, not trying to impress, but more out of fear.

"See here," Isidor said, pointing at the screen again. "They are trapped permanently as wolves – that was their curse."

"They were captured," I whispered to myself as I remembered how Nik had been trapped as a wolf.

"Captured?" Potter quizzed me.

"They can't change from wolf back into human form," Isidor said on my behalf.

"So how do we defeat them?" I asked, for the first time realising the true nature of our enemy.

"Not easily," Kayla answered.

"It will be piss-easy. I've killed plenty of wolves in my time," Potter said, blowing a cloud of blue smoke into the air.

"Don't be so sure," Isidor said, looking back over his shoulder at Potter. "These Skin-walkers have the power to steal the body of any person. So how do you know if you're killing a Skin-walker or an innocent human?"

"Bullshit," Potter snapped. "How do you steal another person's skin? There'd be blood, piss, and snot everywhere. These Skin-walkers would stick out like sore thumbs."

"They don't actually steal the skin and wear it like a coat, silly," Kayla giggled. "By looking into your eyes, they can absorb themselves into you. It's like they take you over – control you and your soul."

"Just like the Lycanthrope could stare into your soul and control you," I said, thinking of how Jack Seth had tried to control my mind with those depraved images of him taking me.

"But they do have a couple of weaknesses," Kayla explained.

"Like what?" Potter snapped, as if eager to know so he could start hunting these creatures.

"They don't like the sunlight very much," Isidor said. "They much prefer the night. And secondly, when they are in human form, they only have the strength of a human."

"So what do they hunt?" I asked Isidor, my stomach tightening as the enormity of what they had discovered became clear.

"Just like the Lycanthrope, they love to hunt children," Isidor said, his already-pale face turning grey.

"Different name, but the same scum," Potter said.

"But what I don't understand," I said, "is if all this information is readily available on the internet, why don't the humans stop them?"

Kayla pulled up a chair alongside me and sat down. "The guy in the store back in that creepy town told us that the humans and wolves – these Skin-walkers – had signed some kinda treaty over two hundred years ago."

"And guess where that treaty was signed?" Isidor quizzed, looking at Potter then at me.

"Where?" I breathed.

"Wasp Water," Isidor said.

"You're shitting me!" Potter exclaimed, cigarette dangling from the corner of his mouth.

"Nope," Isidor said, turning back to face the laptop. "I looked it up and basically the humans fought with the Skin-walkers for as long as is recorded. But a truce was made two hundred years ago between them. The Skin-walkers got tired of being hunted and the humans grew tired of having their children snatched and slaughtered in the dead of night. It seemed that no side could win."

"So what was this treaty that both sides were happy with?" I asked.

"That every five years, the Skin-walkers would be free to take the children from one village of their choice," Kayla explained. "If the parents resisted, then they too would be slaughtered."

"So they just arrive in the village, round up all of the children and kill them?" I gasped in disbelief.

"Not exactly," Kayla said. "There were some rules negotiated during the treaty. The wolves couldn't take children under the age of thirteen or over the age of eighteen. They could pick one village at random, but they couldn't kill the children. There were certain conditions."

"What conditions?" Potter snapped.

"The children would be housed at the nearest school," Isidor said. "Held prisoner, I guess. And here they would be matched."

"Matched?" I asked.

"Because the Skin-walkers are captured as wolves and unable to shape-shift back into human form, they are matched with human children," Isidor said.

"But why?" I asked him.

"Because once the wolves grow from yearlings into juveniles they are the same age as teenage humans," Kayla explained. "So each juvenile wolf that is ready to leave their pack comes to the school and seeks a match – a human child that they can steal the skin from – absorb themselves into. Any human teenagers who aren't matched are set free."

"And what about the ones who aren't freed?" I asked her.

"The wolf spends the rest of its life living inside of them – inside their skin," Kayla said.

"So why every five years?" Potter asked, grinding out his cigarette end on the stone kitchen floor.

"That is the time that it can take a yearling Skin-walker to reach the juvenile stage," Kayla continued, her eyes growing wide. "This is the treaty that the Wolf Man negotiated."

"Who is this Wolf Man?" I asked her.

"I've found a picture of a Wolf Man on the web," Isidor said, clicking on a new page on the screen before him. "I think this could be him. Scary, isn't he?"

Potter leaned forward and stared at the screen, then said, "Are you taking the fucking piss?"

"No, why?" Isidor said staring blankly back at Potter.

"That's Michael Jackson for crying out loud," Potter snapped, his cigarette almost falling from the corner of his mouth. "That's him dressed up in the Thriller video."

"Is it?" Isidor asked, squinting at the screen. "It says he is the Wolf Man."

"Do you think this Wolf Man would run around in a red and yellow jacket, blue jeans, and white socks while he grips his crotch and moonwalks?" Potter asked in disbelief. "This Wolf Man is stealing children's souls, not running around the place in a sequined glove for Christ's sake!"

"He looks pretty scary to me," Isidor said studying the picture that he had found on the web.

Then, looking at Kayla and me, Potter gasped, "Is it just me or is the kid taking the piss?"

"Okay, keep your wings on, Gabby," Isidor shot back. "So I made a mistake, how was I s'posed to know that wasn't the Wolf Man..."

"And stop calling me Gabby," Potter barked at him. "My name's not Gabriela, Gabriel or anything else, it's Potter..."

"But the Elder said your new name was..." Isidor started.

76

"I couldn't give a monkey's toss what the Elders said!" Potter barked, the veins on his neck bulging through his skin.

"Can we just stop this bickering?" I snapped at the both of them. "This isn't helping."

"Well, he winds me up," Potter shot back. "Here we are trying to figure out what the fuck has happened since coming back from the dead and you've got numb-nuts over here Googling the greatest hits of Michael Jackson..."

"It's called Toogling now," Kayla cut in.

"Whatever," Potter hissed.

"Look," I said, taking a deep breath. "So Isidor made a mistake, it's no big deal. He found out a whole bunch of other stuff. But what we really need to know is, who is this Wolf Man?"

"That's the problem, Kiera, no one knows," Kayla said back. "He is believed to be a human. He negotiated the treaty on behalf of the Skin-walkers and in return, they cast a spell that has given him unnaturally long life. He has been around for over two hundred years. The treaty says that if his identity is ever revealed then the uneasy truce is over and the humans win. The Skin-walkers have to return to their caves beneath the Fountain of Souls and leave the humans and their children in peace."

"So I guess we try and find this Wolf Man," Potter said. "Let's be honest, it shouldn't be that hard, we'll spot his sparkling glove a mile off."

Ignoring him, I looked at Isidor and Kayla and said, "So do we know where the children of Wood Hill are being held?"

"In a remote boarding school on the outskirts of the town," Isidor said, bringing up another page on the screen before him. "But I bet you'll never guess what this school is called?"

Then, with a sense of dread falling over me as I remembered my dream of the girl falling from the sky and being chased to that big building, I looked at Isidor and whispered, "Ravenwood."

"How did you know that?" Kayla asked me in shock.

"I had a dream about it," I told her.

"Ravenwood?" Potter cut in. "What's that old fart got to do with this?"

"I don't know," I said back, wondering if Doctor Ravenwood were still alive in this reality.

"What sort of a screwed up world have we come back to?" Potter said, lighting another cigarette. "And I thought things were bad when the Lycanthrope were out on their killing sprees."

"Why do the authorities stand by and do nothing?" I said, feeling numb at what Kayla and Isidor had discovered.

"Like Potter said," Kayla almost seemed to whisper to herself, "we've come back to a different world than the one we knew. And somehow, I think by coming back, we are to blame."

But I knew in my heart that it was my fault. "I'm to blame," I told them.

"How do you figure that?" Isidor asked me.

"If I'd made my choice back in The Hollows like I was meant to, then none of this would have happened," I said, lowering my head in shame.

"You don't know that," Kayla said, placing a hand gently on my shoulder.

"She's right," Isidor said. "Who knows what changes would have happened if you had chosen the Vampyrus over the humans or the other way around. However, had you chosen there would have still been changes to the world. You were in an impossible situation."

"The Elders said that I would be cursed for failing to make a choice," I told them, unable to look in their eyes. "They weren't kidding, were they?"

"It's the Elders who have done this, not you, Kiera," Potter said.

"But it's me who has to put it right," I said, still unable to look at them.

"Not just you," Kayla said, gently squeezing my shoulder. "We're all a part of this. We've all come back. Like you said, Kiera, we've come back for a reason."

"We just need to find out what that reason is," Isidor said softly.

"I think that's obvious, don't you?" Potter snapped at him.

"Okay, keep your halo on," Isidor bit back. "So what is the reason?"

"Like the guy in the shop said," Potter hissed. "We push back. And we push hard."

"But where do we start?" Kayla asked him.

"How about with that email?" he said, pointing at the laptop screen.

The three of us turned our heads to see that an email had appeared in my inbox. The subject line read:

I've been pushed!

Chapter Fifteen

Kiera

Within an hour of receiving the email, the sender was sitting across from me in the consulting room that I had prepared earlier that day. Elizabeth Clarke was in her early twenties and very pretty, something that Isidor had obviously noticed. He sat to the side of me, his mouth open. Elizabeth had blond hair that she had piled on top of her head in a loose-fitting bun. Little wisps of hair lay against her perfectly formed cheekbones. Her green eyes twinkled and her full lips glowed with a faint shade of pink lipstick. She was smartly dressed in a white blouse and light blue pencil skirt and jacket.

"Are you any good?" she asked me.

"At what?" I smiled back, but I knew what she meant. I had advertised my services as a private investigator and she wanted to know if she was going to be wasting her money or not.

She glanced at Potter who slouched against the wall in the corner, lost in a cloud of cigarette smoke, then at Isidor and Kayla who sat on either side of me. "Perhaps I've wasted my time," she said, getting up from her seat.

"You're not married, Miss Clarke," I started, and winked at Kayla. God, this was so easy but it felt so damn good to be back at doing what I enjoyed the most. "However, you are dating someone and he hasn't shaved for at least two days. You're a school teacher by profession. You were raised in the town of Wood Hill but left some years ago and haven't been back for some time. You live in a city that is some distance away. Your journey today was long enough for you to need to stop at a petrol station and refill your car. You've come about a family matter. Not a friend. A member of your family..."

"Okay, you've made your point," Elizabeth said, sitting back down. "How did you know all that stuff about me – have you researched me in some way?"

"All I knew was from what you said in your email, that you had been pushed and that your name was Elizabeth," I assured her.

"So how do you know then?" she asked me. "Are you psychic?"

"No," I smiled, shaking my head.

"She sees things," Isidor added.

"So you are a psychic then," Elizabeth said. "I have no need for one of those."

"You're not married because you don't wear a wedding ring," I smiled. "That was the easy part. You haven't removed one or forgotten to put it on as there is no red mark left on your finger. You are, however, in a relationship with a man who either hasn't shaved for a few days or has a very short beard. He has travelled with you and is probably waiting for you back at your motel."

"How can you be so sure about that?" Elizabeth asked me, looking startled.

With my fingertip, I tapped my cheek and said, "Miss Clarke, your cheeks have a rather healthy glow, as does your chin. That might be due to exceptionally good health, but the redness to the chin – no that looks more like a rash of some kind – like you've been kissing a man recently who hasn't shaved. He has travelled with you today as you've come a long distance and the rash would have faded by now. The spattering of chalk dust on your right sleeve tells me that you have been writing recently on a chalkboard, which suggests that you are a teacher of some kind. The raised pimple of flesh on the middle finger of your right hand tells me that you like to write a lot – more than just the occasional note or two, so I'm guessing your mark a lot of homework."

"And how do you know that I've travelled a long distance today…"

Before she had the chance to finish her question, I said, "By the fact that you needed to refill your car with petrol - you've splashed some on your skirt. You would have only come such a long distance if it was a matter of urgency. For instance, a problem with a family member. I'm guessing by the fact that you are staying in a motel that it is a brother or sister who is working in this area. If it had been a parent, you would be staying with them."

"How can you be so sure that I'm staying at a motel?" Elizabeth asked.

"Because no one would have left their own home on such a wet night dressed like you are now," I smiled at her. "When you set off today, you had no idea that the weather would be so bad once you got here and you hadn't packed adequate clothing."

"Very good," Elizabeth said staring at me.

"Good?" Kayla gasped, "That was awesome!"

Not wanting to waste any more time, I looked at Elizabeth. "You said in your email that you've been pushed. Please explain what you mean by that?"

With the back of her hand, Elizabeth knocked away one of the loose strands of hair and said, "I saw your advert in the shop window and it reminded me of something my sister used to say."

"Your sister?" I asked her. "And where is your sister now?"

"What makes you think that she has gone somewhere?" Elizabeth shot back.

"You spoke of her in the past tense," I smiled. "What was her name?"

"Emily," Elizabeth said, taking a picture from her pocket and sliding it across the table towards me.

I picked it up, glanced at the photo and said, "An identical twin?"

"Yes," she nodded. "We were identical in more ways than just our looks. Emily, like me, was a teacher. I've taught now for the past two years at a school in Linden."

"Don't you mean Lond…" Isidor started and I kicked him under the table.

"Please continue, Miss Clarke," I smiled at her.

"Emily decided against a career in Linden and decided to teach closer to where we were raised in the town of Wood Hill," Elizabeth continued. "She was so happy when she got herself a position at Ravenwood's, a nearby private school. The pay was good and she seemed very happy for a time."

"So what changed all of that?" I asked her, my interest growing in the case on hearing that Elizabeth's sister had been working at Ravenwood School.

"The wolves came," Elizabeth said. "As you well know, we all spend most of our teenage years fearing that the wolves would come to our town to match, but obviously like yourselves, we were lucky and the wolves didn't choose our home town while we grew up. So we escaped the matching. Like everyone else, we heard the stories and the rumours about the schools and the children where the wolves had chosen. That's one of the reasons that both Emily and I decided to be teachers, we wanted to try and help those children should the wolves ever arrive at the schools where we taught. I think somewhere deep inside the both of us, we both prayed that would never happen. As you know, it has been more than five years since the wolves came to match and this time around they chose the school where Emily taught. We have always been close even though we have lived apart over the last few years," Elizabeth continued, and I could see tears standing in her eyes as she recalled her sister. "Within days of the wolves arriving at Ravenwood School, the teachers there started to leave."

"Why?" I asked, curious to know what had taken place there.

"The wolves arrived, but you must understand that they don't look like wolves, they look just like us humans," she explained. "They wear the skins of the children that they matched with years ago. They erected searchlights and towers and covered the tops of the walls with razor wire. Emily called me one night and said that Ravenwood was now more like a prison than a school. She told me that some of the parents had tried to break into the school to free their children, they wanted the treaty that had been agreed to hundreds of years ago ripped up."

"What happened to these parents?" Potter asked, stepping from the corner of the room.

"Emily didn't say," she answered him. "I remember one night that she was very upset and I could tell that she had been crying. A pack of juvenile wolves had arrived wanting to be matched. Emily had been close to all of her students but she had a couple of favourites. Both of these had been chosen for matching and she said that they changed – they were no longer the children that she had once taught. Within days they had left and she never saw them again, nor did their parents."

"How had they changed?" Kayla asked.

"Emily didn't say," Elizabeth said, and I watched as a tear spilled from the corner of her eye and rolled down her cheek. "But I knew she was, at times, terrified of what was happening at Ravenwood. Then, she started ringing me and saying that she had started to be plagued by vivid dreams. In these dreams she saw a different world. At first I thought it was just Emily wishing that things could be different, but she became convinced that the world as we know it had been…pushed…somehow. That's how she described it, Miss Hudson, just like you did in your advert. Emily started to believe that the world had been pushed off course. She told me that the world had once been different. Where there weren't any wolves – Skin-walkers. She described a world not too dissimilar to the one we know, but it was a world where children weren't matched."

"Where is Emily now?" I asked her, wishing that I could speak with her to discover what else she knew.

"She's vanished," Elizabeth said, trying to fight off a stream of tears that were desperate to roll down the length of her face.

"Vanished how?" Isidor gently asked her while handing her a piece of tissue.

"Thank you," she said, mopping away her tears. "I believe she has been murdered."

"What makes you think that?" Potter cut in.

"Emily told me that the Headmaster of the school just left or disappeared," Elizabeth explained. "A wolf by the name of McCain took his place. He was a harsh man and he replaced the teachers with people who wore hoods and gowns. Emily told me that you couldn't see their faces. These new teachers, if that's what they were, were cruel to the children. Emily said that on several occasions their cruelness was something close to brutal. She went to McCain and objected at what she had witnessed. McCain told her that if she didn't like how the school was being run, she was free to leave. But Emily couldn't – she wanted to stay and protect the children, and besides, like most of the other teachers had, she lived on the school grounds, it was her home.

"Then, one night she called me to say that she had woken the night before to find McCain standing in her room, staring down at her while she slept. She asked him what he wanted and what he was doing in her room in the middle of the night, but he left without giving an explanation. Emily said she was now in fear for her own safety and I begged her to leave. But she told me how she had bought herself one of those tiny video cameras. She explained that she was going to try and capture on film some of the cruelty that the children endured at Ravenwood School and then send it to the press. She was also going to hide the camera in her room at night to see what it was that McCain was doing in there while she slept. Emily feared that he had perhaps been into her room before but she hadn't woken."

"And did she capture anything on film?" I asked her, now gripped by the story.

"I don't know," Elizabeth said, that red rash on her cheeks now gone. "I haven't heard from Emily since that last phone call. I've tried ringing her mobile, I've sent emails, but have heard nothing from my sister. I've tried to contact McCain but he refuses to return my calls. So today, unable to continue with my life until I find out what has happened to my sister, my boyfriend, Harry and I drove the long distance to Wood Hill to visit Ravenwood School. We didn't get any further than the main gates, which are locked with chains and padlocks. Emily was not exaggerating when she said that Ravenwood had become something close to a prison.

"Eventually, McCain came down to the gates and told me to go away before he called the police. But I could see in his eyes that he had murdered Emily," Elizabeth said.

"How can you be so sure?" I asked her.

"Because when he saw me standing at the gates, he looked as if he had seen a ghost," she said. "He hadn't known that Emily had an identical twin. For a moment, he thought I was her."

"What did he say?" I asked her.

"After realising his mistake, McCain told us that Emily had left the school some weeks ago, but I knew that was a lie because I'd only spoken to her a few days before," Elizabeth said. "Knowing that McCain would never tell me the truth, Harry and I headed back into town and paid a visit to the local police station. I spoke to an officer there by the name of Banner, but he didn't seem interested. It took me over half an hour to get him to agree to file a missing persons report. So, feeling as if I had wasted my time and was still no nearer to the truth, we decided to stay in town, but we soon realised that the place was like, really weird."

"I know what you mean," Kayla added. "Isidor and I have been there."

"We decided to stay out of town in a motel," Elizabeth continued. "And it was as we made our way back through town to our car, that I saw your advert in the shop window and that word 'pushed' made me think of what Emily had said to me. Do you think you can help?"

Not wanting to give away how much I knew about the world being pushed, I looked across the table at Elizabeth and said, "I think it would be best if you returned straight to Lon...Linden. You can be of little to no help here. And just in case you are wrong about McCain, surely it would be better if you were at home, where your sister knows that she can find you. I will make some enquires at the school and with the local police. Please can you give me your sister's full name, date of birth, bank details, mobile phone number and car index?"

"Why?" Elizabeth asked me.

"It may help with my enquiries."

"Do you think you might be able to discover what happened to my sister?" Elizabeth said, writing down the information that I had asked for.

"I don't know the answer to that question," I said softly.

"But you have my guarantee that I will do my very best to discover the truth for you. But it does seem like a most desperate case where your sister is concerned and it would be wrong of me to give you false hope."

"It's not hope that I'm looking for," Elizabeth said. "It's the truth that I seek."

"Then go back to Linden tonight and I shall be in contact with you as soon as I have some news," I tried to assure her.

Elizabeth stood up and went to the door. Isidor followed her as if to show her out. But at the door, she turned to look back at me.

"Pushed," she said. "You know what my sister was talking about don't you, Kiera Hudson?"

I looked straight back at her, and with half a smile I said, "That's what we do, Miss Clarke. We push back where others can't. Goodbye."

Chapter Sixteen

Kiera

"I'll do it," Kayla said as soon as Elizabeth had left the room.

"Do what?" I asked her.

"Go into Ravenwood School," she said, looking at me straight in the eye. "That's what you want, isn't it?"

"Out of the question," I said, getting up and leaving the room.

"How else are we gonna find out what's happening in there?" she called out, running down the corridor after me.

I reached the great hall as Isidor was closing the door behind our visitor. "Have a word with your sister," I said to him as I made my way back to the kitchen.

"Why, what's she done?" Isidor muttered, sounding lost.

"She thinks she's one of Charlie's Angels," Potter snipped as he followed close behind me.

"I don't think I'm a Charlie's Angel!" Kayla shouted as she stormed into the kitchen.

"You're not doing it," I told her flatly.

"Why not?" she asked, and I could hear frustration simmering just beneath the surface.

"Who's this Charlie dude?" Isidor asked as he wandered into the kitchen.

Potter turned on him and said, "At first I thought the whole dumb thing was just an act, but now I'm beginning to wonder if you're not just a bit thick."

"All I asked was..." Isidor started.

"Whatever," Potter growled, sitting on the corner of the kitchen table where he lit another cigarette. "I don't want to hear it."

"Your sister thinks it would be a good idea if she went undercover into Ravenwood School," I explained to Isidor, feeling a little sorry for him.

He stood by the kitchen door and scratched his tuft of a beard. "That's, like, a really bad idea Kayla," Isidor said.

"Why is it?" she snapped at him, and he almost seemed to flinch backwards. "I'm not a kid anymore and I wish you would stop treating me like one."

"No one is treating you like a kid," I tried to assure her. "It's just that..."

"It's too dangerous," she said, spraying mock laughter. "After everything that we've been through together, everything that I've seen and done and you still don't trust me."

"Steady on," Potter cut in. "This has nothing to do with trust."

"And who asked you, Potter?" Kayla ripped back. "You don't really care about me. I asked you the other day to lend me the money to buy an iPod and you told me to fuck off, so stop pretending that you care."

"What's that got to do with anything?" Potter snapped, blowing smoke through his nostrils. "It's not up to me to provide you with all the must-have gadgets. I'm not your father."

"So stop trying to act like one!" Kayla roared at him. "When my real father died you told me I had to toughen up, remember? You said there was no place for booing and wooing and the only way to defeat the enemy was by being strong and hitting back."

"Did I really say that?" Potter asked me.

"Yes," I nodded, cringing at the thought of how he had broken the news of the death of her father.

"See, I'm not a jerk like so many people believe," he said with a serious look on his face. "I gave you some good advice back there."

"That wasn't good advice," Isidor said in disbelief. "That was cruel. And you said I looked like Shaggy-Doo. I looked him up on the internet and everything. I don't look nothing like a Great Dane!"

"I wasn't talking about the fucking dog!" Potter groaned. "Tell me something, Isidor, have you never watched T.V.?"

"I read," Isidor told him proudly. "I don't watch T.V. I like to use my imagination."

"Don't we know it," Potter grumbled.

"Look, can we please stop talking about Scooby-Doo and God knows what else?" I gasped in disbelief. "It's like living with a bunch of kids."

"He started it," Potter said, pointing at Isidor.

"No, I did not," Isidor shot back. "You said I looked like a cartoon dog."

"Yeah and you keep calling me Gabriela," Potter barked, climbing from the table.

"Gabriel," Isidor said, stepping closer to Potter. "Besides it wasn't me who called you that, it was those Elders and…"

"Please!" I screamed, slamming my fists down onto the table. "Enough already! I can't take any more."

The room fell into silence. It was so quiet that if we'd had hearts we would've been able to hear them beating. I drew a deep breath. Then, turning to look at Kayla, I said, "If you really want to do this, I won't hold you back."

"You really mean that, Kiera?" Kayla asked, her eyes wide. "What changed your mind?"

"You're right," I told her. Then, looking at Potter, I added, "and however much it pains me to say this, Potter was right too. Sometimes it doesn't do any good wallowing in self-pity. Sometimes you have to take the fight to the enemy."

"It sounds like suicide to me," Isidor said.

"Perhaps you should go then," Potter mumbled and I shot an angry look at him.

Then, turning to look at Kayla, Potter said, "Are you sure about this? You've got nothing to prove to any of us. I know how tough you can be and I'd be happy to stand shoulder to shoulder with you in any fight."

"Thanks," she half-smiled. "I know I don't have to go into Ravenwood School, but how else are we going to find out what's happened to Emily Clarke? I mean, what's the worst that can happen? I'm dead already."

"You can still be destroyed," Isidor said, stepping towards his sister and wrapping his arm about her shoulder. "If one of those wolves were to cut off your head, or…what if one of them tried to match with you?"

"Yeah, thanks for your input, Shakespeare," Potter said. "Why don't you go bury your head in a book?"

"No, Isidor is right," I said. "What if one of those wolves tries to match with Kayla – what would happen then?"

"Let's just hope that they don't like the look of me," Kayla half joked.

I didn't want to dwell on the danger that Kayla was putting herself in – the danger we were all placing her in, so I said, "You've got a week in there - max. No more. And one whiff of danger and you fly straight out of there."

"I promise," Kayla said, and I could see the excitement burning in her eyes at the thought of the adventure and mystery that lay ahead of her.

"And if we sense for one moment that you are in danger, we are coming in after you," Potter told her.

"How are we going to know if she's in danger?" Isidor quizzed. "We won't be in contact with her. It's not like she can pop home one evening or give us a call."

Potter reached into his back jeans pocket and pulled something from it. "Kayla can keep in contact with this," he said, throwing whatever it was that he had fished from his pocket across the room at her.

Kayla snatched it from the air and her face lit up. "It's an iPod!" she beamed.

"I got it for you when I went over the wall a few days ago," Potter said. Then swallowing hard, as if what he was about to say was going to choke him somehow, he said, "I'm sorry for telling you to fuck off the other week when you asked me to lend you the money. I was just feeling a bit cranky that day. I didn't mean anything by it."

With a smile spread across her face, Kayla came around the table and threw her arms around Potter. "Thank you," she said.

I could see that Potter didn't know whether or not to hug her back, as his arms hung uncomfortably at his sides. "Yeah, yeah, that's okay. Just remember, I'm not your dad. That thing cost me nearly three hundred pounds, so you can pay me the money back if and when you ever get a job," he said, then winked at me over her shoulder.

Kayla let go of Potter and looked down at the iPod.

"How is Kayla going to keep in contact with that?" Isidor asked.

Before Potter had a chance of saying anything back to Isidor, I said, "Kayla will be able to send emails to my iPod and we can Skype. That way we can talk and see each other." Seeing the look of concern on Isidor's face for his sister, I added, "You'll be able to see and chat to Kayla too."

"Good," he smiled; although I could see that he was still scared for her.

"So what's the plan?" Kayla asked. "How do I get inside the school? Shall I fly over the wall?"

"No," Potter said shaking his head. "They might wonder where you suddenly appeared from. They must keep a register – something like that. We need a good cover story."

"My parents are both dead, right?" Kayla cut in. "So how about, I've been sent here to live with my Uncle Potter. But my uncle can't be bothered with having some spoilt teenager hanging around the place, so he packs me off to the local boarding school?"

"It sounds okay, I guess," I said thoughtfully. "Do you think this McCain will buy it?"

"Why not?" Potter said. "It doesn't sound like this McCain is the sort of guy to turn a kid away. He needs as many as he can get, remember?"

"When shall I go in?" Kayla asked, refusing to let go of the iPod that Potter had bought for her.

"I'll call McCain tomorrow," Potter said thoughtfully. Then, looking at Kayla, he added, "Don't just stand there, go and pack a bag."

Without saying another word, Kayla left the kitchen. Isidor followed her, but on reaching the door, he looked back at the both of us and said, "You better be right about this."

Before I'd had the chance to say anything, he had gone. I turned to Potter to see him light another cigarette. "That was a really nice thing that you did," I said to him.

"Oh yeah, and what was that?" he asked me.

"Buying that iPod for Kayla," I said, moving across the kitchen towards him, needing a hug.

"It was nothing," he shrugged, taking me in his arms.

"It wasn't nothing to her," I told him. "I saw that look of delight on her face. You made her really happy."

Smiling down at me he said, "Fancy making me really happy?"

"And how might I do that?" I smiled back.

"By letting me share your bed tonight, sweetcheeks," he said. "It gets lonely in the gatehouse."

As I led him to my bedroom, I looked at him and said, "So where did you get the cash to be able to afford that iPod?"

"You know that little tin that you have hidden on the shelf in the kitchen back in your flat?" he said.

"Yeah, the tin with my savings in..." Realising where he had got the money, I pushed him hard in the chest. "You are so naughty..."

But before I'd the chance to finish what I was going to say, Potter was leaning into me. "You love it when I'm naughty," he whispered in my ear. Then, throwing open my bedroom door, he pushed me down onto the bed.

The next morning, as planned, Potter found the number of Ravenwood School on the Web and called McCain. Potter explained that Kayla's parents had recently been killed in a boating accident and she had been left in his charge. He said that his niece was fairly wayward and he was too busy and lacked the patience to deal with her. As Potter had suspected, McCain was all too willing to take Kayla into his care. He even waived the school fees. McCain informed Potter that he would send a car to collect Kayla within the hour.

I couldn't help but feel a lump in my throat as Kayla appeared at the foot of the stairs that led into the great hall. In her hand she clutched a small case.

"Are you sure about this?" I asked, giving her a hug.

"I'm sure," she said.

"Remember what we've all agreed. You make contact every morning and every night. If we don't hear from you, then we're coming in to find you," I told her.

"I'll keep in contact," she assured me with a smile.

"We'll be close," I said. "We're going to stay at a nearby farmhouse that Isidor has found on the internet. We'll be renting it for a week, so find out what you can and fast."

"I know what to do," Kayla said.

"Got the iPod?" Potter asked her.

"You bet."

I let go of Kayla and she went to Isidor who stood by the door. "I'll miss you," she told him.

"I'll miss you more," he said, gripping her tightly in his arms. I couldn't help but notice the look of sadness that had come over his face.

"I better go," Kayla told him, and I could sense that if she didn't go now, she never would.

Isidor let go of her, and we all watched as she stepped out into the rain. Kayla pulled the collar of her coat up around her throat. She looked right, then back at us. "I can see the car waiting just outside the gates," she said.

"Are you sure you want to go?" Isidor asked, hiding from view in the doorway.

Then, looking back one last time at him, Kayla said, "See you later, alligator."

"In a while, crocodile," Isidor whispered, closing the front door on his sister.

Chapter Seventeen

Kayla

My journey from Hallowed Manor to Ravenwood School took just over an hour. The driver had spoken little, offering the odd grunt in response to my attempts at conversation. In fact the man had seemed too busy chewing on the end of the cigarette he held between his teeth to say very much at all.

I sat and glanced through the rain-spattered windows as we reached the grounds of the school. The first thing I noticed was the huge search towers that Elizabeth Clarke had described and the razor wire that covered the tops of the walls. I could see that a bunch of hooded figures were watching from the towers as the driver drove the car through the gates and steered it up the winding drive to the school.

With the back of my hand, I rubbed away some of the condensation from my window. But however much I stared up at those hooded figures in their grey robes, I couldn't see their faces. It kinda freaked me out, my stomach started to somersault. It was too late to go back now.

"What is this place?" I asked the driver, keen to make out that I knew nothing of the building that stretched before me.

"A school," the driver said, the tip of his cigarette winking on and off as it dangled from the corner of his mouth.

I watched the blue-grey cigarette smoke squirt from his nostrils and said, "Do you think you could put that out? It smells disgusting."

"Quit complaining," the driver said, and sucked on the end of the cigarette as if in defiance.

"It's bad for my health," I told him.

"Yeah and so is a smack in the mouth, so keep it shut!" the driver replied.

Elizabeth hadn't been kidding when she had described the school staff to us. Ignoring him, I turned and looked back through the car windows at the school, which loomed ahead.

Elizabeth had been right in her description of it. It did look more like a prison than a school.

"Are you sure this is a school?" I asked the driver.

"I'm sure," he coughed.

"It's just that it doesn't look like a school – it looks like some kinda mental institution."

He stubbed out his cigarette in the already overflowing ashtray, and flashing a set of bright yellow teeth he said, "You'll feel right at home then, won't you girlie."

"I thought my uncle had sent me to a place of education," I said.

"Jee-sus!" the driver wheezed. "Don't you ever quit your moaning? No wonder your parents topped themselves!"

I knew that Potter had told McCain that my make-believe parents had died in a boating accident, not that they had killed themselves. This jerk was just trying to be cruel. I looked at the driver and said, "My parents never killed themselves. They died in a boating accident. They drowned."

"Blah! Blah! Blah!" he mocked. "You go on believing that, girlie. Whatever floats your boat!" Laughing, he looked at me and added, "Get-it? Whatever *floats* your boat!"

Just wanting to punch this whack-job straight in the face, I sat on my hands, turned away and looked up at the school. The car tyres crunched over gravel, and it sounded like the car were rolling over a carpet of broken bones. The driver swung the car round the last bend in the driveway and killed the engine in front of the school. Not wanting to spend another moment in the driver's company, I snatched hold of my small case and fled the car. One of the hooded figures stood in the rain and beckoned me forward with a gnarled finger.

"This way!" the figure ordered. "Follow me."

With my stomach churning as if my innards were being strangled, I started after the figure.

"Hey!" a voice called after me.

I spun around to see that the driver had wound down the passenger's window of his car and was now leaning across both front seats. "Good luck, girlie!" he grinned. "You're gonna need it!" Then the driver wound up the window, drowning out the sound of his obnoxious laughter, started the engine, and drove away down the drive.

With rain jabbing away at my face like broken fingernails, I watched the car until it had disappeared from view.

"Follow me!" the hoodie ordered, its voice sounding stern and old.

I gripped the handle of my case over my shoulder, turned on my heels and followed the hoodie into the school.

The school was very old. The building was constructed of cold slabs of grey stone and rock. The corridors the hooded figure led me through seemed never-ending. The walls towered high above me like some ancient cathedral. The sound of my shoes snapping off the cobbled walkways echoed all around me as the hoodie's long robes made a whispering sound as they trailed behind him. Set into the walls were giant stained glass windows and they cast eerie shadows along the corridors.

The hooded figure led me to a small, wooded door. He pushed it open to reveal a dimly-lit room. On the floor was a cardboard box with the words *Poor Box* written along the side in red marker pen.

"Find yourself a suitable blazer then get to class," the figure hissed, its grey robes swishing back along the floor as it made its way up the stone corridor.

Once it was gone, I bent down and rummaged through the *Poor Box*, my hands lost amongst second-hand ties, socks, jumpers, and blazers. The clothes smelt musty – like a tramp that had brushed up too close to me on the London Underground.

"This sucks, don't you reckon?" came a voice from beside me.

I looked up to find a boy about my own age standing next to me. He was thin-looking, with a long face, a mop of black curls, and mischievous blue eyes.

"I guess," I sighed and went back to rummaging through the box.

"You're new here, ain't ya?"

"Yep," I said without looking up.

"Don't worry," the boy said. "This place takes some getting used to, but…"

"Who said I'm worried?" I asked, pulling a dusty-looking blazer from the box and holding it against me.

"You look as if you've just seen a ghost!" he smirked. "Either that or you ain't feeling too well."

I brushed the dust from the blazer, and said, "I'm fine, okay? So if you don't mind, I'm trying…"

"Just look at this crap, will ya?" he groaned, cutting me dead. "How do

they expect anyone to wear this stuff?" he said, yanking a blazer from the box and putting it on. The sleeves dangled over his wrists and covered his hands. I slid my arms through the sleeves of the blazer I had chosen and they stopped halfway up my arm.

Then he looked at himself, then at me. "We look like a right pair of Muppets!"

"Swap?" I suggested.

"You kidding?" the boy grinned. "If they insist we wear this crap, then they'll have to put up with us looking like a couple of dicks."

"But we don't look very smart," I said.

"That's the point," he smiled, poking his fingers from beneath his sleeves.

"But…"

"I'm Brook. Sam Brook," he said, thrusting his hand out towards me.

"Kayla Hunt," I replied, shaking Sam's hand.

"What year you been put in?" Sam asked, kicking the box over and walking away up the corridor.

"Sorry?" I asked, watching the second-hand clothes spill out of the box like a pile of entangled guts.

"How old are ya?" Sam shouted over his shoulder.

"Sixteen!"

"Nice one. You'll be in the same classes as me!" he smiled back at me, and his piercing blue eyes seemed to sparkle with delight. "C'mon, you don't want to be late for Brother Michael's lesson!" And with another wicked grin, Sam mooched away and up the corridor.

I straightened my thick auburn hair and said, "To be honest, I do feel kinda nervous."

"I knew it," Sam smiled at me.

"How? Is it that obvious?"

"You look as if you're gonna shit yourself!' Sam laughed.

"Thanks!"

"I'm just taking the piss!" Sam grinned and slapped me on the back. "Don't worry, you'll get used to being at Ravenwood."

I knew that my time at the school was short, and I needed to find out as much information about it and the staff as possible. So not wanting to waste any time, I said, "The teachers here seem weird – kinda strange."

"The Ravenwood Greys, that's what we call 'em," Sam said, his voice dropping to just above a whisper.

I thought of the teacher who had met me outside of the school and the grey robes and hood that it had worn, and the name seemed to fit. Wanting to know more about these Ravenwood Greys, I said, "You're not reassuring me, Sam. Are they really bad?"

"The old lot of teachers we had – they were pretty safe. But one morning we all tipped up for lessons as normal, and they'd all gone – vanished!" Sam told me.

"What do you mean, vanished?" I asked, thinking of Emily Clarke.

"Dunno," Sam shrugged. "They just disappeared and were replaced by the Greys."

"Where did they go?" I asked him.

"How should I know?" Sam whispered, approaching the door to the classroom and pushing it open. I followed him inside.

Just like my blazer, the classroom smelt old, musty, and of sweat. It was full of teenagers all about the same age as me and Sam. Some looked a few years younger. They sat in rows behind single wooden desks. I followed Sam across the room, and finding a spare desk and seat next to him, I sat down. Along one side of the classroom, windows spewed dreary shafts of winter morning light across the desks and chalkboard.

Glancing out of the windows, I could see one of the turrets that surrounded the school spiralling up into the overcast sky. At the top I could see a hooded figure pacing back and forth as it kept watch over the school and everyone imprisoned within it.

Chapter Eighteen

Kayla

"I thought you said we shouldn't be late for Brother Michael's lesson?" I said to Sam, looking at my watch. "He's five minutes late already."

"Shhh!" Sam said. "He might already be here!"

"What do ya mean?" I asked. But before Sam could explain, something happened.

At first there was a rustling sound, like leaves being carried along the street in a storm. This was followed by a wailing sound and a spray of shadows that flickered across the chalkboard like the silhouette of a giant bird. Then out of the gloom in the corner of the room stepped one of those Greys. His robes fluttered all around him as he made his way to the front of the class.

"Where did he come -" I began.

"Shhh!" Sam said again, prodding me in the ribs with his elbow. "That's Brother Michael."

Brother Michael stood at the front of the class, his giant frame wedged into a grey coloured robe. But it wasn't just his cloak and the hood that he had draped over his head, everything about him was *grey*. His hoodie was pulled so far down over his face that the only part I could see was his mouth. Brother Michael's lips were puckered, cracked, and blistered looking.

"For the benefit of the new student," Brother Michael's mouth hissed, "I will remind you of the entire list of school rules." Then, running his tongue over his lips to moisten them, he began. "You will not leave the school grounds. In fact, you won't have any contact with the outside world until you leave this school!"

School! Is that what he calls it? I wondered.

His tongue snaked from between his lips again and a silver globule of spittle glistened as it dribbled from the corner of his mouth. He looked as if he were about to throw a fit. "If you should see anyone other than a member of staff in the school grounds, you are to report it at once!" Straightening the rope that hung about his waist, he continued. "By that I mean anyone odd – anyone looking strange! Do I make myself clear?" he asked.

What? Stranger than you? I thought to myself. *Not likely!*

"Yes, Brother," the class replied. I sat silently and watched Brother Michael knock away the spit that swung from his chin.

Brother Michael continued to inform the class of the many rules that we must all obey, and as he did, I stole a glance about the room and spied at some of the other students. They sat with their backs straight, faces taut and emotionless, like mindless dummies in shop windows. They looked haunted – lost in some way – like they had given up somehow. Then, as I was turning back to face Brother Michael, I caught someone staring back at me. It was a boy, about my age I figured, with narrow green eyes and a scrunched-up looking face. He had a fierce-looking crew cut like a Marine, and he had his fists on his desk like two giant clubs.

The way he stared made me feel uncomfortable, so I offered him a half smile. In return, he grinned back at me. Then, pointing his thumb and forefinger like a pistol, he aimed it at me and pretended to fire a shot off. I faced front again to find Brother Michael continuing to recite the never-ending list of school rules.

"Apart from the searchlights in the grounds, all the lights will be switched off at nine p.m. After this time, the school will be in total darkness!"

I had no trouble in conjuring up eerie images of Ravenwood at night and as I pictured the long, soulless corridors, a thought came to me. Raising an arm above my head, I tried to get Brother Michael's attention.

"What is it, Hunt?" Brother Michael hissed. "It had better be good!"

I lowered my arm, glanced at the other kids seated nearest to me, then back at Brother Michael. Just above a whisper, I said, "Brother, if the school is in total darkness, how will I find my way to the toilet – you know, just in case I need to pee?"

The class erupted into hysterics. I stared at them, never intending my question to be humorous, it was a genuine concern that I had.

"Silence!" Brother Michael screeched and the laughter stopped. "So we have a comedian in our midst, do we?"

"No, Brother...I was just wondering..."

"You'd better not be trouble, Hunt. I'm not known for my sense of humour and children who break the rules make me laugh even less!" Brother Michael spat, reaching into the folds of his robes and producing a long, black, plastic rod similar in size to a ruler.

Whoosh!

Brother Michael cut the air with the rod, slicing it back and forth. With a malevolent grin, he said, "Children who wish to disobey the rules will receive this!" He waved the rod again, and this time the end of it lit up in an explosion of blue sparks. The tip of the rod fizzed and spat short bursts of electricity into the air, illuminating Brother Michael's chin which jutted from beneath his hood.

I was right – I had been sent to live in a prison! The rod that Brother Michael was waving about was some kind of Taser – like the cops carried before the world got pushed.

I tucked my hands beneath the desk, and wondered if the police knew what was going on here. But then I thought of what Isidor and I had discovered on the Web about how the world was now, and guessed that the police couldn't give a crap as to what happened to me or any of the other kids at the school.

"We take every pleasure in giving you children the odd zap," Brother Michael said, firing up the end of the rod again. "Because on occasions you will need it. And believe me, one day you will thank us!"

Waving the electric rod around in front of the class, I noticed that one of Brother Michael's fingers on his right hand was missing. Where his index finger should have been was a stumpy lump of flesh. But instead of it being grey like the rest of him, the stump was purple in colour and it looked raw like a piece of meat that had been gnawed at. Unable to stop looking at it, the flesh along my spine began to prickle and tighten.

"Want to get a better look at it do you?" Brother Michael asked, and he was now looming over me, thrusting the stump under my nose. I looked up at the shrouded figure before me, and that invisible fist tightened itself around my intestines again, making my stomach cramp.

"Do you want a better look, Kayla Hunt?" Brother Michael spat, the painful-looking stump just millimetres from my face. God, it smelt so bad I thought I might just puke.

I jerked my head away from it, the smell of rotting flesh and decay making me gag. "No, Brother," I whispered.

Nodding beneath his hood, Brother Michael said, "Very well."

I glanced sideways at Sam, and gave him a look as if to say, *What a freak?* But Sam just winked back at me and offered a nervous smile.

Chapter Nineteen

Kiera

Soon after Kayla had left for Ravenwood School, Potter, Isidor, and I packed a bag each and set off for the farmhouse that we had rented on the outskirts of Wood Hill. Potter had wanted to drive the Rolls Royce Phantom that he had found housed in the large garage at the rear of the manor.

"Yeah, and why don't we paint it pink and really draw attention to ourselves?" I said, taking the keys to the smaller Ford Focus that Isidor and Kayla had been using on their trips to and from Wood Hill over the last few weeks.

"You're such a killjoy, Hudson," Potter said, snatching the keys from me and climbing behind the wheel of the Ford.

I got in beside him and Isidor sat in the back. All of us were dressed in jeans, warm sweaters, and boots. None of us stood out and that's what I wanted.

Potter drove us across the Welsh Moors as we made our way through the bleak countryside towards the town of Wood Hill. Isidor had his head buried in a book for most of the journey and Potter chain-smoked, flicking the ash and blowing smoke out of the window.

"Close the window," I groaned. "You're letting the rain in."

With a cigarette held between his teeth, Potter closed the window. At once the car filled with a cloud of blue-grey smoke.

"Better?" He asked, peering through the rain-streaked windscreen as he navigated the narrow winding roads.

"Not really," I said, winding down my own window and drawing in a lungful of clean air.

"I thought you were getting wet?" Potter asked, shooting me a sideways glance.

"It doesn't matter," I said, taking my iPod and placing it into the dock on the dashboard.

Potter frowned in confusion and looked back at the road.

"Fancy some music?" I asked him.

"Sure, why not?" he replied.

"Isidor?" I said, twisting in my seat to look at him.

"Huh?" he said, not taking his eyes from the copy of *Harvey Trotter & the Dragon's Throne* that he had in his hands.

"What do you fancy listening to?" I asked.

"Oh anything," he said, without looking. Then, added, "How about *Voulez-vous* by Abba?"

"You've got to be kidding me," Potter groaned beside me.

With a smile, I said to Isidor, "I don't have that song but..." Then, scrolling through the tracks on my iPod, I found the song that I was looking for and hit the play button. Within moments, *Dancing Queen* by Abba was playing.

A sullen look fell over Potter's face.

"Don't be such an old misery-guts," I said to him.

"Abba?" he groaned again. "Haven't you got any U2?"

"Not in this world," I reminded him.

Isidor started to sing along in the background as he continued to read his book.

Potter glanced at him in the rear-view mirror and said, "I really don't get you, Isidor."

"What's not to get?" he asked between singing the words.

"Well just take a look at you," Potter said, keeping one eye on the road ahead. "You've got the eyebrow piercing, the Shaggy-Doo beard and tattoos up your arms and neck and your singing along to Abba. I mean, what's going on?"

"So what you're saying is that I should be listening to something more gothic – dull and depressing?" Isidor said, still not looking up from his book.

"Well, yeah," Potter said.

"If I wanted that sort of thing, I'd spend more time listening to you, Potter," Isidor said, glancing up from his book and winking at me.

"Very funny," Potter said.

"Leave Isidor alone," I smiled at the sight of Isidor giving Potter a taste of his own medicine.

"Whatever," Potter sulked.

We spent the rest of the journey in silence, until suddenly I noticed that Potter was strumming his fingers on the steering wheel in time and singing along to *Take a Chance on Me.*

It was early afternoon when Potter pulled the car up in front of the farmhouse. The rain hadn't stopped the whole journey, and the sky was so overcast that it could have been night. The farmhouse was situated at the top of a narrow dirt track that was barely wide enough to fit the car. On each side of the track there were slate stone walls that were covered in wild ivy, nettles, and thorns.

The farmhouse itself was neat and tidy and had been looked after. There was a small kitchen and living room downstairs and two bedrooms upstairs with a tiny bathroom that was just big enough to fit a tub. The nicest thing about the house was the real fireplace that was set into the far living room wall. It was surrounded by red coloured brick and the owner had been kind enough to have stacked a pile of freshly cut logs before it.

Isidor took one of the bedrooms and Potter and I took the other. Once we had settled in, I checked my emails on my iPod to see if I'd received a message from Kayla. There wasn't one. Looking out the living room window across the fog-covered moors, I wondered if Kayla was safe. I still had fears about her locked away in Ravenwood, and if I'd had my way, she wouldn't have gone. But Kayla wasn't my sister, although I thought of her as one. I loved Kayla and did feel in some way responsible for her, even though she was only four years younger than me. I understood how Kayla felt, and even though she had been through so much already in her life, I still found her a little naive at times – just like a younger sister would be.

"What now?" a voice said from behind me and I turned to see Potter standing at the foot of the wooden staircase which led into the living room.

"I'm going to drive into town and visit the local police station," I said. "Make some enquires into Emily Clarke's disappearance."

"Her sister has already tried that," Potter reminded me.

"Yeah, but she didn't have one of these," I said, holding up my police badge.

"I'll come with you," he said.

"No, stay here," I told him.

"Why?"

"Because I don't want to go in heavy handed," I said as delicately as I could. "We want to try and get the local coppers on our side. We might need them."

"So what am I meant to do?" he asked me.

"Get that fire going," I smiled at him.

I pulled into the car park of the local police station, killed the engine and made my way inside. With an air of confidence, I flashed my badge to the clerk behind the front desk and asked if I could speak to whoever it was in charge. The clerk told me to take a seat.

I waited for several minutes until a large looking head with a shock of white hair appeared around the edge of the door that led into the station. It was a tired-looking face, a face that had seen too many late nights and long hours.

"Kiera Hudson?" the face asked.

"That's me," I said standing up.

The door was pushed open further to reveal a well-built man, wearing a shirt which was open at the throat, and smart trousers that looked too tight about his waist.

"Inspector Cliff Banner," he said thrusting out one large meaty hand towards me. "What can I do for ya?"

I shook his open hand, which he pumped up and down with such force that I thought he was going to snap every one of my fingers. Once I had the feeling back in my hand, I produced my badge and showed it to him.

"I'm from out of town but I could do with some help."

"Sounds intriguing - follow me." He ushered me through the door from the small waiting area into a sterile and brightly lit corridor. I followed him to his office, where he gestured me towards a seat. We sat facing each other on opposite sides of his cluttered desk.

"Excuse me," he said, "I was just in the middle of my supper." He picked up a half-eaten sandwich which looked small and ridiculous in his huge hand, and took a bite. Peanut butter oozed from it and onto his bushy white beard, which he wiped away with a piece of crinkled tissue paper that lay amongst the other litter on his desk.

"So how can I be of help?"

"A friend of mine, Emily Clarke has gone missing."

"How old is this friend...a kid is she?" he asked as he chewed the remains of his sandwich.

"No, she's an adult, a little older than me."

"What she's vulnerable then...you know...like retarded?"

"No, she's just like you and me," I told him. I knew where he was going with this without him saying anything else.

"Well there's the trick. If she ain't a juvey and no retard then there's nothing we can do about it." He screwed up the piece of grease-proof paper that his sandwich had been wrapped in and threw it at the rubbish bin on the other side of the room. "You should know there ain't nothing we can do about it, you being a cop and all."

"Yeah I know all that, but this is different," I told him.

"Oh, how come?"

"Emily was teaching at the Ravenwood School..." I began to tell him.

"Whoa, whoa, whoa," he whistled through his teeth. "Stop right there. That school has been taken over by the wolves – the Skin-walkers."

I shook my head. "So?"

He stared at me blankly.

"My friend, Emily, told her sister, Elizabeth Clarke before she went missing that..."

"Who did you say?" That name seemed to have grabbed his attention.

"Elizabeth Clarke," I repeated.

"Ah, that's right," he said thumbing through the paperwork strewn across his desk. Then, holding up a sheet of peanut butter smeared paper, he added, "she came in here yesterday spouting on about how her sister had been murdered. Can you believe that? Murdered! Reckons that Headmaster McCain did it."

"Have you had dealings with him before?"

"Never," he said, combing his overgrown moustache with his fingers.

"So how can you be sure that he's not capable of murder?" I said defensively.

"Well damn me," he chuckled.

"Look, I can see that you find this all very amusing, but are you gonna help me or not?" I asked him.

"Listen, Karen..."

"Kiera," I corrected him.

"Kiera, for a cop, you ain't half naive. These people...wolves...Skin-walkers, whatever you want to call 'em...they don't live like us," he warned me in an almost fatherly tone.

"What do you mean?" I asked him.

"You know...they don't live by the same rules as us. People may not like it, but that's the way it is. It's been like it for hundreds of years."

"So they are allowed to get away with murder?" I said sarcastically. "My understanding of the Wasp Water Treaty is that they can *match* with children every five years, although that is bad enough. But are they allowed to murder innocent people? I thought that's what the treaty was brought in for – to end the killing."

"Look, what goes on behind the walls of that school is wolf business," he said.

"So that makes it all okay then?" I argued.

"All I'm saying is that your friend...Emily...has probably found herself another teaching post and moved on."

"So what you're saying is, Emily just woke up one morning and left her home, her job and hasn't been in contact with her sister since?" I pushed him.

Realizing that he wasn't going to change my mind, Banner sighed deeply and said, "What's a pretty young copper like you gone and got herself caught up in something like this for?"

"What, police work you mean?"

"Wolf business," he said, staring at me from across his desk.

Without breaking his stare, I said, "Look, one cop to

another...are you gonna help me or not?"

Banner pulled a notepad and pen from beneath the mountain of rubble on his desk. "Who does she bank with?" he asked.

"What's that got to do with anything?"

"She's gotta eat, ain't she? Fill up her car with petrol?" he said as if he was teaching me something new. "I'll run a few checks to see if she used her bank cards in the last few days; that should tell us where she is." He tossed the pad and pen across the desk at me.

I scribbled Emily's full name, date of birth, address, and banking details onto the pad. I was just about to hand it back when I paused and then added the address of where I was staying. I then pushed it back across the desk towards Banner.

"Thank you," I said.

"I ain't promising you nothing. If it wasn't for the fact you're a cop, I'd kick your arrogant arse outter here!"

I got up and left his office.

Chapter Twenty

Kayla

I was relieved to discover not only was I sharing many of the same classes as Sam, but we had rooms next to each other. Sam seemed friendly enough, and I guessed I would need a friend at Ravenwood. My room was little more than a box, three floors up in one of the school's winding towers. To get to the room, I had to navigate a set of stairs that spiralled upwards like a corkscrew. The stairwell was dark and the steps echoed with each snap of my heel.

A metal framed bed lent against the far wall of my room, and the sheets were rough and made my skin itch. It was like falling asleep in a bed of stinging nettles. The walls were made of stone and a desk crouched in one corner.

I intended to stick close to Sam, as I tried to find my way around Ravenwood and understand many of the odd rules that seemed to be at its heart. On my first night I took my iPod and sent a brief message to Kiera. I told her about the freaky Greys and how I had made a friend who might be able to give me information about what had taken place at the school. I stressed that I needed to be careful as I didn't want to draw attention to myself. Within minutes of sending my message, Kiera sent one back explaining that she and the others had arrived at the nearby farmhouse. I took comfort from knowing that. Kiera also said that she had made a visit to the local cop shop, but wasn't holding out too much hope that they would help her.

Once I had read her message, I deleted it as she had told me to do. Should my iPod be found and the messages read, then that would have given our whole plan away.

Was there a plan? I wondered, hiding the iPod into a gap in the seam of the bag that Potter had sliced open for me with one of his claws. With the iPod hidden again, I reached into the bottom of my bag and took out a bottle of Lot 13. During the day, my cravings had progressed from feeling like a mild itch to an aching need in my stomach. Potter had given me enough bottles of Lot 13 to last me seven days. I unscrewed the cap and gulped down the slimy pink liquid. It coated the inside of my mouth and throat. I swallowed the bittersweet fluid and those cravings for the red stuff eased.

I pulled the blanket made of stinging nettles over my head. The feelings of uncertainty and loneliness that I suddenly felt as I lay in the dark were almost suffocating.

Had I done the right thing by putting myself in the middle of Ravenwood? I couldn't help but now wonder, as I lay and listened to the way off sounds. The background noise seemed almost deafening. None of the sounds were familiar to me – not like sleeping at the manor where I had grown up. I had gotten used to the noises back there. But at Ravenwood, as I lay in the dark, I could hear the sound of the Greys' robes swishing across the cold stone floors as they patrolled the corridors in the dark. I could hear the sound of sobbing as if coming from some far-off place. But above all, I could hear the sound of wolves howling.

Unable to bear it any longer, I reached for my bag, slipped my fingers into the tiny tear in the fabric and pulled out my iPod again. I wore the earphones and scrolled through the tracks I'd downloaded during my last night at Hallowed Manor. I dragged my fingernail down the screen until I found the song that I was looking for. With the blanket over my head and my eyes closed, I listened to *Ugly* by The Sugababes. It was the song that I had often cried myself to sleep listening to during my time spent at boarding school. Ugly and Stickleback were the names that the other girls there had called me. The song was one constant in this new world that I now found myself in. I don't know how long I had lain awake listening to that song, but eventually I fell into a restless sleep where I dreamt of those girls that had bullied me and made my life a misery for so long. I had been their dumping ground. Every school had one, even Ravenwood School, as I was about to find out.

Alan Dorsey was small for his age and very burnt. The

rumour was that his parents had been killed in a house fire, a fire that Dorsey had managed to escape from; but the flames had left their mark, a permanent reminder of what had taken place that night. His face was scarred, the skin stretched tight across his face, and in places it looked as if it had run like melted candle wax. Dorsey's eyes were two narrow slits, his nostrils looked like two puncture wounds in the middle of his face and his mouth was pulled into a permanent grimace. Dorsey knew that the other kids at Ravenwood stared at him, and I guess he didn't blame them. No more than I now blamed those girls who had stared at me. After all, wasn't it human nature to stare at the freaks?

On my first morning at Ravenwood, I had overslept. Fearing that I would be in trouble with the Greys for being late for class, I showered in the communal girl's bathroom and hurried down to join the queue for breakfast, which snaked across the schoolyard. The day was overcast and dull-looking again, but at least the rain had stopped. It was still very cold, though. I found Sam, propped up against a wall.

"What you doing?" I asked him. "Not joining the line for breakfast?"

"Waiting," Sam said, and it was only in the pale winter light that I realised how good looking he actually was. It wasn't only his thick, black curly hair, it was his eyes; they were a brilliant blue that had such a look of mischief in them.

"Waiting for what?" I asked, looking over his shoulder at the other kids on the schoolyard. Some of the girls stood chatting, while a group of boys kicked a scruffy-looking football about.

"For the fight to start," Sam said.

"What fight?"

Sam nodded in the direction of the boy who I had caught staring at me from the back of the class the day before – the one with the scrunched up face and Marine haircut. "See Pryor over there? He's gonna smash Dorsey," Sam told me.

"How do you know that?"

"He's been winding-up that kid for weeks," Sam said. "Pryor's a bully - an animal."

"What makes you think he will -" I started, but before I could finish, Sam stepped away from the wall.

"Watch," he whispered.

I looked at Pryor amongst the crowd of boys with the football. He stood amongst them and watched Dorsey walking alone. I saw Pryor's eyes narrow as he followed Dorsey's progress. Unaware that he was being watched, Dorsey made his way towards the school building, his head bowed, chin almost touching his chest. Pryor broke away from the pack. Slow at first, and I could hear his shoes whispering against the concrete. Then, he was running, narrowing the gap between himself and Dorsey.

"You're dead!" Pryor screamed, leaping through the air and crashing into Dorsey.

The first Dorsey knew that he was under attack was when the back of his head bounced off the ground and the air from his lungs belched out through his burnt and twisted lips. Dorsey looked up to see who it was that had knocked him off his feet, his eyes wide and full of bewilderment.

"You fucking freak!" Pryor roared, straddling Dorsey.

From where I was standing, I could see the loathing Pryor had for Dorsey in his eyes. Dorsey could see the hate in them too and he knew he was in trouble. Throwing his hands in front of his face, Dorsey managed to block the first wave of blows that Pryor threw at him.

"Freaks like you should be caged!" Pryor spat, smacking Dorsey up the side of his head.

"What have I done?" Dorsey cried out.

"You should be in a circus!" Pryor said, punching Dorsey in the face.

I stepped away from the wall. The first thing that struck me was the sound Pryor's fists made as they pounded into Dorsey's face. They didn't make the *crunching* noise that I had so often heard in the movies, but more of a *Whap! Whap!* sound. Seeing Pryor's fists raining down on Dorsey made me feel as if I had a heart that was beating, but not in my chest, in my stomach. Those sounds made me feel sick.

I wanted to stop Pryor. Not for Dorsey's sake but for my

own. I couldn't bear that *Whap! Whap! Whap!* sound. If I had to listen to it for much longer, I believed that I might just go insane, right there on the edge of the schoolyard.

Pryor must have been at least fourteen-stone and over six-foot in height. Although I was way smaller than him, I knew I could kick his arrogant fucking arse all over the schoolyard – but that would've just brought me unwanted attention to myself and my abilities. But I couldn't bear to watch Dorsey taking a beating.

Maybe I could go and get one of the teachers. Wouldn't they put a stop to Pryor? I wondered. But I knew that they probably wouldn't be interested. I glanced at Sam, who stood beside me, his face grim and pale. The spark in his eyes had faded and he looked as sick as I now felt.

"We can't just stand and watch!" I said.

Sam didn't say anything. He stood and continued to watch the fight and the large group of boys and girls who had gathered like vultures around Pryor and Dorsey.

Whap! Whap! Whap!

Pryor looked down into Dorsey's tear-stained face. "What's the matter with you?" Pryor roared. "Why do you have to look like that?" And he punched Dorsey in the face again. *Whap!*

The sound of that last punch made my stomach cartwheel. Without considering what I was about to do or the shit I could be getting myself into, I raced towards Pryor. Pryor's back was facing me, and it looked as broad and as sturdy as a dining room table propped on its side. With my fists clenched so my claws wouldn't spring out, I focused in on my target.

Some of the other kids who were gathered around the fight saw me coming and parted like waves so I could get at Pryor. Raising my fist above my head like a hammer, I swung it down in a swooping arc. But before it connected with the space between Pryor's shoulder blades, a hand gripped my wrist and yanked my arm backwards.

I spun around to find myself looking into Sam's face.

"No, Kayla. Pryor won't give a crap that you're a girl. He'll smash your face in, too."

"But I can't just stand by and do nothing," I told him.

"You might have to," Sam warned.

Then, the air was ripped apart with the ear-splitting sound of the sirens from the search towers. It sounded like an air raid was underway. The kids swarming around Pryor and Dorsey split to the four corners of the yard.

Sam yanked on the sleeve of my blazer and said, "C'mon. They're coming!"

I followed Sam as he darted away across the yard. Before we reached the other side, I glanced back. Several of the Greys were racing towards Pryor and Dorsey. Their robes fluttered like wings as they swooped down on the two boys who still rolled around on the ground. I turned front and followed Sam around the corner of the school wall and the *Whap! Whap! Whap!* sound was replaced by *Zap! Zap! Zap!*

Chapter Twenty-One

Kayla

Sam and I ran round the side of the school building with the *Zap! Zap! Zap!* sounds fizzing behind from the schoolyard. Without even noticing it, a Grey pounced from a doorway like a shadow detaching itself from the wall. From beneath its flowing robes, the Grey produced one of those sticks and fired it up. Coils of blue-mauve electricity snapped from the end of it and lit up the mouth of the Grey which protruded from beneath its hoodie like a jagged cliff edge.

"*STOP!*" the Grey roared, pointing the stick at me and Sam.

Sending up plumes of dust from beneath our shoes, we both skidded to a halt, stopping inches from the sizzling electric sparks.

"Follow me," the Grey ordered us.

"We haven't done anything wrong!" Sam insisted.

"Stop your noise, Brook, or I'll fry you," the Grey grinned from beneath his hood.

"But..." Sam started.

Zzzzzzz...the Grey waved the stick under Sam's nose and he staggered backwards like a tightrope walker.

"Get going!" the Grey cried, pointing in the direction that we had come.

We made our way back onto the yard, the Grey inches behind us.

What have I done? I wondered. *Perhaps Sam had been right, I shouldn't have tried to get involved.*

Pryor was bent double on his knees and he looked sick. Dorsey was knelt beside him, and he was wringing his hands together in his lap. Behind them stood two of the Greys. One of them was huge and towered over the other, and although I couldn't see his face, I knew it was Brother Michael.

Sam and I joined Pryor and Dorsey as a giant of a man strode onto the yard. Without him even having to introduce himself, I knew that this was McCain, the self-appointed Headmaster. His hair was black and slicked back over his brow. He was incredibly thin, borderline anorexic-looking. His cheeks were so sunken that it looked as if he was permanently sucking in mouthfuls of air. His nose was so bulbous and red; it was like something a circus clown would have been proud of. But it was his eyes. I had seen eyes like that before - Jack Seth had had a set. They glowed a brilliant yellow from within two sunken eye sockets. McCain was a wolf – a Skin-walker.

"Get up!" he barked at Pryor and Dorsey.

Pryor was the first to stand, although his legs looked as if they might buckle under him at any moment sending him crashing back onto the ground. His eyes brimmed with pain, but even so, he eyed McCain with defiance.

Dorsey was slower to get up, so I stepped forward and looped my arm through his and dragged him to his feet.

"Get off me," Dorsey groaned. "I don't need your help."

I let go of him, startled at his ungratefulness. Dorsey swayed from side to side like a drunk.

McCain walked amongst them like a caged tiger. "Well, well, well!" he said. "Time after time it's the same old faces lined up before me."

"Excuse me, sir, but I've never -" Sam began, but was cut short as the Grey behind him dry-stunned him in the back with his electric stick.

"*Aaaarrrgghh!*" Sam cried out, locking up on the spot and going rigid. I glanced at Sam, his thick, black curly hair had straightened like he had just stuck his fingers into a wall socket. The effects were momentary, and Sam unlocked and loosened up.

"Wow, that hurt!" he groaned under his breath at me.

"Just keep your gob shut," I whispered back, just wanting to get out of this situation without drawing any attention to myself. Jeez, I'd been at the school less than twenty-four hours and I was already in the shit with the Headmaster.

McCain stepped forward and said, "Even when you're lined up before me, you don't know when to keep quiet do you, Hunt?"

I looked at him, surprised that he knew my name already. McCain's nostrils flared in and out, they looked red and sore.

"Well?" McCain said.

"Well what, sir?" I asked. "I don't know what you mean, *sir*."

McCain's lips contorted into a bloodless grin. "I can tell that you think you're a real smartarse, don't you, Hunt? You've only been here five minutes and I can tell we're going to have trouble from you."

"I don't know what you mean, *sir*," I said again. I wasn't really scared by him. I had dealt with werewolves before. I had met Jack Seth and he had been a complete and utter freak, a screw-up, but dangerous. He could teach McCain a thing or two.

McCain eyed me with suspicion and said, "You even say *'sir'* like a smartarse. Well, let me make myself clear. In here, you're mine. I own you. You are no one and you have no one." Then, stepping away from me, McCain looked at the four of us who stood before him. "The lot of you have been given over to me by your parents or you were orphaned and the state gave you to me to look after. And this is how you show your gratitude, by behaving like wild animals?"

McCain strode towards Pryor, and Pryor looked away.

"Look at me, Pryor!" McCain roared, grabbing hold of his face and snapping it towards him. "Don't think you can throw your weight around in here. No wonder your mother and father ran out on you. God knows if I'd had a son like you I might have been tempted to disappear!"

I watched Pryor clench his fists into two meaty clubs.

"You're nothing but an animal so you'll be treated as such," McCain roared. "Brother Michael, take this vermin to the rat-house."

Hearing this, Pryor loosened his fists and said, "Not the *rat-house*. I spent most of last week in there!"

"You shouldn't worry, Pryor, you'll be in good company – the Addison twins are serving a fortnight in there. Now get going!"

Brother Michael stepped forward, and taking hold of Pryor

by the arm, he marched him across the yard.

"What's the rat-house?" I whispered at Sam.

"Some rat-infested shack," he whispered back.

"Please, Mr. McCain!" Pryor pleaded over his shoulder. "Anything but the *rat-house!*"

Then, there was the *zapping* sound and Pryor crumpled to his knees. Taking hold of him by the tails of his blazer, Brother Michael dragged Pryor off the yard and out of sight. McCain approached Dorsey and looked down at him.

"You need to toughen up, boy, or no wolf will ever want to be matched with you," McCain told him, like Dorsey would be missing out on some sought after honour. "What's your problem? That house fire melt your backbone along with your face?"

Dorsey stood staring down at the ground and said nothing.

"Answer me," McCain said, rummaging in his trouser pocket.

"Can't you leave the kid alone?" Sam suddenly said from further down the line. "Can't you see he's got...*issues?*"

"You'll have *issues* in a minute, Brook, if you don't keep your trap shut!" McCain barked, and he nodded at the Grey who stood behind him.

"*Aaaarrrgghh!*" Sam shrieked as he was zapped again from behind.

"Brother Vincent, take this *jellyfish* Dorsey to the pool and don't let him leave until he has swam a hundred laps. It might help him develop a spine," McCain said. Then taking a bottle of sinus spray from his pocket, he rammed it up his own right nostril and breathed in.

"But I can't swim," Dorsey whispered.

"Then it's about time you learnt," McCain sniffed, screwing the cap back onto the bottle and putting it away.

Brother Vincent took Dorsey by the scruff of the neck and marched him back into the school. McCain waltzed in front of me and said, "It would appear that *your* parents were in need of some swimming practice, Hunt."

I met McCain's cruel stare and said, "My parents were excellent swimmers."

"That's not what your uncle told me when we spoke on the telephone. Didn't your mother and father drown?"

You know they drowned and I'm not going to give you the satisfaction of thinking that you're hurting me, I smiled to myself.

"So it would seem, *sir*," I said, emphasising the word 'sir', knowing that it pissed McCain off.

McCain wiped the tip of his bulbous nose with his forefinger and stared hard into my eyes.

"Give me your stick," he said, holding out his hand towards the Grey who stood behind me. The Grey passed him the stick and straightened the folds of his robes.

"Put out your hands, Hunt," McCain said, his voice just above a whisper and his eyes never leaving mine.

I did as he asked and held out my hands, palms facing upwards. Bracing myself for the pain, I tightened the muscles throughout my entire body. McCain raised the stick and I could hear it humming, like the sound of a cat purring in the sunshine. Except there wasn't any sunshine. The sky was the colour of gunmetal and full of clouds.

McCain fired up the stick, and hues of blue and pink flashed in his eyes. I clenched my jaw and gritted my teeth.

Here comes the pain! I thought.

But yet it didn't. McCain thrust the sparking end of the stick into the palm of my hand and I felt nothing. The stick hissed and spat and the smell of burning skin wafted up into the air. I was startled by the sweetness of its scent – like roasted pork glazed with applesauce.

McCain's eyes widened, not because of the smell of my roasting flesh, but the fact that I seemed to feel no pain. Yanking the stick away, McCain pressed down as hard as he could onto the fleshy ball of skin beneath the thumb on my other hand. Again the stick hissed and spat, sending tendrils of smoke up into the air. But again, I felt nothing. I didn't even flinch. I just stared hard into McCain's eyes.

What's happening here? This should be frying me! I thought. *But then again, I was dead – did I not feel pain now?*

More out of frustration than spite, McCain bore the end of

the electric stick down into the palm of my hand again. I looked up at McCain and couldn't help but notice that his nose had started to bleed.

Staring at him, I said, "Your nose is bleeding, *sir*."

McCain removed the stick from my hand and he wiped the end of his nose against his suit sleeve. Looking down, I could see blood smeared up his wrist. McCain touched the tip of his nose with his fingers and looked at the globules of red that now covered them. He glanced at me and wiped his nose with the back of his hand, spreading the blood across his upper lip like a crooked crimson moustache. I looked down at my hands, they were blistered and raw. The skin around my fingers had turned black and crisp in places, and streams of white liquid-fat oozed from the fleshiest parts of my hands.

McCain looked at them too, and realising that I wasn't in any pain, he turned to the Greys standing behind Sam and me and said, "Get them out of my sight. Send them back to their rooms."

Chapter Twenty-Two

Kiera

I was woken by the sound of the telephone ringing. Potter groaned beside me and rolled over. Without surfacing from beneath the bed covers, I fumbled blindly about the bedside table as my hand tried to locate the phone. I plucked the receiver from its cradle and dragged it under the covers with me.

"Hello," I groaned, still partially asleep.

"Hudson! Hudson, is that you?" an irritable and obnoxious voice asked.

"Speaking," I mumbled, rubbing sleep from my eyes with my free hand. I felt Potter's hand brush against my thigh and flicked it away.

"It's Inspector Cliff Banner," he barked down the phone at me. He didn't sound happy.

As soon as I realised who it was on the other end of the phone, I yanked the blankets from over my head and sat up.

"I've got some good news and bad news for ya," he snapped.

"Okay," I said as I tried to focus on what he was about to tell me.

"The good news is that your friend Emily Clarke is still in the land of the living, walking around as pretty as you like!"

I felt relief and shock all at the same time to hear this piece of news. I had convinced myself that Emily had been murdered by McCain.

"So, what's the bad news?" I asked cautiously.

"You've been wasting my fucking time! That's the bad news!" he roared down the line at me. "I got onto the bank first thing this morning - gave 'em your friend's details. Within the hour they had faxed me back with a list of transactions she's made in the last week!"

"Oh…" I started to say, but he cut me dead and continued

to rant.

"How long did you say she's been missing?"

"About four days."

"Jeezus wept! According to these bank records, she was buying Cadbury's chocolate fingers in the local Seven-Eleven at ten-thirty yesterday morning for crying out loud!" he bellowed.

I felt Potter's hand brush against my thigh, and again I brushed it away.

Then it hit me. Banner hadn't actually spoken to or physically seen Emily Clarke. He was just going on a computer printout from credit card transactions. Credit cards which were rightly in Emily Clarke's name, but not necessarily being used by *her*.

"Has anyone been to the store and spoken to staff or checked out the CCTV?" I asked Banner.

"Has anybody been...?" he sounded exasperated with me. "Listen, I'm up to my frigging neck in shit down here and you expect me to go running around town on some fantasy...looking for your friend who is supposedly missing! Jeez, if this is her idea of going missing, I'd hate to see what happens when she gets fucking lost!" he bellowed.

"I just thought you could send someone down to the store to check..." I started

"Listen here, smartarse, you've got a badge...fucking use it!" and he hung up the phone.

"Who was that?" Potter groaned from beneath the blankets. Then, snaking one arm around my waist, he tried to drag me back under the covers with him.

"Banner," I said, taking his arm from around me. "The copper I spoke with at the police station yesterday. The one who couldn't give a shit about what's happening at Ravenwood."

"What did he want?" Potter asked, poking his head from beneath the blankets.

"He reckons Emily Clarke is alive and well and buying chocolate in the local Seven-Eleven," I told him, throwing on my dressing gown and heading for the door.

"How does he know that?" Potter mumbled, still half asleep

125

but already reaching for his cigarettes and lighter.

"He doesn't know for sure," I said looking back at him. "But he's too lazy to go and check it out."

"Do you want to check it out?" Potter asked, peering at me bleary-eyed through a haze of blue smoke.

"Straight away," I said, heading out of the room and across the landing to the bathroom.

I shut the door and ran a shower. As the water warmed, I dropped my dressing gown and stood naked in front of the mirror. I didn't want to release my claws, fangs, or wings, but I had to know. With my wings fluttering behind me, and those little black claws rolled into three-fingered fists, I stared at my reflection. I felt sick as the cracks appeared around my eyes and the corners of my lips. They spread like wild ivory down my neck, over my shoulder, and across my breasts. They covered my stomach, my hips, and the length of my legs down to my toes. I looked like an ancient statue, like the one outside the summerhouse back at the manor. As I stepped closer to the mirror, I felt a slight relief to see that the cracks weren't as deep and ragged as they had been. The blood I had sucked from Potter's neck had worked in filling the cracks for a while, but now the effects were fast wearing off.

Then, from behind me, I heard a noise and gasping out loud, I spun around. Potter was standing naked in the bathroom with his back to the door. Without saying anything, he came towards me. He held his wrist up to my mouth. I looked down and could see the green and blue veins beneath his skin.

"I can't," I whispered, tears beginning to stand in my eyes. "I feel like some kind of drug addict."

"Stop thinking of it like that, Kiera," Potter said gently, holding out his arm. "Are the living addicts because they need air to survive?"

"But they're not hurting anyone by breathing in air," I said, looking into his black eyes.

"And neither are you," he said back. "You can't hurt me, Kiera, I'm already dead, remember?"

"But you might not always be here," I said. "What happens

then? I might have to hurt someone to survive."

"Kiera, I'm never going to leave you," he whispered, brushing his wrist against my lower lip, and the smell of blood was almost intoxicating. It made me feel as if I was losing control – losing my mind. He looked into my eyes and said, "Kiera, the cracks are back and they will only get worse. Then what? They become so bad that you crumble into a pile of dust. What happens to me? I wouldn't want to spend the rest of eternity here without you. I couldn't do that. I know taking my blood isn't perfect, but until we figure this whole thing out, it's the best that we can do."

"And what if we don't figure it out?" I whispered, the smell of his blood driving me half-crazy.

"Tiger, you have the knack of figuring everything out," he half-smiled. "You're Kiera Hudson."

Then, unable to fight the urge anymore, I lunged forward, sinking my fangs into the fleshy part of his wrist. His blood exploded into my mouth and I gulped it down. It felt hot as it splashed over my tongue and down the back of my throat. I heard Potter making a hissing sound, as if in some small way he was in pain. But even though I knew that, I just couldn't stop until I was full.

With my head feeling dizzy and light, I loosened my jaws around Potter's wrist and withdrew my fangs. He gripped his arm with his free hand and held it high above his head to slow the flow of blood that oozed between his fingers.

"Did it hurt?" I asked, wiping his blood from my lips with my fingertips.

"I'd be lying if I said it didn't sting a bit."

"You didn't say it hurt last time," I said, feeling a little guilty.

Then looking at me, Potter smiled and said, "Sweetcheeks, the last time you did that to me, we were making love and I was so turned on, you could've ripped my freaking head off and I wouldn't have felt a thing."

"It didn't hurt me, either," I winked back at him.

Potter glanced at the shower then back at me. "Fancy having your back washed?" he asked me.

Then, pushing him gently in the chest and guiding him back to the bathroom door, I smiled and said, "I'd rather have a coffee."

I closed the door and stood alone, those little black claws opening and closing at the tips of my wings.

Although what Banner had told me wasn't conclusive proof that Emily Clarke was still alive somewhere, it did raise my hopes that she was perhaps safe and well. Perhaps she had rented a room? But what I couldn't understand was why she hadn't contacted her sister, Elizabeth.

With these thoughts clawing away at me, I took my shower and got dressed. Potter had made me a coffee and he sat at the kitchen table smoking. I took my iPod and checked it for any messages from Kayla. There weren't any. Should I be worried? Not yet, perhaps. It was just short of ten o'clock, so maybe she had been in class all morning? Did these 'Greys,' as Kayla described them, even bother to teach the kids at Ravenwood?

Isidor came into the kitchen and waved away the smoke that lingered like a cloud above Potter and the kitchen table. "What's the plan?" he asked me.

"I've got a lead I want to follow up in town," I explained. "I thought Potter and I would go and check it out."

"Okay," Isidor shrugged. "What do you want me to do?"

"Use the laptop to Toogle for any information on Ravenwood School." I said. "Find out its history. We all used to know Doctor Thaddeus Ravenwood and he was a friend of your father's. See if you can't find a connection between Ravenwood and this school."

"Do you think it might be connected to my father in some way?" he asked me.

"I don't know what to think," I told him honestly. "But have a look and see what you can dig up on McCain."

"No worries," Isidor said, booting up the laptop.

"And if you come across any pictures of werewolves wearing sparkling gloves, try not to get too excited," Potter said, getting up from the table and heading for the door.

"You're so funny," Isidor sighed.

"I know," Potter smiled without looking back. "It's one of my many charms."

I crossed the kitchen, and pecking Isidor on the cheek, I said, "Keep safe."

"Why, are you expecting trouble?" he asked, cocking the eyebrow with the piercing.

"That copper, Banner knows that we're staying here," I explained. "I'm not sure that I can entirely trust him."

"Don't worry about me," Isidor said, suddenly brandishing his claws and fangs. "I know Potter thinks I wander around with my head up my own arse, but I can look after myself."

"Want to know a secret?" I whispered.

"What?" he whispered back, his fangs and claws disappearing.

"Potter was cut up real bad when you were murdered back in The Hollows," I told him, leaving the room.

Chapter Twenty-Three

Kayla

"I've never seen anything like that before," Sam whispered as the Greys led us back through the maze of winding corridors to our rooms.

"Like what?" I whispered back, checking out the burns on the palms of my hands.

"The way you stood there and got zapped without even making a sound. I mean, you took some pain there!" Sam said, heading up one of the narrow, winding staircases.

I tried to hide my hands from him, but I knew he could see the inflamed skin and the liquid-fat, which had started to congeal and harden between my fingers.

"Doesn't it hurt?" he asked, wincing just at the sight of them.

"Not really, I can't feel anything," I told him.

"Are you crazy?" Sam said, as the Greys led us higher up into the gloom of one of the school's many turrets. I couldn't help but wonder about McCain and wanted to question Sam about him, but he wouldn't stop going on about my hands.

"Crazy - how?" I asked.

"This whole thing is *crazy*!" Sam said.

"Oh," I replied, starting to pick away at some of the scabs that had already started to form on my hands.

"Is that all you've got to say?" Sam whispered, keeping one eye on the Greys who walked only a few feet ahead of us. "We're living in a prison run by a bunch of freaky-looking hoodies, there's search towers and sirens, a sadist for a headmaster, and I've just witnessed the new girl get her hands fried without so much as a whimper and all you can say is 'OH'!"

I lowered my hands and looking at Sam, I said, "What do you want me say? I thought you were the one who said I'd get used to being at Ravenwood."

"Look, Kayla," Sam said, "I was ball-crapping ya, okay? You ain't ever gonna get used to this place – you just kinda look away – pretend it's not happening – it's all just a bad dream. But what I saw today wasn't no bad dream. I was wide awake and I had that Grey prodding me in the back with that sizzle-stick just to remind me."

"To be honest, I'm not too bothered about my hands," I said. "Okay, so I didn't feel anything – maybe I was in shock or something. I don't know. But what does bother me is how McCain..." But before I'd a chance to say anything more, one of the Greys stopped outside my bedroom door and was shoving me inside.

"I'll catch you later, Kayla," I heard Sam shout as he was thrown into his room next to mine. The Grey slammed my door shut with such force that it rattled in its ancient frame.

I pressed the side of my head against the door and listened to the sound of the Greys' robes whispering over the stone floor as they made their way down the corridor. When I was happy that they had gone, I went to my bag, which I had stuffed beneath the rickety-looking excuse of a wardrobe that lent against my bedroom wall.

I took out the iPod and hurriedly typed a message to Kiera. *Met McCain for the first time this morning,* I wrote. I wanted to tell her about how he had Tasered me, but I decided against it. I didn't want to see Potter smashing down the school walls – not just yet, anyhow. I needed to find out more about Ravenwood before that happened. *I've made a friend called Sam,* I wrote. *Seems okay – pretty hot as it goes! I'm going to try and get him to tell me more about Ravenwood and what's going on here. I will update you later. Kayla X*

I kept hold of the iPod just in case Kiera got right back to me. But before I'd the chance to find out, I heard someone outside my door. I threw the iPod back into my bag and kicked it back beneath my wardrobe. My bedroom door opened a gap, just big enough for Sam to creep inside.

"I've got to get outta here!" he said.

"What do you mean?" I asked. "Escape?"

Shaking his head, Sam said, "Not escape, I've got nowhere

to go. I mean just get out of Ravenwood for a few hours."

"What, right out of the school grounds?"

"Yeah, why not?" Sam said.

"I can think of one good reason," I told him.

"What's that?"

"This place is like a fortress! I've only been here five minutes and even I can see that. Besides, even if we did get past the Greys, the searchlights, and all that razor wire, where would we go? What would we do?"

"I dunno – anything!" Sam said. "I've been shut up in this place for months now and I know it's not going to be too long before I'm matched with a wolf and then things will never be the same for me again."

"How does the whole matching thing work?" I asked, sitting on the edge of my bed and watching him cross my room to the window.

"You mean you don't know?" he asked, sounding shocked.

"No, not really," I said shaking my head.

"Where have you been your whole life?"

Not wanting him to grow suspicious of me because of my lack of knowledge of how the world now worked since being pushed, I said, "I mean how does it work here?"

"Every Friday night, McCain holds the matching ceremony in the chapel at the back of the school," Sam started to explain, silhouetted by the milky winter light which poured in through the window behind him. "McCain watches us – studies us – as he looks for suitable students to be matched with the juvenile wolves who arrive each Friday evening. As far as I understand it, each of us are chosen carefully to make the right match. It has more to do with our personalities than how we look."

"How come?" I asked him, needing to know as much as possible about how this whole matching thing worked.

"Just like us, I guess each wolf is different," Sam said. "Each one has a different personality. If they're gonna spend the rest of their lives looking like a human, it makes sense, I s'pose, that they feel comfortable in that skin. From what I can figure out, the wolves are looking for teenagers who will succumb to the wolf that takes them other. I've heard that if the human host is quietly strong – rebellious by nature - then it's harder for the wolf to take over their soul and take complete control."

I thought of the fight I had witnessed that morning and said, "So someone like Pryor wouldn't make a good match?"

"How do you mean?" Sam asked me.

"Well he seems like a rebel – someone who rocks the boat – stronger willed," I explained. "I guess a wolf would have a job trying to crush his soul once inside him."

"Yeah, perhaps you're right," Sam said thoughtfully. "Maybe that's why he's such a jerk, like it's some kind of act so he isn't matched. But if that's what his game is, it could backfire on him."

"Why?"

"Because the wolves want to match with as many of us as possible," Sam said. "Remember they only get to pull this crazy shit every five years and only in one town at a time, and they only get six months to do it. Those of us who aren't matched get to go home – back to our families. See, Pryor can kick off as much as he likes, but McCain will just beat it out of him – break him. There are very few kids who aren't eventually matched."

"Does it scare you?" I asked Sam.

"Does the thought of being matched scare you?" he shot back.

"I don't know," I said honestly. I really didn't know how I felt about matching as I believed it really had nothing to do with me. I'd come from another place – another reality. But now that Sam had asked me the question, I realised now that I was living at Ravenwood, I ran the risk of being matched just like he might be.

"Like me, you've probably just grown up accepting the fact that one day it might happen to you," he said. "A bit like getting cancer, I guess, that's how I came to see it. The odds weren't in your favour, but you just prayed that you'd never get it."

"I guess," I said, pretending I'd had similar thoughts while growing up. In a way I felt like I was tricking him. Sam seemed like a nice guy, and I really didn't understand what it must have been like to grow up knowing that one day you ran the risk of having your soul taken by a werewolf. I'd had to grow up

133

coming to terms with the fact that I was a half-breed and that had been bad enough, but whatever I turned out to be, I was still going to be Kayla. I was never going to lose my identity – have my soul taken away from me. "Don't you hate your parents for letting them take you?" I asked him.

"Do you hate yours?" he shot back.

"It's different for me," I told him. And keeping up the pretence, I said, "My parents both died in a boating accident so I had little choice."

"I'm sorry that your mum and dad died," he said. "My parents died too."

To hear him say that made me wonder how much longer I could keep lying like this to him. I had no idea how he was really feeling. I wondered what the penalty would have been if the parents refused to let their child go, but I couldn't ask for fear of blowing my cover. I was meant to know all this stuff if I'd grown up in this world just like him. So I said, "When the wolves turned up in Wood Hill, did some of the parents try and hide their children or smuggle them away?"

"What would've been the point?" he asked, looking at me as if I'd lost my mind. "The wolves know exactly who does and doesn't have children in town – the government gives them access to the census. Anyway, a few weeks before McCain arrives in town, everyone knows that he sends spies, wolves that have previously been matched and look human. You must have heard that?"

"Something like that," I nodded briefly.

"And you must have heard what happened years ago in that town...what was it called now?" he said scratching his head and looking at me as if I might know the answer. But of course I didn't. "It doesn't matter. Anyway, some parents did try and resist and the wolves did that thing with their eyes. They looked into those parents' eyes and drove them half mad. They were never the same again, like vegetables I heard."

As I sat and listened to Sam talk, I remembered the people of Wood Hill and understood why they tried so hard not to make eye contact with those who passed them on the street. Then, I thought of the woman I had seen with the pram and the doll which had had its eyes removed. As if reading my thoughts, Sam started talking again.

"If any of the kids resisted being taken, the wolves would just stare into their eyes and they would be driven half mad with what they saw in them," he said. "I heard about this woman from one town, I think it was some years ago now, who was so desperate for her child not to be taken, that she cut her son's eyes out then removed her own, so neither of them could be brainwashed. How bad is that?"

"Awful," I whispered, feeling numb as I finally began to understand the devastation that the wolves – Skin-walkers – were causing to these people.

"Some of the teachers at Ravenwood tried to object to what was happening," Sam told me.

"What, the matching?"

"No, not that," he said, coming away from the window to sit next to me on the edge of the bed. "Like our parents, most of them realise that they don't have a choice in matching, but it's the way that McCain goes about it – that's what some of the teachers objected to. The brutality of the man, that's what the teachers didn't like. Isn't the matching bad enough, why does he have to be so cruel about it? Look what he did to you this morning."

I glanced down at my hands and was surprised to see that they had almost healed. There were a few black scabs where McCain had stuck his Taser, but nothing more. The purple swelling had gone and so had the streams of liquid-fat. Sitting on my hands, I looked at Sam and said, "Did you know a teacher by the name of Emily Clarke?"

"Yeah, why?" he asked me, sounding surprised.

"Oh no reason," I said, breaking his stare. "I just heard a few girls talking about her in the bathroom this morning. They were saying what a great teacher she was and how much they missed her."

Accepting my lie, Sam said, "She was a nice lady and a good teacher. She wasn't cruel like the others. Miss Clarke stood up for us. McCain hated her. But now she's gone, just like the other teachers."

"What do you think happened to her?" I asked, trying to make my questioning sound as casual as possible.

"McCain probably killed her," Sam shrugged.

"You're kidding me?" I said, again trying to sound as laid back as possible.

"Yeah, I'm just messing about," he said staring at me with those blue eyes, which in the fading light looked almost turquoise. "I don't mean this in a sick way, but part of me wished that he had murdered her."

"Why?" I asked him, surprised by what he had just said.

"Because he would have broken the conditions of the treaty, don't you see?"

"Would he?" I said.

With his eyes open wide, Sam looked at me, and said, "Kayla are you from this planet or what? You must know that if just one wolf kills – murders – a human, then the treaty is broken. And if that happens then the matching comes to an end and we're free!"

"What if McCain did murder Miss Clarke and the other teachers?" I whispered, not taking my eyes from his.

"McCain wouldn't be that stupid," Sam said.

"What if he's not stupid?" I said. "What if McCain is a killer?"

"You'd never prove it," Sam sighed.

Then, thinking of how Elizabeth Clarke had told Kiera how her sister had hidden a secret camera in her room, I looked at Sam and said, "We'll never know if we don't look."

"Look for what?" he asked, frowning at me.

"Clues," I said back.

"And where are you going to start looking for clues?"

"Do you know where Miss Clarke's room was?" I pressed.

"Yeah, why?" he said and the look of fear I could see in his eyes told me he had guessed what I was going to say next.

"We go and check it out tonight," I whispered.

Chapter Twenty-Four

Kiera

The store where Emily Clarke had supposedly used her credit card to buy chocolate, amongst other items, was on a road which lay about two miles north of Wood Hill. We didn't go straight to the counter and speak with the staff. Instead, Potter and I wandered around the store and looked to see what CCTV they had, if any. The only camera I could see was positioned behind the counter and looked out into the store and down at the cash registers. I looked at Potter, and we didn't have to speak to one another to know that if Emily had been in the store the previous morning, she would be on camera.

I threw some items into a basket, junk food mainly, and went to the cash register with it. The spotty youth who was working began to process my groceries. Once he had placed everything into a bag, Potter asked for a pack of cigarettes.

The guy working the cash register threw them into the bag and said, "That will be thirteen pounds twenty, mister."

Potter rummaged through his jeans pockets and pulled out a roll of twenties. At the same time I took my warrant card from my jacket pocket, opened it, and realised that I hadn't any money. I looked at the cash in Potter's fist. *My savings?* I wondered and looked at him. Potter shrugged his shoulders at me with a guilty grin.

I looked at the spotty youth behind the counter and I could see that he was eyeing my badge "Sorry, but my boss says I can't give discounts to the law anymore – not since one of you guys issued him that ticket for running a red."

"What?" I asked surprised. "I don't expect any discount."

"You can't be from around here, then," he said back.

"No, we're not," Potter cut in.

What kinda police department are they running down here? I wondered. Potter handed over the money and looking at the CCTV camera above his head, he looked back at the clerk and asked, "is there any chance we could take a look at the CCTV footage for yesterday?"

"No, you can't," he said.

"How come?" I asked him.

"Doesn't work. It's been broken for months," The clerk explained.   "The boss says it costs too much to get fixed. He'll be screwed if we ever have a robbery, insurance company will never pay out."

"Do you have any other cameras in store?" I asked.

"Nope, just that broken one. Why you want to know?" he asked, looking at me, then at Potter.

"It doesn't matter," I said, picking up the groceries and leaving the store.

I threw the bag onto the backseat of the car and slammed the door shut in frustration. Potter popped one of the cigarettes between his lips, lit it, and inhaled deeply.

"When are we going to get a half-decent break?" I asked him.

Potter looked at me and blew a lungful of smoke into the air.

"We're running around in circles," I said, more to myself than him.

"Something will turn up," he said, leaning against the side of the car and enjoying his smoke.

"And what if it doesn't?" I snapped, sounding more frustrated than cross. "Kayla is inside that school, werewolves are free to take children at will, we've got a young woman who has suddenly vanished or worse, and the local cop couldn't give a crap because he's too busy screwing the local Seven-Eleven for a discount!"

Potter didn't say anything back, he just puffed on the cigarette and squirted jets of smoke out through his nostrils. When he had finished, he flicked the cigarette into the gutter and got into the car. I climbed in next to him, feeling more frustrated than ever. Potter started the engine and it spluttered and wheezed to life.

"We need some petrol. We're nearly empty," he said.

On the other side of the road, there was a small petrol

station with two pumps on the tiny forecourt. "Over there," I said, jabbing my finger in the direction of the petrol station.

Potter swung the car out of the car park and crossed the road to the petrol station which stood opposite the Seven-Eleven. He drew level with a pump, got out, and began to fill the tank. I watched him through the car window, and it was then that I saw it. There was a CCTV camera attached to the underside of the petrol station canopy facing out across the forecourt.

While Potter finished filling the tank, I climbed from the car and walked over to where the camera was fixed. I looked up at it and studied the position it was facing. I turned my back to face it and looked out at the view that the camera had. I could see the whole of the forecourt and beyond, where to my delight, across the street was the entrance to the Seven-Eleven.

"I wonder?" I whispered. "I wonder?"

Chapter Twenty-Five

Kiera

We went into the kiosk and Potter paid for the petrol in full from my savings. I didn't show my badge before the petrol had been paid for, as I wasn't sure if this was something else Banner and his merry men expected discount on. The girl behind the counter was chewing obnoxiously on a piece of gum. I showed her my badge. She raised her eyebrows as if to say '*What now?*' and then said, "What can I do you for?"

"I'm investigating a missing person enquiry and I was wondering if I could view your CCTV footage for yesterday."

"How's that?" she mumbled, removing the gum from her front teeth with her tongue.

"How's what?" Potter glared at her.

"Why do you want to watch the CCTV?" she asked him.

"Because we've had information that she may have been in the area yesterday, so we need to check it out," he said bluntly.

"What, she came in here did she?" the girl asked.

Potter sighed and managed a false smile as if he was fast losing his patience. "I don't know. That's why we need to view the CCTV."

She eyed us momentarily and blew a large pink bubble from between her lips. It popped and she sucked it back into her mouth.

"Sure, it's all in the back," and she nodded towards a door that had *PRIVATE - STAFF ONLY* written across it.

"Thank you," I smiled and headed towards the door.

The backroom was poky and smelt strongly of stale tobacco smoke. There was a table and a rubbish bin that was overflowing with empty cans of Coke and cheeseburger wrappers. The table was littered with crumpled magazines and newspapers. Fixed to the wall was a TV monitor which showed the gas station forecourt. I watched it and could see a car pulling in. In the distance, I could see across the street and customers entering the Seven-Eleven. It wasn't the clearest picture in the world but it would do. I guessed that if Emily Clarke was in that store yesterday, I would be able to make her out on the footage. After all, she looked just like her sister, Elizabeth. On the wall beside the monitor was a shelf which housed a bunch of discs in plastic CD cases. I ran my fingers along their spines and stopped when I had found the previous day's disc. I plucked it from the shelf and placed it into the DVD player beneath the TV.

The monitor went blank then flickered into life and once again I was viewing the gas station forecourt from the previous day. It was like going back in time. In the right-hand corner of the screen flashed yesterday's date and time. It read 07:13 hrs. I held my finger down on the fast-forward button and whizzed through the next few hours of footage. Banner had told me that Emily's credit card had been used in the Seven-Eleven store at 10:30 am, so I let the DVD run at normal speed from 10:25 am just to make sure and take into account any timing discrepancies.

We stood in the staffroom and glanced anxiously up at the screen, both hoping that we would see Emily. The clock on the film ticked round to 10:30 am and we still hadn't seen her.

"Come on," I breathed, hoping for just one break.

"Take it easy, tiger," Potter said, sensing how anxious I was becoming.

By 10:31 am there was still no sign of her. The minutes seemed to take an eternity to pass. Now 10:32 am - nothing. Then, as the clock turned to 10:33 am on the screen, I saw something. I quickly pressed the pause button and the image froze. I moved closer to the screen until my nose was almost pressed against it and I screwed up my eyes and stared at the screen. I didn't recognise the person leaving the store a few moments after Emily's credit card had been used but it definitely wasn't Emily Clarke. Even through the grainy black and white image on the screen I could see that it was a man. He was tall, with black, swept back hair, wearing a black suit.

"Who do you think that is?" Potter asked me.

I had never seen McCain, but from the grainy picture on the screen, the image of the man looked just how Elizabeth Clarke had described him.

"McCain," I said, unable to take my eyes from the TV.

"How can you be so sure?" Potter asked, peering over my shoulder.

"I can't," I told him, taking the disc from the DVD player. "Let's just hope that Isidor has done his homework in researching this McCain."

"Let's hope," Potter said, sounding unconvinced.

"But one thing's for sure," I said, looking at him. "Emily Clarke didn't use her credit card yesterday. So where is she now?"

"Beats the shit out of me," Potter said, heading back through the kiosk.

"Did you find what you were looking for?" the girl with the gum called out as we headed out of the door.

"Maybe," I smiled, leaving the kiosk.

Chapter Twenty-Six

Kayla

We waited for lights-out, and for the school to fall into silence before we dared leave our rooms. With his head bent low, and crouched over like a crab, Sam made his way down the narrow staircase at the end of the corridor. I followed him down the spiral stairwell and into the bowels of Ravenwood. The school was in darkness, and I felt my way down the staircase by brushing the tips of my fingers against the stone wall, listening to the *snap-snap* sound of Sam's shoes ahead of me. Reaching the ground floor, Sam crept through the passageways which stretched throughout Ravenwood. I followed.

Ahead, oblong shards of moonlight fell through the corridor windows and lit our way. I could hear the sound of Sam's racing heart and it was almost deafening in the desolate corridors. My stomach tightened and I felt sick. Back in my bedroom, the idea of searching out Emily Clarke's bedroom seemed exciting, but Sam hadn't mentioned anything about how creepy the school was during the night and in the dark. Every shadow we passed I eyed with dread, fearing that a Grey would appear from within the gloom and come racing towards me, sizzle-stick in hand, its end pulsating with shocks of electric blue light.

The hallway windows looked out across the grounds of the school. As we neared each one, Sam would flap his hand in a downwards motion, signalling for me to drop. Crouching as we passed beneath the windows, the white light from the search towers flooded the hall then swooped away again. Standing, with backs arched, we moved off again. Ahead, the hallway veered to the right and I followed Sam down it. Not once did Sam falter or stop to wonder what direction he should take. He seemed to know where he was heading. As we rounded the bend, I stopped, threw my arm out against Sam's chest and pressed him to the wall.

"What?" he said, looking startled.

"Shhh!" I hissed. "Can't you hear that?"

"Hear what?" Sam whispered.

Then, the sound of crying – no pleading – that I could hear, seeped up from below.

"That!" I said, my eyes wide like saucers.

The sound came again. But this time it sounded more like whimpering than sobbing.

"Where's it coming from?" Sam asked, taking one of my hands in his. It felt nice to be holding his hand, but his flesh felt cold like a corpse. Sam glanced to his left and then to his right, as he tried to find the whereabouts of the noise in the pitch blackness of the school.

It came again, but this time words could be heard between each sob and whimper.

"*Nooooo....Pleeeaaassee stop! I beg you!*" The voice sounded like the person was being strangled. Whoever had muttered those words was in complete agony.

I followed the voice in the darkness and it led us to the top of a narrow wooden staircase fixed into the corridor wall. The stairs led down beneath Ravenwood.

"I've never seen these stairs before," Sam whispered behind his hand.

"I think we should head back..." I started, just wanting to contact Kiera and tell her what I had discovered. But what had I discovered? Not much. No proof yet of what had happened to Emily.

A splash of light from the search towers illuminated the corridor. It fell across our face. And seeing the fear in Sam's eyes, I knew what he had meant when he said I looked as if I were about to shit myself. We dropped to the floor and lay on our stomachs. I could hear a scratching sound from beside me and I rolled onto my side.

"What's that noise?" I whispered.

"What? The scratching noise?" Sam asked.

"Yeah."

"That's me," Sam said.

144

"What are you doing? Someone will hear!" I groaned.

"Shhh!" Sam said. "I've found something."

"What?"

"The reason why I've never seen this stairwell before," Sam told me.

"How come?"

"They've had it hidden behind this bookcase," Sam whispered. "They just slide it aside when they want to go down..."

"You're hurting me," the voice from below came again, and it sounded weak and petrified. *"I don't know anything about any....no! Pleeeaaassee stop!"*

"I think we should get outter..." Sam started.

"No - wait. I want to listen to this," I whispered, my head tilted towards the top of the stairwell.

"Are you out of your tiny mind?" Sam whispered.

"Shhh!" I told him, putting a finger to my lips.

"*...I don't know what you're talking about...*" the voice echoed up from below again and this time I got the sense that the voice belonged to a woman. "*...Just let me go...I promise I won't say anything!*"

We were so intent on listening to the woman's pitiful voice that neither of us heard the sound of footfalls climbing the stairwell which led up from the basement. Searchlight flooded the corridor again and poured down the stairwell. In the flash of brilliant white light, I saw a shadow creeping along the wall of the stairwell as someone came up from the depths of Ravenwood towards us.

"Go!" I cried, scrambling to my feet.

"Say what?" Sam asked, sounding surprised.

"Someone's coming!" I hissed.

And then, as if being kicked in the ribs, Sam jumped to his feet and raced away down the corridor, as I clambered at his heels. I glanced back over my shoulder, but the searchlight had swept away, and all I could see was darkness. I didn't know what was worse, not being able to see what it was that had come from beneath the stairs or the terrifying images my mind would create later while I lay in the dark on my own.

Without warning, Sam stopped ahead and I nearly crashed into him.

"How much more noise are you planning on making?" Sam groaned in the darkness. "You'll have the whole goddamn school awake in a minute!"

"Oh stop your moaning. It wasn't me who was moving pieces of furniture about back there! Anyway, why'd you stop like that all of a sudden, its pitch bla -"

"Cos we're here, that's why," Sam whispered.

"Where's here?"

"Miss Clarke's room," Sam whispered, and as he swung open the door, a burst of searchlight splashed against the corridor walls again. Sam grabbed my hand again, and pulling me into the room he closed the door behind us.

Chapter Twenty-Seven

Kayla

The searchlights swept back and forth across the lawns outside Emily Clarke's bedroom window. I glanced around the room and in the odd flashes of light from outside I could see that the room was furnished very similarly to my own. There was a single bed in the corner, a wardrobe, desk, and a bookshelf, which looked like it was going to collapse under the weight of the books crammed on its shelves.

"That was close," I sighed, looking into Sam's eyes.

He stared straight back. His breathing sounded shallow and I could hear his heart racing in his chest again, but something told me that it wasn't through fear this time. Feeling a little embarrassed by his gaze, I pulled my hand from his, and stepped away.

"So what are we looking for exactly?" Sam asked.

Not wanting him to know that I was looking for the camera that Elizabeth Clarke had told Kiera her sister had hidden, I stepped towards the wardrobe and said, "I'm not sure."

The room lit up again as the searchlights swept passed the window outside. It was then that I saw the blood. It looked like someone had gone crazy with a paint brush that had been dipped in red paint. Dried blood stained the walls, the ceiling, and the wooden floor in thick streaks and splashes.

"What the fuck...?" Sam breathed in horror seeing the blood for the first time.

I had seen enough of the red stuff to last me a lifetime, but the sight of it made my stomach knot as I thought of how good it tasted. For just the briefest of moments I felt dizzy and swayed backwards, as part of me wanted to start licking the walls clean.

Sam caught hold of me in his arms and held me close. I could hear his heart again and I could tell that he enjoyed holding me. "Are you okay?" he whispered. "I don't like the sight of blood either."

If only he knew, I thought to myself as the dizziness faded along with my cravings. "Yeah, it's something like that," I told him, glancing around the room at the blood. I wished that Kiera was here, because within moments she would be doing her thing – crawling around the room on her hands and knees, seeing stuff that no one else could. Kiera would have been able to tell me exactly what had happened in this room. Just by glancing at the amount of blood that had been spilt, I knew that someone had died in here – they had been butchered. I could guess that it had been Emily Clarke who had died here, but how and who had murdered her, I didn't know.

"Are you okay?" Sam asked again, as he watched me looking around the room at all the dried blood.

"Sure," I said, pulling gently away from him.

Sam crossed the room to the desk and started to rummage through the paperwork that was placed there. "Well that's a surprise," he whispered into the dark.

"What is?" I asked, peering into the wardrobe.

"Miss Clarke had given Pryor a "D" on his last piece of homework," he said, thumbing through a workbook. "He really is thick as shit."

I smiled to myself as I closed the wardrobe door and looked back at the room. Elizabeth had said that Emily had woken to find McCain standing at the foot of her bed. *So where would have been the best place to hide a camera?* I wondered. *Where would I have hidden it?* I looked around the room and if it had been me waking to find McCain watching me as I slept, my first instinct would have been to rip his balls off, but Emily didn't do that – she wasn't me. But if I were her...then, I guessed where she would have hidden a camera. The bookshelf!

I crossed the room towards it and started to pull aside the books. Then, I came across a small green light shining from amongst the row of books, which lit up my face like a Halloween mask. The green light seeped from behind a thick leather-bound book. I pulled the book from the shelf, and there was the camera.

"Wassa-matta?" Sam asked, looking over his shoulder and seeing me staring at the bookshelf.

The camera was very small and was one of those that could have easily been hidden in the palm of my hand. It was the type of camera that didn't take a disc or memory card, but one which you downloaded straight to your laptop. If I could take it without Sam noticing then that would be great. It wasn't that I didn't trust him, but the fewer people that knew about it, the better.

"Wassa-matta?" he asked again.

"I'm listening, just in case someone comes down the corridor," I told him.

"Chill out, will ya? You're making me nervous," Sam said.

"I'm making *you* nervous?" I half-smiled back at him. "How do you think McCain's gonna make you feel if he catches us in here?"

"He ain't gonna catch us. You don't think he lives here, do ya?" Sam scoffed. "He's probably got some right nice drum somewhere. It's just us mugs that have to put up with living here. He won't be back 'till the morning."

Sam turned back to the desk. I slipped my hand between the books and tried to free the tiny camera. I could feel wires leading from the back of it. I tried to loosen them with my fingertips, when I heard someone in the corridor outside. Sam must have heard the footsteps too, as he hissed, "Hey! Someone's coming!"

I drew breath and it made a shallow wheezing sound in the back of my throat. I had been so close to taking that camera. I turned to look at Sam. His eyes were wide.

"What are we gonna do?" Sam panicked.

I scanned the room, searching for a hiding place for the both of us. From the corridor, the sound of approaching footfalls grew louder.

"Under the bed!" I whispered.

"You're kidding me?" Sam groaned.

"Get under the bed!" I spat and I could see terror in Sam's eyes, and seeing it only heightened my own sense of fear.

Sam seemed to freeze, unable to do anything. Knowing that

my friend had become cemented to the spot, I rushed forward and pushed Sam hard in the chest.

"How you ever talked me into this, I do not know!" Sam groaned.

"Get under the bed!" I hissed.

Sam dropped to the floor and rolled underneath, and I followed. Wrapping his arms about himself, Sam curled up, his knees were against his chest and he was taking small, shallow breaths.

"Budge over!" I whispered. "I need some room."

"Perhaps you'd like to sit on my lap?" Sam said.

"Yeah, very funny. Now move!"

I forced my way into the space and made myself as small as possible. I screwed my eyes shut and prayed that whoever it was coming down the corridor would walk straight past.

Please go right past! Please don't come in here and find me and Sam hiding under the bed curled up like a couple of babies!

The sound of approaching feet stopped outside the door.

Please!

I peeked through my fingers and watched as the bottom of the door swung open. A pair of gleaming black shoes entered the room. I knew who was wearing them. I could hear him sniffing as if his nose was blocked. McCain closed the door and came inside. He stood in the middle of the room and sniffed the air. Then, crossing over to the wall on the opposite side of the room, he did what I had fought the urge to do. He rolled his tongue from his mouth and licked the congealed blood that covered the wall. He licked it like you would a lollypop, in long, drawn-out movements as if he was savouring every moment. I watched as he pressed his nose into the dried blood and sniffed. He sniffed again, and he seemed to become agitated as if he couldn't smell the blood in some way, like his nose was stuffed with snot.

McCain crossed the room and sat down on the edge of the bed.

How did I get into this? I cursed at myself. *Should've listened to Kiera.*

I heard McCain sniff again and then rummage through his

trouser pockets. Empty. He sniffed again. I guessed he was looking for his nasal spray. McCain squirmed on the edge of the bed as he bent forward. Sam flinched beside me and rammed his fist into his mouth as one of McCain's shoes brushed against him.

He's gonna find us! I screamed inside.

Sam lay on his side, eyes closed. If he had popped his thumb into his mouth, the image of a baby in its cot would have been complete. McCain shifted above us again, and the springs in the bed groaned.

"Where is it?" I heard McCain curse under his breath.

I can't breathe! McCain's feet were now so close to us, I could smell the leather that they had been cut from and see the stitching that was holding them together. Then, something landed on the floor just inches from where we were hiding. Sam jumped and looked at me. Seeing what it was that had fallen beneath the bed, Sam's eyes bulged in their sockets like hardboiled eggs and he pointed at it with one trembling finger. I looked in the direction that Sam was pointing, and could see McCain's bottle of nasal spray lying between us beneath the bed.

Suddenly, McCain's hand appeared. It scurried about like a bony spider, as it felt for the medicine beneath the bed. To my horror, his hand began to scuttle towards me. And with no room to manoeuvre beneath the bed, I might well end up in Sam's lap. McCain's hand inched nearer and nearer, in search of the bottle. Sensing that I was only seconds from being caught, I leant forward and pushed the medicine towards McCain's hand with my fingertips. McCain's spidery-like hand curled around it and snatched the bottle away.

I looked sideways at Sam. He closed his eyes, then tilting his head as if looking up at the ceiling, he mouthed the words, "Thank you."

I felt McCain stand up, and from our hiding place we watched him head over towards the bookcase to where the camera was hidden. I watched McCain unscrew the cap, like a desperate drunk opening a bottle of beer, then ram the bottle into his right nostril. Throwing his head back, he squeezed the bottle between thumb and forefinger and breathed in deeply. He then thrust the bottle into his left nostril and did the same. Shaking his head from side to side, tears began to trickle from the corners of his eyes, and his nose began to dribble snot onto his top lip. He replaced the cap and put the nasal spray back into his pocket. There was a small mirror attached to the wall next to the bookshelf. From our hiding place, we watched as he pushed up the end of his nose and tilted his head from side to side as he glared up his own nostrils. Then with his right forefinger, he pulled a bloody length of snot from his nose. After inspecting it, I gagged as McCain rolled it between his fingers then popped it into his mouth.

Forget being discovered under the bed with Sam, if he ever found out we saw him do that, we'd get more than a few zaps with a sizzle-stick – we'll be doing twenty years hard labour in the Rat-House, I thought and rammed my knuckles into my mouth to stop myself from puking.

I looked at Sam, who was pretending to throw-up. He was putting two fingers into his mouth and grinning. Turning away, I watched McCain stand in front of the bookshelf and my stomach scrunched up in fear.

The camera! He'll see the camera! I screamed inside my head.

Then, a high-pitched wailing sound broke the silence and McCain turned away from the bookshelf. The noise was ear-splitting and I placed my hands over my ears. Spying from beneath the bed, I could see the green light from the camera peeking between the spines of two books.

"I don't believe it!" McCain groaned. "How many more of those *things* are gonna freak out?" McCain left Emily's bedroom, slamming the door behind him.

No sooner had the door closed then Sam and I were scrambling out from beneath the bed.

"C'mon!" Sam said, heading towards the door.

"Hang on," I told him, knowing that I would never be able to sneak the camera out of the room now without him seeing me. But I needed that camera – that's what I had risked everything for – and I wasn't leaving without it. I pushed aside the books and grabbed the camera. It wouldn't come free; the wires attached to it were still holding the camera in place.

"What are you doing?" Sam hissed from the doorway.

"I think I've found something," I said back, tugging the camera free of the wires.

"Have you lost your mind?" Sam snapped. "We don't have time for this. Can't you hear the sirens? This place is gonna be crawling with Greys."

I yanked one last time on the camera, and it came free of the wire. The green light went out. "I'm good to go," I said, trying to conceal the camera in my hand.

Sam looked at it, then glancing at me he said, "Whatever is on that camera had better be worth the shit we're gonna be in if we get caught."

Then, sneaking from the room and back into the darkness of the corridor, we crept with speed through the labyrinth of passageways. Not wanting to be caught by McCain, who we feared might still be close by, we headed back towards our rooms as quickly as we could.

Racing through the hallways and corridors, the searchlights whizzed frantically back and forth. No longer were they controlled, sweeping movements, but desperate and erratic as if searching for something that was now loose in the grounds of Ravenwood. Sam charged down the passageways. Almost halfway back to the safety of our rooms, the air raid sirens grew louder. It was like I had been transported back in time to the Blitz. The noise was deafening, and with the sudden flashes of light illuminating the corridors from outside, both Sam and I became disorientated.

We raced on, every part of my being urging me forward. Sam's arms pumped beside him, and he ran so hard and fast that his knees looked as if they might just touch his chin. Reaching a bend in the corridor, we sprinted around it, stalling in fright as a Grey sprung from the shadows.

"Whoa!" Sam shrieked as the Grey took hold of him by both shoulders.

Light flashed into the corridor and in that instance, I recognised the Grey to be Brother Michael. The light darted away again, leaving his large frame shrouded in darkness.

Brother Michael made a rasping sound in the back of his throat, like he was gargling blood or something. His tongue smacked off his chin, spraying spittle through the air. Brother Michael screamed, tilting his head to one side as if waking from a nightmare. His screams were hideous, gut-wrenching, and filled me with dread. I wanted to get far away from Brother Michael but he had Sam trapped. Without thinking, I grabbed at Sam. Taking hold of his shirt, I yanked him back and away from the Grey. Brother Michael released his grip, and then shook all over, as if he'd just received an electric shock.

Spinning round, Brother Michael charged into the corridor wall, smacking his head against it. He staggered and then fell backwards. The sound of his head striking the wall was a dull, sickening thud and I half expected to see the Grey's brains explode out of the back of his head. Somehow, Brother Michael managed to stay on his feet as he began to spin around and around, his arms flapping up and down on either side. We watched in disbelief as Brother Michael bounced off the walls like a ball in a pinball machine. He reached the end of the corridor, where he crashed through a set of doors and out into the grounds of the school.

Seizing our chance, Sam and I dashed up the stairs, taking two at a time until we had reached the landing outside our rooms. At the top of the spiral staircase, I looked out of the window. I watched as several of the Greys wrestled with something on the lawn beneath the window. Whatever it was, it was screaming. The noise that it made sounded like it was having its throat slit.

Sam crashed into my bedroom, and I followed close behind. I slammed the door closed, lent against it, my chest pumping up and down, trying to suck mouthfuls of air into my burning lungs.

"That was close...*too* close!" I gasped. "I guess Brother Michael will be sending us to the Rat-House when he catches up with us!"

Sam collapsed onto my bed and lay there panting for breath like a tired dog.

"Are you taking the piss, Kayla?" Sam wheezed.

"No."

"He ain't going to be sending us to no Rat-House. We won't be seeing him again. Didn't you see him? He's freaked out – gone bat-shit!" he puffed. "Have you still got that camera?"

"Yes," I said, not wanting to let go of it.

"What do you think is on it?" Sam asked, getting his breath back.

"I don't know," I said, collapsing onto the bed next to him.

"Maybe it will show us what really happened to Miss Clarke," Sam said. Then he added, "It might show us where all that blood came from."

"It might," I said, wondering now if I really wanted to watch what had been recorded on the camera. Did I really want to see Emily Clarke being butchered?

"Well, let's have a look then," Sam said, propping himself up on one elbow. We lay so close to each other that our heads nearly brushed together.

"We can't," I said, holding up the camera. "I left the power cable behind."

"You're shitting me, right?" Sam gasped in disbelief.

"You were rushing me," I insisted.

"You're telling me we nearly got busted to get that camera and we can't even watch what's been recorded on it?" he asked me.

"Looks like it," I said, looking at the camera.

It was then Sam started to laugh.

"What's so funny?" I asked him.

"Us," he laughed. "We must be out of our freaking minds."

Staring down at the camera and knowing there was no way I was going to find out what was on it, I started to laugh too. It wasn't just a giggle or snigger. We lay next to each other and laughed great big belly laughs until tears streamed from our eyes.

With his laughter under control, Sam turned his head so he could look at me and said, "You know, Kayla Hunt, I've never met a girl like you before."

"Oh," I said. I didn't know what else to say.

"You're different," he smiled. "It's kinda exciting being with you."

"Is that a compliment?" I asked him, his blue eyes burning into mine.

"A big compliment," he smiled again.

I didn't know what to say. I had never had a boyfriend before and the last guy who paid me a compliment ended up murdering me. With those memories in the front of my mind, I sat up and said, "I think you should go back to your own room now."

"I didn't mean to upset you," Sam said, sounding concerned.

"I'm just tired," I lied.

Sam went to the door and opened it. Before he left, he looked back at me and said, "There is something different about you, Kayla. I don't know what it is, but you're definitely not like other girls." Then he was gone, closing the door behind him and leaving me alone.

Chapter Twenty-Eight

Kiera

On arriving back at the farmhouse, Potter and I found Isidor sitting before a roaring fire with the laptop on his knee. The late afternoon was cold, and the sky looked as if it was threatening to snow. Isidor sat with his back arched and his eyes fixed on the screen before him. The fire flickered in the grate, casting warm-looking shadows across the walls. The room felt cosy, and sinking onto one of the old armchairs next to Isidor, I stretched out in front of the fire.

"Had any luck?" he asked us without looking up.

"I don't know yet," I said, taking the disc from my jacket pocket. "Put this in."

Isidor looked at the disc. "What's that?" he asked.

"A disc," Potter said.

"I know what it is," Isidor said. "What I meant is, what's on it?"

"It's CCTV from a petrol station which looks across the street at the store where Emily Clarke's credit card was used yesterday," I explained.

"Nice," Isidor smiled, taking the disc and sliding it into the side of the laptop. "What about CCTV from the store?"

"Didn't have any," Potter said, perching on the arm of my chair.

We all sat and watched the screen as the disc loaded. In seconds the shot of the petrol station forecourt flashed onto the screen.

"Wind forward to ten-thirty-three," I told him. Isidor found the place on the disc. I stared at the screen and waited for the man to appear from within the store. The image looked clearer on the laptop than it had on the TV back at the station.

"There!" I said, jabbing my finger at the screen. "Stop right there."

Isidor hit pause and the image froze as the man I suspected

to be McCain left the store.

"It's not great," I said. "Is there any chance you can get a bigger image?"

"Give me a second or two," Isidor said, and I could see that he was enjoying showing me, more likely Potter, that he could be of use. Isidor took a screenshot, then opened it with the paint programme, where he enlarged the picture.

"That's McCain," Isidor said, looking at me.

"Are you sure?" Potter asked him.

"You asked me to do some research on the guy," Isidor said, ignoring Potter and looking straight at me. "I searched the net for info on the guy, but it was hard because there are loads of McCain's all over the place, so it was difficult for me to track him down. But I eventually found this article on a Morris McCain. He is known as the *Matcher* by the wolf community."

"The *matcher*?" I breathed.

"It would seem that Morris McCain has spent his life organising the matching of wolves into human skins. He is meant to have a nose for it. And I'm not trying to be funny about the whole nose thing either. Apparently he has this amazing sense of smell, a bit like my own I guess," Isidor explained. "That's how he matches wolves to humans – he matches them by smell. But over the years, it has been rumoured that his sense of smell has weakened and some of the matches that he has arranged recently haven't been entirely successful."

"How come?" Potter asked him, sounding interested in what Isidor had discovered.

"It seems that for there to be a successful matching, the human host has to be very similar in attitude, temperament, and spirit to the wolf. If they're not, then there can be problems."

"What sort of problems?" I asked him.

"From what I've read, it's almost like organ donation," Isidor said. "If you don't get a perfect match like blood type and stuff the body rejects the organ. If this happens in *matching*, the human rejects the wolf. It's like they have an internal clash – a battle – if you like."

"What happens then?" Potter asked, taking a cigarette and twiddling it between his fingers instead of lighting it.

"They go kind of crazy," Isidor said, looking at us.

"How crazy?" I asked him.

"Put it like this," Isidor said, "The crazy ones are known as the Berserkers. They either get humanely destroyed like rabid animals or get locked away. They are too dangerous to be allowed to just wander around the place."

"So what about McCain?" Potter quizzed.

"Well, he seems to be quite high up in COW."

"Cow?" I asked him.

"The Council of Wolves. It's a self-regulating body of Skinwalkers who make sure that the Treaty of Wasp Water is adhered to. The humans have the same kind of thing, it's called UNCOW. United Nations Control of Wolves," Isidor explained, stroking the little beard that jutted from his chin. "Both organisations monitor the treaty. McCain is a prominent figure who is in charge of matching wolves with humans. He is highly thought of amongst the wolves and some humans."

"Only some?" I asked, as a flurry of sparks from the fire disappeared up the chimney.

"There have been reports that he is brutal with some of the children he chooses for matching. The treaty says that although the matching of wolves with humans is a necessary evil to maintain peace, it has to be done humanely and with as little suffering to the child as possible. Those who aren't chosen have to be returned unharmed to their families within a reasonable time. They can't be held indefinitely."

"That's good of them," Potter said dryly, then lit the cigarette he had been playing with.

"I can't believe what you're telling me, Isidor," I said. "I know the world has been pushed...but this is nasty."

"It gets worse," Isidor sighed. "McCain is also rumoured to have murdered parents and teachers who have uncovered his cruelty and threatened to expose him. But it has never been proved. Witnesses have either retracted their statements or gone missing."

"Just like Emily Clarke," I said thoughtfully.

"But this time he just might not get away with it," Isidor said, turning to face the laptop again. "Take a look at this."

He brought up a page on the screen which contained an article about Morris McCain. In the top right hand-corner was his picture. Although the CCTV footage was grainy, I could see that it was McCain who had left the Seven-Eleven just moments after Emily Clarke's credit card had been used.

"We have him," Potter said grimly.

"Not quite," I cautioned him. "We have a piece of dodgy-looking CCTV of a guy who looks like McCain leaving the store. Even if we could prove that it was him, we don't actually have proof that it was him who used Emily's credit card. How many other people were there in that store? Any one of them could have used that card."

"We could go back and get a statement from the dude with the zits," Potter suggested. "He might remember serving him."

"What, and have another witness go missing?" Isidor cut in.

"Okay, Velma Dinkley," Potter said, "what do you suggest this time? Perhaps we fire up the Mystery Machine, storm the school, and torture a confession out of this piece of shit?"

"No," I cut in. "We pray that Kayla finds that camera."

Chapter Twenty-Nine

Kiera

I could see him lying there, his face white, bruised, and featureless. I moved towards him in my mind, feeling nauseous and not wanting to look at him at all. But despite my fear and repulsion, I edged forward, half expecting him to sit bolt upright. I stood over him, his hard, cold, grey body looking like stone. I couldn't tell how old he was, but there was something – I didn't know what - but I had seen him before.

Who would sculpt a statue lying down, hidden amongst a pile of wild bushes? I wondered.

I leant over him and just like I feared, he sat bolt upright. I screamed and staggered backwards out of the bushes and into the woods. He crawled on his broken hands and knees into the clearing, parts of him falling away into grey, powdery dust.

I had seen that before. But there had been a girl. Hospital beds...

"C'mon, Kiera, come on in out of the cold!" the statue suddenly said, beckoning me with one cracked-looking hand, back to the shelter of the bush, "I have so much to tell you."

"What do you have to tell me?" I whispered, stepping away.

"Come on in out of the cold," he said again, not through his mouth as he didn't have one. His voice seemed to seep from the crevices and breaks in his stone flesh.

"I'm not cold," I lied, shivering in the snow-covered wood. "What is it that you have to tell me?"

"I need to talk to you about Alice," he said, crawling forward, two of his fingers crumbling away as he grabbed at the woodland floor.

"Who's Alice?" I asked him.

"The girl in the hospital bed," he said.

Then there was a noise. It was shrill and sounded like a far-off alarm. I looked back into the wood, the snow seesawing down in giant white flakes. The sound of the alarm was coming from *back there somewhere. I faced front again and screamed. The statue was standing inches from me, it's broken hand outstretched.*

"What's that noise?" someone asked from beside me.

I turned to see Potter.

"Kiera, it's Kayla," he said...

"Potter?" I whispered, opening my eyes.

"Kayla is Skyping you," Potter said, shoving my iPod into my hand.

I looked around me, half expecting to see the statue in the snow-covered wood. But I wasn't in the wood; I was curled in the armchair before the roaring fire, where I had drifted asleep.

"It's Kayla," Potter said, thrusting the iPod towards me again. Hearing his sister's name being mentioned, Isidor came into the room and looked at me.

I took my iPod from Potter and looking down I could see her pretty face staring out of the screen at me. Wherever she was, it was dark, as the light from the screen of her own iPod lit up her face in eerie shades of blue and green.

"Kayla," I said, raising my iPod so she could see me. "Are you okay?"

"I guess," she half-smiled back at me, her voice sounding faint and distorted. "I needed to speak to you."

"Where are you?" I asked her. "It looks dark where you are."

"I'm in my room," she explained, her voice just above a whisper. "Lights go out at nine at Ravenwood. I daren't put the light on or it might attract the attention of one of those Greys. They've gone crazy tonight."

"How come?" I asked her, Potter and Isidor now standing behind me so they could see Kayla.

"I don't know, but something spooked them," she said, bringing the iPod closer to her face. "These alarms were ringing and Greys were running around everywhere. One of them nearly caught us."

"Us?" I asked her, wondering what was happening in that school.

"Me and Sam went walk-about tonight," she whispered, her face ghostly looking as she stared back at me.

"Why?" Isidor asked, leaning over my shoulder.

"Hey, Isidor," Kayla said, catching a glimpse of her brother. "I miss you."

"I miss you too," he said back, sounding a little choked. "But why did you..."

Before he had a chance to finish, Kayla said, "I'm not going to find anything out unless I actually go and investigate, am I?"

"Who's Sam?" Isidor asked, sounding like a concerned older brother.

"Just a friend, he's really nice," she said, and I heard her voice soften slightly at the mention of him.

"So, did you find anything out on this little trip of yours?" Potter suddenly cut in.

"Hey, is that cranky-pants?" Kayla asked, and I could hear her giggle back in her room.

"Watch it," Potter said but he didn't really sound angry with her, he knew she was just teasing him. "So did you find anything or not?"

"I found out that McCain is a complete and utter whack-job," she said.

"What do you mean?" I asked her, fearing that he might have hurt her in some way. We sat huddled around my iPod as Kayla told us about her visit through Ravenwood to Emily Clarke's bedroom. She described in detail the blood that covered the walls and how she and Sam had hidden when McCain had come to the room. On hearing how he had licked the walls, my stomach lurched as it made me feel sick, but not as ill as when Kayla described what he had done after that. Kayla told us in a whisper how McCain seemed to have a permanently blocked nose, and Isidor told her why.

Kayla seemed to know little about the matching other than it took place at a disused chapel and that McCain was responsible for the matching of the wolves with the kids at the school. Hearing her description of Emily's bedroom, I feared that this was how Emily had met her death. I asked Kayla if this is all that she had managed to discover.

Then, for just a second she disappeared from view, then was back again. She held something up before her and said, "Look what I found."

It took me a moment to figure out exactly what it was she holding. "Is that the camera Emily had hidden in her room?" I breathed.

"Sure is," she said, sounding pleased with herself.

"Have you watched what's on it?" Isidor cut in, sounding excited.

"Does it show her being murdered?" Potter asked next.

"Shhh!" I hissed. "Let Kayla talk."

"No, I haven't been able to watch it," she said. "It's one of those cameras that downloads straight to a laptop. Besides, I had to leave the power cable behind."

"Why?" Potter asked.

"I was in a mad rush to get out of that room before McCain came back," she explained.

"So how are we gonna ever know what's on there?" Isidor inquired.

"I'll go and get it," Potter said, standing up as if he was going to leave right now.

"No, don't do that!" Kayla insisted. "I'm not allowed visitors until the matching is over and they drill it into the kids that if they see strangers or anyone who looks odd, to report it."

"I don't look odd," Potter snapped. Then, looking at me, he said, "Do I look odd to you?"

Ignoring him, I looked down at the screen and said, "What do you suggest, Kayla?"

"I'll try and sneak away tomorrow somehow," she said. "But the place is pretty guarded, what with the searchlights and towers. But I've got the advantage that no one here knows what I truly am. I can move fast and I can fly so I should be able to figure something out."

"Don't take any unnecessary risks," I warned her. "This world is screwed up enough without throwing a winged half-breed into the mix."

"I'll try and leave the camera on the other side of the school walls," Kayla suggested. "I'll find a place to hide it, somewhere that you can find it. I'll leave a marker of some kind. Then, I'll send you a message, Kiera, to let you know where I've hidden it."

"Okay," I agreed. The plan wasn't great, but I couldn't think of what else to do, and we didn't have time on our side. "As soon as the camera is in place, let me know and I'll send Isidor to collect."

"Why not me?" Potter asked, sounding offended.

"Because we stand a better chance of Isidor getting close to the school and getting the camera without drawing any attention to us," I explained. "If we lose that camera then we lose everything. Besides, Isidor will be able to follow Kayla's scent to wherever she leaves the camera. Right, Isidor?"

"You bet," Isidor said proudly and sniffed the air.

Then, not wanting to debate it further, I looked back down at Kayla's ghostly image and said, "Good work, Kayla. You've done a good job. Be careful and we'll wait for your message."

"I miss you guys," Kayla said one last time before she ended the call.

I slipped the iPod into my pocket and looked at the others.

"I don't like this one bit," Potter said.

"Neither do I," Isidor said, and it was the first time that I had ever known them to agree on anything.

"We get the camera," I said. "We see what it's got to show..."

"And if it does show McCain killing the Clarke woman?" Potter asked.

"We get Kayla out of there," I said.

"Then what?" Isidor said.

But before I'd had the chance to reply, Potter said, "We push McCain so freaking hard, that he never gets up again."

Chapter Thirty

Kayla

I arrived for the class the following morning only to discover that Sam had been right, Brother Michael had taken ill. As I sat down next to Sam, he couldn't wait to tell me that rumours were rampant that our new teacher, Sister Margaret, had actually gone berserk herself and freaked out a few weeks before. Hearing this, my heart sank. Another *freak*!

"What happened?" I whispered behind my hand, as Sister Margaret sat slumped in a rocking chair at the front of the class. Just like the other Ravenwood Greys, her face was covered by the hood of her robes.

"Listen to this," Sam whispered back. "I heard she started to eat a book she was reading!"

I looked at him and said, "That's just a bunch of crap. That never happened."

"Honest," Sam said. "I'm not faking. She started to rip the pages from her book – then eat them, until she puked her guts up all over the classroom floor."

I had seen a lot of crazy stuff in my life, but this story seemed
too strange to believe. The class as usual was in silence, there hadn't been much work set for us. I guessed it was art class or something, because on each desk had been placed a jug of cloudy water with paintbrushes. It almost felt like we were killing time until we were either chosen by McCain for matching or we were set free. The class had been sitting quietly. As I spied around the room, I could see that some weren't painting at all, but just staring into space like freaking zombies, while others sat and painted pictures.

Dorsey was sitting in front of me. I peered over his shoulder and could see that he was painting a picture. I couldn't see what it was, but his small, narrow shoulders were slumped forward, his burnt face almost touching the paper in front of him.

Sister Margaret continued to sit at the front of the class, with a book open, but facing down in her lap. Her head was bent forward with her hood concealing her face, and all the while she just rocked slowly back and forth in her chair. I thought of the conversation that I'd had with Kiera, Potter, and Isidor the night before and knew that I had to find a way of sneaking out of the school and hiding the camera.

Dorsey suddenly stood up and went to the front of the class. He stopped at the sink and filled a jug with water. It was then I noticed Pryor. He was sitting next to two other boys. The three of them looked pale and gaunt, as if they hadn't seen daylight for a while. The last time I'd seen Pryor, he was being dragged across the schoolyard by Brother Michael on his way to the Rat-House. By the look of the two emaciated-looking identical twins sitting on either side of Pryor, I guessed that they were the Addison twins that McCain had mentioned. By the look of them, their time spent in the Rat-House hadn't been great. They looked dirty, scruffy, and haunted.

I watched Pryor lean over and nudge one of the Addison brothers. The twin began to snigger and he turned to his brother and laughed. His twin winked back at him. Dorsey made his way back from the sink holding the jug of water and some paintbrushes. As he approached Sister Margaret, Pryor stuck his leg out and sent Dorsey pin-wheeling through the air. The jug he was holding flew from his hand and I watched as it spun towards Sister Margaret. It crashed into her left shoulder and shattered on impact, as if it had just been thrown into a brick wall. Water sprayed everywhere, covering Sister Margaret's head and chest.

For a moment she didn't move, she didn't even flinch, as if she had been totally unaware of what had just happened. Sister Margaret continued to sit, rocking back and forth several more times until she suddenly stopped. The class sat in silence as we stared at her. Dorsey got to his feet and began to brush himself off with his burnt and twisted fingers. Sister Margaret slowly rose out of her chair and loomed over Dorsey. For what seemed like the longest time, she just stood there, completely motionless. Then, without warning, her tongue rolled from between her lips like a fat, grey worm and she licked the water from her chin. Once she had soaked up every drop, her tongue crawled back into her mouth. She then raised one of her arms and pointed at Dorsey. Then as quickly as she had raised her arm, she lowered it and then freaked out.

She darted across the room, colliding with chairs and tables, until she reached one of the Addisons' desks. Here, she snatched up his jug of dirty paint water, which he'd cleaned his brushes in, and raising it to her mouth she gulped down the lot. Thick coloured water spilled from the corners of her mouth and dribbled off her chin. She threw the empty jug onto the floor where it smashed into tiny pieces. Sister Margaret then headed towards another kid's desk. Here she took hold of his glass of dirty water and hurriedly swilled it down. As she drank, I could hear the revolting sound of her slurping and choking as it washed down her throat.

Chucking the empty glass to the floor, she was off again and heading straight for me. She took hold of my paint jug in her grey hands, tilted her head back on her neck, opened her mouth wide and poured the muddy-looking water in. She spluttered and coughed as water appeared around the creases of her mouth in tiny bubbles. Once the water had gone, she sighed as if her thirst had at last been quenched. Sister Margaret then let out the longest and loudest belch I had ever heard, wiped her mouth with the sleeve of her robe, turned and left the room. As she disappeared into the depths of the school, I heard her start to scream.

The class remained silent. I glanced at Sam.

"I told you," he whispered.

It was so still and quiet that I could hear the racing heartbeats of those that sat nearby. The silence was broken as Pryor jumped up, knocking his chair flying. He grabbed hold of Dorsey with one meaty hand and with his other he scooped up a paintbrush and dangled it in front of Dorsey's face.

Dorsey flinched away, but he wasn't quick enough and Pryor began to daub his face with paint.

"There you go! You look a lot better already. Let's cover up those hideous burns," Pryor teased.

Some of the others in the class began to laugh and jeer at Dorsey, as he was humiliated in front of us.

Although it wasn't me who was being bullied, I felt for him and was furious inside. The feelings I'd had the day Pryor had attacked Dorsey in the yard came flooding back. I had wimped out that time and I'd felt ashamed ever since. Those memories of how I'd been tormented came flooding back and I felt sick for Dorsey.

"Let's see if I can't make you look more human," Pryor jeered, lurching forward with the paint brush again. Dorsey made a whimpering sound as he cowered before Pryor.

I felt rage explode inside of me like a bomb going off in a confined space. Then, before I even realised what I was doing, I leapt at Pryor, swinging my clenched fists at him.

"Leave him alone, you fucking arsehole!" I screamed.

Pryor looked up, saw me, ducked out of my way and as I shot past him, he punched me around the back of my head. Sam had been right, Pryor didn't give a shit that I was a girl. He would beat up on anyone weaker than him, or so he thought. I lost my footing and clattered heavily into a table, sprawling it and myself across the floor. With my head throbbing from where he had struck me, I scrambled to my feet and launched myself at him again.

"Pick on someone your own size!" I roared at him. Then, all of a sudden, I felt a hand grip my shoulder and yank me backwards. I tried to whirl around to see who had taken hold of me, when I realised that it was Sam.

"Leave it, Kayla. He's not worth it!" he shouted at me.

"Come on!" Pryor taunted me, his huge fists swinging before him.

I wanted to break free from Sam. I wanted to hurt Pryor, like he had hurt Dorsey, like I had been hurt before.

"Leave it, Kayla. Leave it!" Sam warned me.

I turned to face him. He looked me in the eyes and I could feel myself shaking with rage. I just wanted to rip Pryor's fucking head clean off. I knew that I could do it, too. In a blink of an eye, his head would be spinning from his shoulders, and I would be on him, sucking the warm blood from his twitching corpse. But if I did that, the pleasure – satisfaction – would be short-lived. Everyone would know that I wasn't really one of them – human. However angry I felt, I had to stay focused on the real reason I was at Ravenwood and that was to discover what had happened to Emily Clarke. I wouldn't be able to do that from the Rat-House or worse.

"There'll be another time, I promise," Sam said, his crystal blue eyes looking into mine. I looked away and glared at Pryor.

"Chickenshit," he said, then laughed and picked up his chair.

Suddenly the door was thrown open and McCain came bursting into the classroom. His lips were drawn tight, looking as if someone had just run a purple coloured marker pen across his face. McCain marched to the front of the class and screamed at us.

"Get yourselves in the courtyard right now!"

On his command, the class began to slowly exit the room in single file and I followed.

"Move it! Move it! Move it!" He wailed, his voice shrill and annoying.

We quickened our step, our heads down and fearing the worst. On reaching the courtyard, we stood in line and waited for McCain.

"I promise if any of you grass on me, I'll rip your fucking heads off!" Pryor threatened the rest of us.

"But…" one of the Addison twins began.

"Shut the fuck up!" Pryor spat as he stepped out of line. He jabbed Addison in the face with his fist to illustrate what would happen if we so much as breathed a word. Addison placed his hand over his lip, which had already begun to swell and I could see a trickle of blood ooze through his fingers. My stomach somersaulted and I clenched my fists. Sam must have seen me do this, as he placed his hand on my arm as a warning that this was not the right time to get into a fight with Pryor.

The door to the courtyard was thrown open and McCain came striding out across it, Taser – sizzle stick – in hand. His emaciated face shone an angry crimson. I half expected it to explode right there and then on top of his neck, sparing us the beating we were all expecting. He paced furiously back and forth before us like a caged beast.

"Which one of you idiots is responsible for throwing water over Sister Margaret?" He seethed, trying to keep his obvious anger under control.

We all remained silent.

"Who was it?" his voice barely a whisper, as if his anger was fighting its way up his throat, causing him to lose his voice.

Again we remained silent.

"Answer me, goddamnit!" he screamed.

Dorsey visibly flinched beside me on hearing his screeching voice. We continued to remain silent, stupidly refusing to give up Pryor's secret.

"Right, seeing as not one of you has the moral decency to own up, I take it then that it was a team effort?" he asked, his anger reined in momentarily, but still bubbling under the surface.

Silence.

"If that's the way you want to play this unfortunate game, then so be it. Each and every one of you will be sent to the Rat-House."

On hearing McCain's threat, I immediately felt sick with fear. Not for myself, but for Dorsey. I couldn't stand back and watch him being punished for something Pryor had done. Dorsey had put up with enough from Pryor and his friends. I could see that he was frail and at a breaking point.

So I stepped forward out of line and said, "It was me. I did it."

McCain looked at me, "Well, well, well!" he said as if swallowing a mouthful of bile. "Hunt, come here." He pointed to a spot on the floor within a couple of feet of him. I moved towards it.

"Do you have any idea of the consequences of your actions?" McCain roared at me, his anger now completely unleashed and uncontrollable. "Do you even care?"

I said nothing and stared at him.

"Answer me!" He screeched.

His eyes glowed yellow and spun in their sunken sockets. I knew it didn't matter what I said – what excuses I gave – the outcome was inevitable, he was still going to send me to the Rat-House. As I stared back at him, all I could think of was what Potter might say if face to face with McCain. Then, by accident and without thinking, I said, "Let's get this over with shall we, McCain?"

On hearing my remark, some of the other kids began to snigger and McCain's head turned a darker shade of crimson. I was convinced I saw his head actually swell in size, and I wondered if it might just go *bang!* right in front of me. A deep greeny-blue vein appeared in the centre of his forehead and began to pulsate like a deformed heart.

"Goddamnyou!" he cried one last time as he gripped me by the arm and shoved me across the courtyard and back into the school. As he led me away, I turned and looked at Sam. He looked scared for me. I then caught sight of Pryor who smirked.

I mouthed the word *coward* at him, then looked away.

McCain dug his fingers deeply into my flesh. But instead of taking me to the Rat-House like he had threatened, McCain forced me through the winding corridors and up the stairs to my room. Pushing me against the door, he shoved me inside. He closed the door behind him, and stood looking at me.

"There is something different about you," he whispered, taking a step closer towards me.

"I'm not sure what you mean?" I said, pulling my blazer tight about me. I wasn't scared of him hurting me, I was scared that he might realise that I was different – different from the others at the school.

He came closer still, so he was brushing up against me. Then, leaning over me, he rested his cheek against mine. I flinched away at his touch. McCain pressed the tip of his nose into my cheek. It felt wet, like a dog's. I thought of how he had sniffed at the bloodstains on Emily Clarke's bedroom wall and I felt sick.

"Who are you?" he whispered in my ear, his breath hot against my cheek. "*What* are you?"

"I'm Kayla Hunt," I said. "I'm human."

"You don't smell like any human I've smelt before," he sighed, as if he was actually getting a thrill out of sniffing me. The urge to kick his arse was unbearable.

"I thought I was going to the Rat-House?" I asked him, as he ran his nose through my hair.

"No, no, no," he breathed. "There is something about you."

"What?" I asked, closing my eyes, not knowing for how much longer I could bear his touch.

"I don't know," he said, his voice now sounding soft – dreamlike – as if he was being intoxicated by my smell. "You have courage. You're fearless and have an anger that I admire. I've never tried to match someone like you before." McCain pulled back from me, his yellow eyes glazed-looking. He stared at me. Then, taking his nasal spray from his trouser pocket, he shoved it into each nostril and breathed deeply.

"You'll stay where I can keep an eye on you, Kayla Hunt," he said. "You interest me. I'm not sure, but I might have the perfect match for you."

"And who is that?" I asked him.

McCain went to my bedroom door, opened it and looked back at me. "She's very special. I shall be telling the Wolf Man all about you."

Then, without another word, he slipped from my room and closed the door. With a huge sigh, I collapsed onto my bed. I needed to get that camera to Isidor and quick. Hopefully the camera held all the evidence that we would need to nail McCain and I could get out of Ravenwood before he got this *special* wolf to match with me.

Chapter Thirty-One

Kayla

Lying alone in my room, I knew that I wouldn't get a better opportunity to try and sneak from the school grounds and leave the camera on the other side of the wall for Isidor to find later. The rest of the kids were in lessons along with most of the teachers. All I had to do was get across the main grassy area in front of the school, to the cover of the trees that grew against the wall circling the school grounds.

I took the camera from my bag which was hidden beneath my wardrobe and tucked it inside the pocket of my blazer. The camera was small, and the front of my blazer didn't stick out too much. I placed my iPod in my trouser pocket, planning on taking a picture of the place where I finally hid the camera, which I could then send to Kiera to help Isidor locate it.

The corridor was quiet and empty, so closing my bedroom door behind me, I snuck from my room. I made it with no problem down the winding staircase. I listened intently for any noise that might suggest that a Grey was nearby or that I was being followed. Like I had hoped, the corridors and passageways were empty and only twice did I have to hide in the shadows of a nearby stairwell or doorway as a Grey shuffled past me. Before long, I began to feel disorientated and wished that I had Sam to show me the way. But I wouldn't have been able to take him with me as he would've wondered why I was placing the camera outside of the school grounds. I couldn't tell him about the others – just in case.

In case of what? I wondered. Sam seemed like a good guy and I hoped that I could trust him. After all, he had risked everything last night leading me to Emily Clarke's room. But I had trusted a man before and I'd ended up dead. So just for now, I would go on alone.

I reached a side door that led out into the grounds of the

school. Crouching in the shadows, I looked left and right to make sure no one was around. When I was sure that I wasn't being watched, I made my way as quickly as possible across the grassy area to the trees. I'd only got about halfway, when I heard someone call my name.

"Hey, Kayla!"

Hearing my name being shouted, I froze just like the statue I had seen in the forbidden wing back at Hallowed Manor. I turned around to see Sam trotting across the lawn towards me.

"Where are you going?" he asked.

"Nowhere," I lied, feeling flustered. "I'm just going for a walk."

"I thought you'd be in the Rat-House by now," he said with a look of concern on his face.

"And I thought you'd be back in class by now," I said back, annoyed that he had seen me.

"McCain gave us the rest of the morning off," he explained. "Hasn't got a replacement Grey."

"Oh," I said.

"Do you want some company?" he asked me.

"I'd rather be alone," I smiled, hoping I didn't hurt his feelings. Sam had been a good friend to me since arriving at Ravenwood.

"Don't be like that," he half-smiled. "I've got nothing to do. Let me hang with you. Stuff always happens when I'm with you."

"What sort of stuff?" I frowned.

"Crazy stuff," he smiled. Then, he was heading away towards the trees.

I followed him until we were hidden by the crop of trees that stretched away from the school building.

"So how come McCain didn't chuck you into the Rat-house?" he asked me, thrusting his hands into his trouser pockets. It was cold amongst the trees.

"He said he thought there was something different about me," I explained.

"See, didn't I say you weren't like any other girl that I'd ever met?" he smiled, eyes twinkling.

"He said that he wants to match me with some wolf," I told him. "Apparently this wolf is kinda special. You wouldn't know what he is talking about, would you?"

"How should I know?" Sam shrugged. "The guy's a freak. Who knows what he's talking about."

We walked amongst the trees in silence; the only sound was the leaves rustling in the wind overhead. Before the silence became uncomfortable, Sam glanced sideways at me and said, "Why did you stick up for Dorsey?"

"I had to," I shrugged.

"But why?" Sam asked again.

"If I had stood back and watched Dorsey take another beating from that jerk, I don't think I would've been able to ever look at him again without feeling ashamed," I told him.

"Ashamed of what?"

"Myself," I said back.

Sam looked thoughtfully at me. "Sometimes, Kayla, I just don't get you!"

"I was bullied for years," I blurted out.

"Why would anyone want to bully you?" Sam asked, sounding confused.

"They said I was ugly," I mumbled, unable to look at him.

"Who said you were ugly?"

"Just a bunch of girls at this boarding school I used to go to before my parents died," I said.

Sam stopped walking and looked at me. "Kayla, you are not ugly. I don't know how anyone could ever say that."

Still unable to look at him, I pictured those black bony lumps that had once jutted from my back, but I couldn't tell him about those. "Thank you," I said softly.

There was a moment's silence in which I could hear Sam's heart start to race again, as if he was nervous about something. Then, taking a deep breath, he said, "I don't know how to say this, Kayla, but I think you are..." He paused and I looked at him.

"Are what?"

"It doesn't matter," he said, his cheeks flushed red with embarrassment. Then, changing the subject, he said, "C'mon, I've got an idea that will cheer you up!" That twinkle was back in his eyes again and glowing fiercely.

"What is it?" I asked.

"We're gonna get outta this place and have some fun!"

"What do you mean we're going to get out of here?" I asked, going after him as he dashed off through the trees.

"I've found a way out of here," he said over his shoulder.

"But the Greys will notice that we've gone," I said.

"We'll be back in time for lunch," he smiled back at me.

"But..." I started. Although my plan had been to leave the school grounds, Sam tagging along hadn't been part of it.

"No buts," he said. "I know what your problem is; you need to get outta this place. God knows I do, I've been here for months."

I looked at Sam, and he had that wicked glow in his eyes again, as if his brain was burning inside his skull and the flames were licking at his eyeballs.

Trying to put him off the idea so I could go on alone, I said, "How we gonna get out of this place? Just look at it." I then pointed at the high stone walls and search towers, which were just visible through the trees.

Grinning, Sam said, "Come with me."

I followed him into a nearby clump of undergrowth. Branches and brambles reached out for us. I brushed them away. Sam crawled out of the bushes and edged his way along the wall that surround the school grounds. With shoulders rounded, I made my way after him. Sam came to a sudden halt next to a huge chestnut tree, and looked at me.

"What?" I asked him.

"What d'ya see?"

"A *tree*," I sighed.

"Not just any old *tree*," Sam stressed, pointing skyward while keeping his eyes fixed on me.

I looked up and could see that Sam was pointing at our bridge to freedom.

"You're amazing," I whispered. The branches of the chestnut tree were spread out like a giant web. One of the branches reached out further than the others and had worked its way over the top of the wall. Seeing this, I looked back at

Sam and smiled.

"I discovered it a few weeks ago," he explained. "But I've never had the guts to go over the wall."

"Why not?" I asked him.

"I've been too scared," he said sheepishly.

"So what's changed?"

"You're with me," he smiled. Without saying another word, Sam turned and began climbing. I watched Sam shin his way up the trunk of the tree, then like a monkey, he took hold of the nearest branch and swung himself up. I glanced back at the school to make sure that we weren't being watched. Through the shrubs and trees, I could just make out the search towers and the black outline of the school turrets that corkscrewed up into the morning winter sky.

"Are you coming or what?" Sam said from above.

Looking up, I could see him inching his way across the branch that draped over the top of the wall like a broken arm. I ran to the foot of the tree and began to climb. Hoisting my way up into the branches, I made my way towards my friend. By the time I'd reached the branch, Sam was crouched on top of the wall. Clenching my teeth, I placed one hand in front of the other and crawled across the branch.

Flying would have been so much easier, I secretly thought.

Halfway across, the branch began to sway, then creak. I stopped and gripped the branch until my knuckles were gleaming white through my skin.

"What you waiting for?" Sam hissed, balancing on top of the wall.

I looked down, and the ground seemed miles away. "The branch is gonna break!" I said through gritted teeth.

"If you stopped swinging on the thing like some demented monkey, then you might get across without it snapping. Now quit messing about and get over here!" Sam moaned.

Closing my eyes, I crawled the last few feet, using my hands to feel my way across the branch. Then, just as I reached the end of it, Sam leapt into the field on the other side of the wall. I peered over the edge and could see him waving up at me, a huge grin nearly cutting the lower half of his face in two.

"C'mon! Jump, Kayla!" Sam said.

Shutting my eyes, I threw myself from the branch. I hit the ground and rolled onto my back. Air belched from my lungs and up my throat. Sam stood above me, his hand outstretched.

"C'mon, this way!" Sam said, pulling me to my feet. Then, holding hands, we charged across the field and headed towards a large wooded area in the distance.

Chapter Thirty-Two

Kayla

We raced across the field, tiny white plumes of breath escaping from Sam's mouth and floating like tiny clouds up in to the cold sky. As we neared the woods, Sam let go of my hand and disappeared amongst the trees.

I left the field and darted after him. The woods were dark, and slanted shafts of grey light cut through the branches overhead and formed patterns on the leaf-covered ground. The woods were quiet and the trees stood close together, twisted and moss-covered. The only sound was the branches creaking above and the odd flutter of wings, as birds swooped between the trees. There was an oppressive atmosphere inside the woods and I began to feel claustrophobic. I looked between the trees for Sam, and called out.

"Sam? Sam? Where are you?"

Silence.

I went further into the woods, the sound of twigs breaking beneath my shoes.

"Sam, are you there?"

Silence.

What was he playing at? I wondered.

"Sam, if this is your idea of a -"

But before I'd had a chance to finish, something had clattered into me from behind, knocking me from my feet and sending me sprawling onto the ground.

"Gotchya!" Sam grinned, standing over me.

I rolled over and looked up at him.

Laughing, Sam said, "You've got that look on your face again!"

"What look?" I groaned, brushing damp leaves and fern needles from my blazer.

"Like you're gonna shit in your pants!" Sam laughed.

"You dickhead," I moaned, getting to my feet.

Holding his sides, Sam continued to laugh, tears welling in his eyes as he watched me pluck twigs and leaves from my hair.

"Ha-Ha, how very amusing!" I said. "I nearly wet myself, thanks to you!"

"Don't…please…stop…please…" Sam said through his tears.

I glared at him and said, "Freaking jerk."

"Oh c'mon, Kayla, I was just trying to have some fun with you," he said. "We could both do with having some laughs."

Then, seeing the funny side of what had happened, I began to laugh too. It felt good to be laughing again. We stood spraying laughter into the quietness of the woods – sounding like a couple of honking donkeys. But it wasn't just the laughter that felt so good – it was being out of Ravenwood. It felt fantastic.

It was freedom!

Giggling like a couple of little kids, Sam led me deeper into the woods. The further we went, the darker it grew, as if the light filtering through the branches was being turned down with a dimmer switch. And although it was January, the air inside the wood felt warm and clammy. Sam loosened his tie and opened his shirt at the throat.

"How come you know these woods?" I asked him.

"I grew up in this area. I used to come down to the woods with my mate, John. We made a camp in some bushes over there somewhere," Sam said, pointing in the direction of a thick shrubby area that sat on the bank of a bubbling stream.

"Who is John?" I asked.

"You mean, who *was* John."

"What's that s'posed to mean?"

"I knew John all my life. When the wolves came to Wood Hill and we became prisoners at Ravenwood, it didn't seem so bad because I had John with me. We used to share a room. He was my best mate. But he got chosen for matching within a few weeks, and I've not seen him since," Sam said.

"Where do you think he is now?"

"Dunno," Sam shrugged. "He went into that old chapel and

that was it. I've heard that you never know if you're going to the chapel to be matched or released."

"But if you were going to be released, why go to the chapel?" I asked him.

"Either way, McCain throws a party in there," Sam explained. "The party is meant to celebrate your freedom or your matching."

"It sounds a bit sick to me," I said. "How can anyone celebrate being matched with a werewolf – Skin-walker?"

"I don't think it's the humans that are celebrating - it's the wolves," he said. "After all, they've got a lot to celebrate. They've just got themselves a human skin to walk around in."

We walked in silence, ducking low-hanging branches and climbing over fallen tree trunks. Sam wiped his face with the back of his hand, his damp black hair sticking to his forehead in dark lines. I felt as if there was something on the tip of his tongue but he just couldn't bring himself to say it. Glancing at Sam, I said, "What are you thinking?"

Sam looked over his shoulder as if someone might be listening. Then, in a voice just above a whisper, he said, "We don't have to stay at Ravenwood, we could run away. I've been thinking about it a lot lately."

To hear this upset me, because if I was in his position, I would've wanted to run away, too. But I wasn't in the same situation as him. I wouldn't be around for any matching ceremony. I would be gone as soon as we had the evidence against McCain. I would be leaving Sam behind. It hurt me to say what I said next, I felt like I was cheating him in some way, and I hated myself for it.

"Sam, I understand what you're saying, but you need to get those crazy thoughts out of your head."

"How come?" Sam asked, looking confused. "I thought you would feel the same. I thought we could escape together."

"Okay, so we escape, but where we gonna go? We can't go back to friends and family because that's the first place the wolves would come looking. We've got no money. We'd probably last for a couple of days until the wolves caught up with us. Then what? They'd bring us straight back here!" I said.

"But we could tell the police what it's like here, all the weird things that go on," Sam insisted, and I could tell that Sam was desperate for me to go along with his plan – but it wasn't my plan.

"Do you really think they'd believe us?" I asked him.

"It's worth a..." Sam started.

"Sam, it's not gonna be forever. And who knows, we might not even get chosen for matching," I tried to convince him.

Looking at me, Sam said, "Ravenwood might not be forever, Kayla, but having your soul taken over by a wolf will be." Then, as if knowing that he wasn't going to change my mind, he said, "I'll show you the camp where me and John used to hang out as kids. It would be nice to see it again."

Hating myself for convincing Sam to stay at Ravenwood, whereas I knew I wouldn't be, I watched him stride towards the bushes by the stream. At first, neither of us noticed the swarm of flies that hovered around the entrance to Sam's camp. Crouching on all fours, Sam crawled in amongst the branches and leaves and I followed. This isn't what I'd had planned. By now I had hoped to have hidden the camera for Isidor and be back at Ravenwood before McCain noticed that I had vanished. But I felt like I had to see where Sam and his friend, John had hung out. It seemed important to him and it was the least that I could do.

We worked our way amongst the barbs and nettles until we came out into a small clearing. Almost at once, I was struck by a putrid smell. Covering his nose with his hand, Sam gagged at the stench. It smelt of rotten meat that had been left out too long in the sun. I looked at Sam, who had shoved his fist into his mouth, as if fighting the urge to puke. Even in the shadowy light of the bush, I could see that Sam's face had drained to the colour of soap. His eyes were bulging in their sockets as he looked at something ahead in the clearing.

I followed his gaze and looked at whatever it was which stank so much. Lying on its side in the middle of the camp was a dead body.

Chapter Thirty-Three

Kiera

My iPod didn't leave my hand all day. I paced up and down, waiting for Kayla to get in contact with me as to the location of the camera. She had done well to find it, but I wanted her out of that school as soon as possible. I hadn't been happy about her going in there in the first place. As soon as I knew what was on the camera, she was coming out.

From what little Kayla had managed to relay to us, the school sounded weird, to say the least. What were these "Greys" that Kayla had mentioned? Were they the wolves, waiting to be matched, or something more sinister? But what could be more sinister than that? And why did they hide their faces? But it was McCain; the more I heard about the guy, the more I sensed that Kayla and the other kids at the school were in danger. Why terrorise the kids with cattle prods, or *sizzle-sticks,* as Kayla had called them? That was no way of keeping control. It was cruel and barbaric.

As I paced through the kitchen and the living room, Potter sat quietly in a chair by the fire and smoked. Once he had finished one, he threw the end into the fire and lit another. He had told me once that the craving for nicotine masked his cravings for blood. I could understand that in some small way, as my own cravings for the red stuff where always there. Taking blood from Potter helped but I knew that wasn't the answer. Even if I resorted to drinking Lot 13, there was only so much of that left at the manor, and it would soon run out as Isidor and Kayla were drinking it every day. I'd rather them have it than me. I didn't want them resorting to drinking blood – not ever.

"Are you okay?" I asked Potter as he flicked his cigarette ash into the fire.

"I'm sick and tired of all this hanging around," he said. "We should be doing something."

"Like what?" I asked him, kneeling by his chair and stroking his forearm.

"I dunno," he sighed. "But anything has got to be better than sitting around here waiting for something to happen. You know me, Kiera, I'm not happy just sitting around, I need to be in the thick of it."

"As soon as we see what's on that camera, we'll be in a better place to..." I started.

"And what if there isn't anything on that camera?" he asked, looking at me. "We know that arsehole McCain killed that woman, so why are we just sitting here?"

"Things are different now," I said. "We're not part of this world; we can't just go storming about the place like we did before. We've got to take a back seat and wait. We can't afford to bring attention to ourselves."

"So why were we brought back then?" he asked me.

"I don't know that," I told him. "But McCain, Elizabeth, and her missing sister have something to do with the reason why we were."

"What makes you so sure?" Potter asked, sitting forward in his seat.

"Because I'm being punished," I told him.

"By who?"

"The Elders," I said as I looked into the fire. "They told me that I would be cursed. Something tells me that this whole thing – the world being *pushed* – is like a big puzzle that needs putting back together again. Once we have all the pieces we'll understand why we were brought back."

"And you think that McCain, the Clarke twins, and whatever is on that camera are all pieces of this puzzle that the Elders have created for us?" he asked me.

"We're pieces of that puzzle too," I whispered. "We fit in somewhere."

Before Potter had a chance to say anything else, Isidor came down the stairs and stepped into the living room. He wore his long, black coat with jeans and boots. His collar was turned up, his eyes were hidden by a pair of sunglasses, and in his hand he held his crossbow.

"Jesus, Isidor, you scared the shit out of me," Potter sniped. "For a moment, I thought you were the Terminator!"

"Very funny," Isidor said. "How do I look, Kiera?"

"Erm, like the Terminator," I smiled at him. "What are you dressed like that for?"

"I'm on standby to go and get that camera as soon as we get the message from Kayla," he said. "I want to look inconspicuous, but if I do get spotted, then no one will recognise me again."

"I don't believe what I'm hearing," Potter groaned. Then, looking at me, he barked, "I thought you said we had to take a back seat, not draw attention to ourselves! So you don't think the locals are going to notice one of the *Men In Black* strutting his stuff through town?"

I looked at Isidor and I did feel for him. It seemed that he always tried to do the right thing, but somehow got it wrong. Not wanting to hurt his feelings, I said to him, "Perhaps you should lose the shades."

"Do you think so?" he said, taking them off and putting them in his pocket. "I just thought..."

"Well, do us all a big favour and don't think," Potter cut in. "Because when you start thinking, we tend to end up in the shit."

"Okay, keep your wings on," Isidor said.

"And if you make one more jibe about me being an angel, I'm gonna start swinging," Potter snapped.

"Okay, let's not get into a fight about it," I said, standing up getting ready to jump between them. "Isidor, you were right about not wanting to be noticed, but just keep your crossbow tucked away and you'll look fine."

"I know where I'd like to stick that fucking crossbow," Potter muttered, glaring at Isidor.

Ignoring his remark, I looked at Isidor and said, "As soon as we hear from Kayla, get going and collect the camera. The sooner we see what's on it, the sooner we can get Kayla out of the school and solve this case."

Chapter Thirty-Four

Kayla

The body was lying on its side with one of its arms bent beneath it. The other was splayed out to one side and the hand that dangled from the end of it was fingerless. The body was dressed in a long, brown coat and faded blue jeans. On its feet were dirty, brown boots. Although I couldn't see its face, I could tell by the shape and size of the body that it was a young male. His face was covered by a large-brimmed hat, which looked as if it had been made out of stiff, black leather.

"Do you think he's dead?" Sam asked, not taking his eyes off the body in the middle of the camp.

Although I knew that he was, as I couldn't hear a heartbeat, I shrugged my shoulders and said, "Dunno."

"I've got to know," Sam said. "He might still be alive." And he inched towards the figure on his hands and knees.

"No...wait!" I said, but Sam had picked up a stick and was prodding the figure's leg with it.

"Hey, are you alive?" Sam said, and then leaning forward, he pushed up the brim of the hat to reveal its face. "What the hell...?" Sam gasped, sounding as if he had just been kicked in the stomach.

I moved forward an inch and then recoiled. The face had no eyes, not even sockets for them to fit into. He had no nose, mouth, or ears. It was blank like a canvas made of skin which had darkened and looked bruised.

"Let's go!" I yelled, already turning and heading back through the bushes. The face reminded me of the featureless statue I'd seen in the forbidden wing at the manor.

"I think you're right," Sam groaned, coming after me.

Nettles and thorns scratched at our faces and snagged our school uniforms as we fought our way out of the bushes. Desperate to be away from the body and the bush, Sam raced forward, shoulder-barging me out of the way. I pushed back, and both of us collided, falling in a heap outside the entrance to the camp. We lay on our backs, arms flapping as we fought to untangle ourselves from each other. Once separated, we stood panting and sucking in air.

"Kayla, there's a dead man in my camp!" Sam gasped.

"You're not kidding," I wheezed, catching my breath.

"Do you think he's been murdered?" Sam asked me.

"How should I know? And I don't think we should hang around long enough to find out!" I told him.

"Did you see his face and hand?" Sam asked.

"What face? He didn't have one, did he?"

We stood in the woods, which seemed to be darkening by the minute, and looked at each other, both of us waiting for the other to say something. Sam spoke first.

"What should we do?"

"Get back to school," I said. "We've been away long enough. Someone might realise that we're missing."

"Don't you think we should go and tell the police?"

"Police!" I gasped. "Have you lost your mind?"

"What do you mean?" he asked, looking confused. "We've just found a dead body, Kayla."

"We can't go to the police. If we get the police involved they could cause all sorts of problems," I warned.

"For who?"

"For us. Who else do you think? If we go to the police they'll want statements and God knows what else!"

"So?"

"So that will lead them back to Ravenwood and McCain and he'll know that we've been over the wall!" I explained.

"We can't just leave that body in there," he said, hooking his thumb in the direction of the bushes. "It wouldn't be right."

"He's *dead* – in case you hadn't noticed!" I yelled. "It's got nothing to do with us. Don't get involved, Sam. Please, for both our sakes."

Sam looked at me, and he seemed almost disappointed, as if he had expected more from me somehow.

"If you don't want to get involved, go back to Ravenwood," Sam said. "If this gets back to McCain, then I'll say that I came out here on my own. I won't mention you."

I stood and watched Sam start to walk away.

I couldn't let him go on his own.

Birds sprung out of the trees above me, their wings sounding like shotgun fire as they beat together in the stillness of the wood. *How did I get myself into this?* I wondered. I just wanted to leave the camera for Isidor and get back to the school. With Sam heading away from me, I took the camera from my pocket and hid it beneath a pile of dead leaves by the entrance to the camp. Then, seizing the opportunity while I was alone, I quickly sent the following message:

Kiera, camera hidden on south side of school near to stream and huge pile of bushes. If Isidor can't track my scent then he should be able to smell the dead body! Will have to explain later. Got to go! Kayla xx

Happy that I'd hidden the camera, I headed after Sam, hoping that I could change his mind about going to the police. I hadn't taken more than a few steps, when I heard a rustling noise come from the bushes behind me. I spun round to see the faceless figure crawling out of the bushes.

I jumped in fear at the sight of him. He now had one eye, and it was fixed on me. It was blue and cold, and bore right into my skull. His second eye wasn't quite formed yet, just a wet socket and it oozed pussy tears onto his cheek.

"Sam!" I shrieked. "Wait up! I'm coming with you." Then turning, I ran as hard and as fast as I could through the woods. I didn't dare look back, not even once. Sam turned around at the sound of my voice, and seeing the figure coming after us, he started to run. Branches and brambles tore at our faces and clothes as we darted blindly away. We flew over fallen logs, crawled under broken branches, and splashed through the stream. Then, Sam fell flat on his face. I glanced back over my shoulder and he looked as if he had been shot in the back. He lay face down amongst the pine needles and leaves, his nose buried in the dirt.

"Sam!" I called breathlessly. "Are you okay?"

He didn't move. I looked quickly around to see if the

faceless figure was close. I scanned the surrounding area but couldn't see or hear anyone. I gingerly made my way over to Sam and knelt down.

"Sam, wake up!" I pleaded, shaking him.

Nothing.

I rolled him over and he flopped lifelessly onto his back. His eyes were closed and I could see that he had a large gash across his forehead. I shook him again.

"Sam! Please wake up!" I begged.

Then, without warning his eyes opened. He looked up at me and began to scream. I snapped my head around and glanced over my shoulder. Standing about two feet away was the faceless man. He stood there silently - not moving. The wet eye socket winked at me and my stomach lurched as if I were going to be sick. I looked back at Sam and dragged him to his feet. I threw his arm around my shoulder and screamed at him.

"Run! Run!"

I dragged Sam back to the tree by the school wall. He dropped to the ground and let out a mindless groan. I bent down and shook his shoulders with all the strength I had left in me. His eyes rolled in their sockets and I slapped his face.

"Sam! Wake up!"

He groaned at me again. I looked back over my shoulder and caught a glimpse of the faceless man approaching the tree line.

Snaking my arm through Sam's, I dragged him back onto his feet.

"Get up!" I ordered at the top of my voice. Once he was standing, I gripped hold of his face and he blearily looked at me.

"Do you want to fucking die?" I screamed at him.

Looking back again, the figure was now striding towards us. I shoved Sam towards the wall and he began to moan at me.

"Please, Sam!" I begged him. "I can't do this on my own!"

Sam started to sway slightly then straighten. He looked at me and I could see his pupils begin to sharpen and focus. I turned him to face the fast approaching figure and roared into his ear, "If you don't get your freaking arse over that wall in the next two seconds, we *are* gonna die! *Now move it!*"

At last, realising his impending fate, Sam turned to face the wall and began to scramble up it. I followed close behind. If I'd been on my own like I'd planned, I would have just flown over the wall and been well away from that freak. But I couldn't do that now – I couldn't risk anyone in this world that had been *pushed*, finding out I was a half-breed. We hoisted ourselves up onto the branch and shimmied across it. Sam reached the other side of the wall first and without any hesitation, he threw himself from the branch and to safety. I got myself into position to jump, but the urge to look back one last time was too strong to resist. I glanced over my shoulder to see the faceless figure looking up at me, his one good eye staring into mine.

Then, he whispered something from a gash in his cheek. His voice was faint, but I heard what he said.

"Where's Alice?"

"Who's Alice?" I whispered back.

"Sister," he said.

Then, he started to change. It was like his skin was turning grey. Cracks began to appear on his face and hands as he slowly turned to stone. Within seconds he stood motionless, like a statue that had been standing beneath the giant tree for hundreds of years.

Swinging myself from the branch, I landed with a thump in the grounds of Ravenwood.

Back in my room, I placed a wet towel across the cut on Sam's forehead as he lay on my bed.

"I thought that man was dead!" Sam whispered, still not really believing what he'd just seen.

"So did I," I whispered back, dabbing gently at the cut on his brow.

"What the hell is going on?" he asked, as if I had all the answers.

"I don't know," I replied, wiping away his blood. My throat began to turn dry, and my stomach knotted. I glanced over at my bag tucked beneath my wardrobe and pictured the bottles of Lot 13 hidden within it.

"I think you know more than you are letting on," Sam said, taking my hand from his brow and holding it in his.

"Say what?" I asked him.

"There is something about you, Kayla," he said, looking up at me. "I know there is some crazy shit going on and I'm not just talking about the wolves and the freaky faceless dude in the woods."

"I don't know what you mean," I said, trying to break his stare.

"I have dreams, Kayla," he said. "Dreams about the world – but it's not like this – it's different somehow. Do you know what I'm talking about?"

I shook my head.

"I'm going to tell you something, Kayla," he said, his voice dropping. "I've never told this to anyone before 'cos people would think I'm mad."

"So why are you going to tell me?" I tried to smile.

"Because I reckon you'll believe me," he smiled. "I get the feeling that you know there is something wrong with this world, too."

"I don't know what you mean..." I started to lie, but he began to talk over me.

Chapter Thirty-Five

Kayla

"Both of my parents were strong swimmers," Sam said, getting up and crossing to my bedroom window. "I don't think they loved me very much, but they were strong swimmers."

"All parents love their kids, don't they?" I said, acting surprised by what Sam had just told me. I knew that not all parents loved their kids, but I was still trying to do the whole 'let's play dumb' routine. "I'm sure your mum and dad did love you."

"Nah, they didn't," Sam said, still looking through the window. "They loved me enough to feed me and put clothes on my back – but it always felt as if they were just going through the motions. There was never any heart put into it. It was like they always expected more of me – as if they were waiting for something to happen."

"Like what?"

"It was like I had disappointed them in some way," Sam said and this time he did look at me. "I thought perhaps they wanted me to be captain of the school football team or get better grades, but that just wasn't me. My thing is drawing. I draw comics – but it wasn't enough. Not for them, anyway."

"What's wrong with drawing?" I asked. "I think that's cool."

"It's nothing," Sam said, changing the subject back to his parents. "They were away a lot of the time. I never understood what they did, but my dad always seemed to be flying off here, there, and everywhere for meetings and my mum would go with him. People would often visit the house – men in smart suits. I never really got a good look at their faces as I was always ushered up to my room and the door would be closed. I would try and listen to what was going on, but they would always speak in hushed voices. So I spent most of my time escaping. You know, like in your head. I'd make up characters and would bring them to life in comic books."

"So apart from your mum and dad being a bit secretive, what was so weird about that? All parents have secrets – don't you think?" I said, thinking of how my dad had kept the fact that he was a Vampyrus from my mum for years and the fact that she had a son called Isidor. That was a secret that he had kept from me, too.

"It was what happened when they drowned that day – that's what was so weird,'" Sam said.

"What was weird about it?" I asked him, and in the back of my mind all I could really think about was if Isidor was already on his way to collect the camera. But Sam had been a good friend to me and I liked him, so I wanted to hear him talk about himself for a while.

"My dad stood and looked at me sitting in the sand. He was mad again. He was always mad about something. I'd been drawing again – even on the beach, I'd been drawing.

"'Are you coming on this boat trip with me and your mother or what?' he asked me.

'Nah, I think I'll stay here and finish this picture, if you don't mind,' I said, not looking up from my drawing pad.

'Actually, I do mind,' my dad said, reaching down and yanking the pad from my lap. 'For once in your life you're going to take your head out of those goddamn clouds and do something worthwhile.'

'But...' I started; he wasn't in the mood to listen.

'Don't you dare argue with your father!' Mum shouted. I remember she was dressed in a swimming costume," Sam said.

'We didn't bring you all the way to Cornwall just so you could sit here doing those ridiculous drawings!

'I told you we should've left him at home, Sue,' dad groaned as he chucked my art pad into the sea. 'I don't know, we try and do the kid a favour and this is the thanks we get.'

"I looked up at my dad, then at my art pad as it floated away," Sam said, and I couldn't help but feel sad for him.

What kind of dad would do that to his son? I wondered.

Sam stood and looked out of my bedroom window, and I could tell that he wasn't watching the school kids who wandered about below or the Greys, he was reliving the day

194

that his dad had thrown his pictures into the sea like they were little more than rubbish.

"I followed my mum and dad up the beach. The boat sat alongside a short jetty. It was packed with tourists. There were two empty seats and my mum and dad took them. I kinda felt uncomfortable and left out again. My mum said that I was standing in her way and blocking the sun, so I was to go and stand someplace else.

"Without saying anything, I moved away from them. What was the point in inviting me along if they couldn't even bear me standing next to them?" Sam explained, and I felt really upset for him.

"I leant over the edge of the boat and looked back at the beach. There were hundreds of people sunbathing. Everyone seemed to be having a good time, except for me.

"The boat left the jetty and we made our way out to sea. Peering over the edge of the boat, I glanced back at the beach as it slipped into the distance and I saw something odd," Sam said, turning to look at me.

"What did you see?" I asked him.

"It wasn't a something, but a *someone* who had caught my attention. Standing on the shoreline was a figure, their feet were half in and half out of the water."

"So what was so odd about that?" I asked Sam.

"It was really hot and this person was dressed in jeans and a blue hoodie, with the hood pulled up over their head. I tried to see their face but I couldn't, as it was covered by the hood. Then, the screaming began and I turned away," Sam said.

"Screaming?" I asked him.

"'*Man overboard!*' someone screamed," Sam explained. "I made my way to where the other passengers were standing. I could see that the seats which my mum and dad had taken were now empty. I couldn't see them anywhere.

"'They fell overboard! They just jumped!' said this big guy," Sam said, coming back across the room and sitting next to me on the bed.

"Some woman started shouting that a man and a woman had jumped overboard and this other guy said that they had just flipped over the side of the boat.

"I pushed through all the people, and saw my dad's shirt floating on the waves. Then it disappeared beneath the boat. The captain raced towards us. He was telling people to get out of his way. He wanted to know who it was that had fallen over the side of the boat. I told him it had been my mum and dad," Sam said.

"What happened then?" I asked him.

"The captain stood and stared at me," Sam explained. "Then, he put his hands on my shoulders, and the captain asked, 'you sure about that, kid?'

"I just nodded, Kayla. I didn't know what to say. I was in shock or something," Sam said, and I took one of his hands in mine. "My parents' bodies were never found. And in the end the captain decided he should take the boat back to shore. We were met on the jetty by police officers, paramedics, and Life Boat crew.

"The captain spotted me standing alone in the crowd and pointed me out to a police officer. Everything seemed to slow down and I felt my knees begin to buckle beneath me. But before I fell down, an arm was snaking around my shoulders and holding me up," Sam explained and his eyes had grown wide.

"Who was it, Sam?" I asked him.

"I looked sideways to find I was being supported by the hooded figure I had seen standing on the beach," Sam breathed. "My eyelids felt heavy, and I had to fight to stop them closing. But the figure held me tight, then lent forward and whispered into my ear."

"What did he say?" I asked, totally wrapped in Sam's story.

"'Everything is going to be okay. I promise.' That's what the figure said. 'Who are you?' I whispered back, unconsciousness nearly taking me. But I managed to tilt my head back just a fraction, in the hope I could see who it was beneath the hood. Then, the police officer came forward and took hold of me. He asked the stranger if they knew my name.

"'Brooke. Sam Brooke,' the stranger said, letting go of me.

"'Do you know him?' the police officer asked the stranger.

"'Kinda,' the stranger said, then stepped away. The police officer tried to support me with one arm as he fumbled for the radio attached to his belt. I slumped in the officer's arms, and then fell to the ground. Rolling onto my back in the sand, I struggled to open my eyes. I needed to see who it was beneath that hoodie, Kayla."

"What did you do?" I asked Sam.

"I called out as the stranger walked away up the beach," Sam explained. "Turning, the figure looked back at me. Then, pulling back the hood, the stranger revealed their face to me. All I could do was stare in wonder – they were beautiful."

"Who was it?" I gasped, almost ready to pee myself.

"It was you beneath that hood, Kayla," Sam whispered. "You winked at me, then you pulled the hood back over your face and disappeared into the crowd. It was then that I slipped into unconsciousness and everything went black."

"It wasn't me," I said, jumping up. "I've never seen you before and I've never been to a beach in Cornwall."

"It was you, Kayla," Sam insisted. "I couldn't believe it the first day I saw you rummaging around in the Poor Box. It was like seeing a ghost. I didn't want to...I *couldn't* say anything, but that's how I know you are different."

"This is getting really weird..." I started.

"Don't you see, Kayla? You were there the day my parents died, and then you show up here...and your parents drowned, too."

I wanted to tell Sam that my parents hadn't drowned, that it was lie created by Potter, but I had to keep the pretence up. "Sam, I don't know what you're talking about..." I tried to convince him that he was mistaken, but he wasn't listening to me.

Then, gripping me by the shoulders, and staring me straight in the eyes, he said, "Don't you see, Kayla, you've been sent to help me again."

"Help you?" I breathed in disbelief. "What are you talking about?"

"You must realise that you are different from everyone else here," he said excitedly. "Don't you remember what McCain did

with your hands – how he burnt you? You didn't feel a thing."
Then, grabbing my hands and staring down at them, he said,
"See, there are no scars, Kayla – your hands have healed
already – that's impossible."

"They weren't as bad as they looked," I stammered. "I used
cream..."

"Cream!" Sam cried. "There is no cream in the world that
could get rid of burns like you had. You're different, Kayla –
even McCain has sensed it. You're here for a reason."

"And what's that?" I snapped, just wanting him to leave my
room so I could contact Kiera and get out of Ravenwood.

"You've been sent to help me," he said, tears standing in his
eyes. "You've been sent to get me out of here."

I pushed him away from me, not wanting to hear any more.
"I'm sorry, Sam,
but I haven't been sent here to save you or anyone else."

"But you have, Kayla," Sam said. "You just don't see what
you are."

"What am I?" I almost screamed at him.

"You're an angel, that's what you are," he breathed. "You're
an angel, Kayla – a dead angel!"

"Dead angel?" I mumbled, and if I'd had a heart it would
have been racing. "I'm not dead!"

Then, reaching into his trouser pocket, Sam pulled out a
folded piece of newspaper. "I came across this, Kayla, not long
after I saw you on the beach that day," he said, unfolding the
paper.

"What is it?" I asked, my hands starting to tremble.

"It's about you, Kayla," he said, handing me the torn piece
of newspaper.

I took it from him, desperately trying to steady my hands
as I looked down at the headline:

Murdered Girl Found on Side of Cumbrian Mountain

I read the words underneath and it described how sixteen-
year-old school girl Kayla Hunt's naked and mutilated body
had been found partially covered by snow on the side of a

mountain. With tears of my own beginning to well in my eyes, I screwed up the piece of newspaper when I saw the picture of myself staring back at me and read the part which described how the killer had cut off my ears.

"That's not me," I said, sniffing back my tears. "You're mistaken."

"That's you, Kayla," Sam said softly, almost caring. "I know it's you."

"It can't be me," I said looking at him. I tried to smile, as if brushing away what he had just said as being nothing more than nonsense. But I was in danger of being discovered. I just wanted to run – get out of Ravenwood. I wanted to talk to Kiera. I wanted to be with her – she always knew what to do – she made me feel safe. Why hadn't I listened to her when she had warned against me coming to Ravenwood? Kiera said it would be too dangerous for me to come here and she had been right. So, looking Sam straight in the eyes, and trying to be as confident as Kiera, I said, "You're mistaken, Sam Brooke. That can't be me in that newspaper article because I'm not dead."

"You are dead, Kayla," he said, tears running down his face. "You're my dead angel. I just have to prove it to you."

Then, reaching into his trouser pocket he pulled out a long bladed knife. "Please forgive me," he cried as he thrust the knife into my chest.

I looked at him, then down at the knife which protruded from me. I felt a crushing feeling inside of me, as if I were shrinking in some way. I staggered away from him. I just wanted to lie down. My whole body felt weak, and as I curled my numb-feeling fingers around the hilt of the knife, I noticed that my skin had started to turn grey and crack just like those statues I had seen.

"Kiera," I mumbled weakly, dropping to my knees and into a black pool of my own blood. "Kiera – I'm sorry I failed."

Then, everything went black.

Chapter Thirty-Six

Kiera

I just couldn't rest until Isidor came back. Potter sat in a cloud of cigarette smoke in front of the fire and we didn't speak, both of us were lost to our thoughts and concerns. But, if I were being honest with myself, I was more than concerned. I feared for Kayla's safety.

What was this body she had discovered? I wondered. *Was it the body of Emily Clarke?*

What I couldn't be sure of was if there had been another murder committed. If so, had McCain done it like he had murdered Emily? But we didn't even know that he had murdered her. Okay, so we know he used her credit card, but did that mean he had been involved in her murder?

I could feel my stomach cramping and it wasn't through nerves, it was the cravings again. I looked at Potter and he stared at me through the smog that his constant smoking was creating in the room. Turning away, I went to the window and checked again to see if there was any sign of Isidor. The sky was almost black and night was drawing in.

"Where is he?" I muttered to myself. "He's been gone ages."

"I told you that I should've gone," Potter grumbled from the corner of the room. The fire in the grate hissed and spat, the coals glowing red and hot.

"Isidor will be able to track her," I said, looking at him.

"You better hope you're right, because..."

"He's coming!" I almost screamed with relief, spotting Isidor heading across the field that stretched before the farmhouse. Through the darkness, I could see that his hands were empty and I feared that perhaps he hadn't been able to find the camera after all. But at least he had come back and hopefully with some news. I ran to the front door, and throwing it open, I waved my arm in the air and shouted, "Hey, Isidor!"

Seeing me, Isidor ran the last few hundred yards to the farmhouse and Potter joined me at the door.

Before he'd had the chance to say anything, I said, "Did you find the camera?"

"Yes," he nodded, stepping into the warm and closing the door behind him. Then, reaching into his coat pocket, he pulled out a small silver coloured video camera. I took it from him and as I looked into his eyes, I could see that they were dark and fearful.

"What's happened, Isidor?" I asked him. "Are you okay?"

"Yeah, I'm fine," he said.

"Are you sure?" Potter smirked. "Because if any of those school kids picked on you I'll go and speak to their teacher."

"Yeah, very funny," Isidor said, and went into the kitchen where he switched on the laptop.

I glared at Potter who shrugged and said, "I'm just messing about with the kid."

Ignoring him, I followed Isidor into the kitchen where we all sat around the table. As Isidor connected the camera to the laptop, I said, "So, what happened?"

"I got to the school okay," Isidor started to explain. "I crept around the outskirts of the school and it was a while before I caught a whiff of Kayla's scent. I tracked it to a place by the wall where there was a large chestnut tree. The branches spilled out over the top of the wall, and I figured that Kayla must have used the tree to climb over and get out of the school grounds. But there was another scent."

"What kind of scent?" Potter cut in, his face now a mask of concentration, and for all his piss-taking, I knew that he did really care for Kayla and somewhere, deep down, for Isidor too.

"I could smell that a boy had gone with her," Isidor said, jiggling a wire that he had attached to the camera and the laptop.

"Do you think it was this boy, Sam that she has spoken about?" I asked him.

"I can't be sure, but whoever it was, Kayla felt comfortable with him," Isidor said.

"How do you know that?" Potter pushed.

"Because they headed across the field together to a nearby wood," Isidor said. "Their scents were side by side, which told me that they walked together – they were very close. Kayla definitely trusted him. Anyway, I followed their scent through the woods, and it wasn't long before I picked up another."

"What kind of smell was it?" I asked him.

"A corpse," Isidor said, as he figured out how to use the camera.

"The dead body that Kayla mentioned in her message," I breathed.

"I followed Kayla's and the boy's scents which ran alongside a stream, until I came to a massive clump of bushes, just like she said I would," he explained. "I sniffed about a bit and checked the bushes and then found the camera."

"What about the corpse?" Potter asked, reaching into his pocket for his smokes.

Peering over the laptop at Potter, Isidor said, "Now that's where it all gets a bit strange."

"Strange?" Potter asked, glancing at me.

"The smell of the corpse was really strong, so I followed the scent into the bushes," he said. "I'm no Kiera Hudson, but even I could see where the body had been lying – but it wasn't there anymore."

"So somebody had moved the body?" I asked him, feeling confused.

"No," Isidor frowned. "I could only smell the three scents; Kayla's, the boy's, and the corpse's. Which makes me wonder how the body got there in the first place because who brought it there? There were no other scents. It was like the body had fallen out of the sky, but that doesn't happen, right?"

"I don't want to put a downer on things," Potter said, lighting his cigarette, "but if you could only smell three scents, perhaps the boy and the corpse were one in the same?"

"What are you trying to say?" Isidor asked him.

"Maybe Kayla got hungry – needed the red stuff?" he suggested, blowing smoke out of his nostrils. "You know what I'm trying to say, perhaps Kayla killed the boy?"

"Never," Isidor hissed. "She wouldn't do a thing like that!"

"Don't be so sure," Potter came back. "Your sis can be real feisty when she wants to be."

"She would only kill in self-defence," Isidor said.

"Maybe it was in self-defence," Potter suggested. "All I'm trying to say is, we don't know anything about this kid she has gone and hooked herself up with. Haven't we all learnt by now that people don't always tend to tell us the truth? People have a habit of talking bullshit around us."

"She still wouldn't have killed a human," Isidor insisted. "Kayla knows that if she ever fed from one of them, she'd be creating another vampire."

I sat silently for a moment and thought of the dream that I'd had of the girl falling out of the sky and landing in a wooded area near to Ravenwood School. Her face had been deformed somehow, but she had been chased away by wolves and ended up at Ravenwood.

"Are you okay, Kiera?" Potter asked me. "You look kind of lost."

"I'm fine," I said back, forcing a smile. "I was just thinking about what Isidor has just told us. So what did you do next?"

"The smell left by the corpse led out of the bushes and back in the direction of the school. So I followed it. I picked up Kayla's scent again, and the boy's. It was like the corpse was chasing them back to the school."

"Sounds like a freaking vampire to me," Potter cut in.

"It wasn't a vampire, because the boy was still alive and he bled," Isidor said.

"Oh this just keeps getting better and better," Potter groaned.

"There was blood?" I gasped, my concern for Kayla's safety growing with every passing moment.

"Only a little," Isidor explained. I hardly got a whiff of it, it was very faint. If Kayla had fed on the boy, there would have been blood everywhere and the smell would have been stronger. I'm guessing that the boy fell over and got up again, because both he and Kayla made it back to the school. I followed their scents back there."

"And the corpse that was running around, what happened

to it?" Potter snapped.

"Well that's the strangest thing of all," Isidor said, finally figuring out how to use the camera.

"What do you mean?" I asked him, feeling anxious.

"The corpse did make it as far as the school wall and the tree. The scent was really strong there, like it had stayed rooted to the spot for a while. But then, the smell moved off again. I followed it back across the field, the scent becoming stronger and stronger the whole time. It led me back into the woods and then suddenly, it stopped."

"What did you find?" I asked him.

"Well this is the craziest part of my story," Isidor said, his voice dropping to a whisper. "The smell stopped by a statue."

"Statue?" I breathed, glancing over at Potter.

"Crazy, right?" Isidor said. "It was like the statue had been the corpse that had chased after Kayla and the boy!"

"Crazy," Potter whispered and looked at me.

"You don't know what that could mean, do you?" Isidor asked.

I looked at Potter, who stared back at me.

"Was the statue of a girl?" I asked Isidor.

"No, the statue was of a male, although it was hard to tell as it didn't really have a face. But it was dressed like a man."

Hearing this I thought of the nightmare I'd had in which the statue of a male had crawled from some bushes in a wooded area, and asked for someone called Alice.

"We've seen one of these statues before," I told him.

"Where?" Isidor frowned.

"Back at the manor," I said.

"So why didn't you say anything?"

"What could I have said? I couldn't explain why it was there myself," I answered, but really I had wanted to forget the statue, I was scared that I was becoming one, too.

"What do you think they are?" Isidor asked me.

"I don't know, Isidor," I whispered. "I really don't know."

Sensing that I was beginning to feel uncomfortable, Potter flicked his cigarette end into the sink and said, "So have you managed to get that camera working yet or not, Einstein?"

Isidor looked away from me and back at the laptop. "Sure, I've got it working. Take a look."

The screen flickered on but only showed a picture of darkness. In the top right-hand corner of the screen was the time and date in neat white text. It had been recorded seven days ago and the time read 23:43hrs. Nothing seemed to be happening on the screen, so Isidor fast-forwarded the image. He stopped the picture at 02:17hrs, when suddenly the image on the screen burst into life. The video showed a wide-angled shot of Emily's bedroom and I could see her lying asleep on her bed. Even from the angle that the camera had been set at, and the gloom of the room, I could see that she was identical to her sister, Elizabeth. The covers had come away and I could see she was wearing jogging bottoms and a t-shirt. The image had burst into life, because out of camera shot, someone had obviously entered her room and switched on the light. Emily stirred slightly on her bed and rolled over, then fell back to sleep.

Morris McCain then walked into the frame. There was no mistake – it was him. I glanced at Potter then back at the screen and watched as McCain crossed the room and began to shake Emily violently. I could see Emily was stunned or maybe it was shock. Although there was no sound, I could see by McCain's actions and body language that he was shouting at Emily.

Emily appeared to be motioning him away by waving her hands at McCain and shaking her head. McCain then began to wave his arms and hands in the air and point angrily at Emily. I snatched another quick look at Potter and he looked coldly at what was unfolding before him.

I looked back at the screen and it looked as if Emily was trying to get off the bed. She was shaking her head and trying to move McCain out of her way, who was now standing directly in front of her and shaking his fists in the air. I watched as Emily managed to get free of her bed by pushing McCain in his chest to move him out of her way. McCain then punched Emily straight between the eyes. All of us flinched in our seats. Emily stumbled backwards, landed on her bed, then rolled off onto the floor. I watched as she shook her head wearily from side to side, as she tried to fight off oncoming unconsciousness.

Watching the video made me feel sick. I stared as McCain then set about Emily in a frenzy of kicks and punches. He repeatedly punched Emily about her head and I struggled to hold back my tears as I watched Emily desperately try to fight him off. She paddled her arms in a vain attempt to protect herself. Then, sitting astride her on the floor, McCain began to change. It was his hands that I first noticed. They seemed to grow into the shape of giant paws. His back arched and his clothes began to fall away in strips as his body took on the shape of a giant wolf. McCain rolled his head back, as his neck began to thicken, and his slicked, black hair which covered his head, started to cover him. His already bulbous nose twitched then protruded from his face forming a wet snout. Raising his giant paws into the air, he opened his vicious-looking jaws and lunged at Emily who lay beneath him. From the amount of blood that jetted from her and splashed the walls, her death was quick and within moments she had stopped struggling and lay motionless on the floor of her bedroom.

"That fucking animal," Potter hissed.

Emily was dead, her eyes wide open. I looked at the screen and I felt goose flesh run up my back as I looked into her eyes. She had died looking straight up at her secret camera. It was like she lay there staring straight into *my* eyes.

We continued to watch as McCain leapt from Emily and stood there looking down at her for a short time, his giant tail swishing back and forth. He then sauntered out of camera shot, leaving Emily dead on the floor. Isidor forwarded the video again until McCain re-entered the bedroom. This time he was back in his human form, but someone or something had returned to the room with him.

"What the fuck is that?" Potter said, squinting at the screen.

"It looks like some kinda elf with a melted face," Isidor suggested.

"That's a small boy," I gasped. "It's a boy who's suffered horrific burns to his face and hands."

"This just keeps getting weirder and weirder," Potter said. "I thought the world was pretty screwed up before it got pushed – but this takes the piss."

We watched as the small boy with the burns yanked the blankets from Emily's bed. Together, McCain and the boy laid them out on the floor. Then between them, they rolled Emily face down onto the blankets and covered her. They then rolled her over until she was wrapped tightly. McCain then took one end of Emily, and the boy took the other. They then carried her out of camera shot.

There was nothing else recorded on the camera. Isidor switched it off and turned to look at me, his face ashen. "What now?" he asked me.

"We go and rip that fucking arsehole's lungs out," Potter cut in.

"No!" I snapped and raised my hand. "We can't do that. It won't solve anything. We need to do this by the book if we are going to get justice for Emily and her sister Elizabeth."

"I don't know if you've noticed," Potter spat, "but there doesn't seem to be too much justice in this new world that we now find ourselves in."

"It doesn't matter," I told him. "We follow the rules and do it properly."

"I was wondering when Kiera's rule book was going to come out," Potter sighed. "When are you going to get it, huh? These animals don't follow any rules – they're nothing but dog shit."

"Kiera's right," Isidor said. "We should tread carefully – we don't want people to find out what we really are…"

"Says the Terminator impersonator!" Potter growled at him. "I should've guessed that you would side with Kiera. Why don't you show some backbone for once…"

"It has nothing to do with what Kiera thinks or about how much backbone I have," Isidor said, jumping up from his seat. "In case you've forgotten, my sister is trapped in that school with that animal. And if it hadn't have been for Kayla's backbone, you wouldn't even have that tape. So back off, Potter, because you're beginning to get on my fucking nerves!"

"Okay, enough already," I said. "This constant bitching isn't going to get us anywhere, nor is crashing into that school and killing McCain."

"So what do you suggest?" Potter snapped. "We sit and wait for McCain and the Munchkin lookalike to rip apart another young woman?"

"No," I said staring back at him. "We take this video to Banner and..."

"Are you for real, sweetcheeks?" Potter barked. "You said yourself that Banner was a waste of space. If we go marching into his station with that video, he is going to make us feel about as welcome as a fart in an elevator!"

"We have to try, Potter," I snapped. "Isidor is right. We can't risk revealing who and what we truly are. This place is messed up enough without throwing Vampyrus and half-breeds into the mix. We take the camera down to Banner and if he's not willing to help us..."

"Then what?" Potter asked me.

"We deal with McCain ourselves," I said.

Chapter Thirty-Seven

Kayla

I wasn't in pain, but I could feel myself going taut as if I were turning brittle somehow. My throat was burning up and my stomach was cramping. I had the flat of one hand pressed against my chest, and I could feel the blood pumping from the wound was already starting to congeal. Feeling the sticky red stuff between my fingers made my stomach ache and I wanted blood more than ever. But I felt so heavy, like I was made of stone somehow.

"Oh my god, what have I done?" someone said close by me. "What have I done?"

I forced my eyes half open, and I could just make out Sam hovering beside the bed. "Kayla what have I done to you? You look like you're turning to stone," he cried.

"My bag," I whispered. "Get my bag."

"Bag?" he asked confused. "What bag?"

"Beneath my wardrobe," I mumbled. "There are some glass tubes – pink stuff in them."

I closed my eyes again and listened to Sam rummaging around beneath my wardrobe. I heard my bag slide across the room and the zip open. "There aren't any tubes," he panicked. "What are you talking about?"

"There is a cut down the side of the bag..." I wheezed. "Look in there."

I heard the sound of the glass tubes clinking together as he fumbled for them. Then he was at my side again. "Open one," I gasped, the cramps in my stomach now agony. The sound of the cap being unscrewed beside me was almost deafening.

"Now what?" he gasped.

"Give some of it to me," I whispered.

I felt Sam's hand slip behind my head as he tried to raise it off the pillow, but it seemed too heavy for him to budge. So he placed the brim of the tube against my lips. I opened my mouth and he poured in some of the Lot 13. It tasted bitter and sweet as it rolled over my tongue. I swallowed, then took some more. Almost at once, the cramps in my stomach began to ease, and I felt my whole body begin to soften. The blood from the wound in my chest dried beneath my fingers.

"Is it helping?" I heard Sam ask, taking the empty tube away from my lips.

I lifted my free hand off the bed and it no longer felt like it were tied to a giant weight. The knife that Sam had plunged into me was still sticking from my chest, so wrapping my fingers around the handle I pulled it out.

Sam made a gasping sound. Then, before he knew what had happened, I had sprung from my bed. Without being able to control the change within me, my fangs were out, as were my wings and claws. I sprang through the air towards him. With a look of horror on his face, I pushed him in the chest, sending him smashing into the wall. Then I was on him, one claw around his throat and the other holding the knife just an inch from his heart.

"Don't you ever do that to me again!" I hissed into his terrified face.

"What are you?" he wheezed, my claws so tight about his throat that it was difficult for him to him breathe.

"You don't really want to know what I am," I warned. "You don't really want to know the truth – you couldn't handle the truth."

"You looked like you were turning to stone, just like that statue that chased us," he gasped. "What happened to you?"

"I don't know," I said, feeling scared.

I loosened my grip on him, and rubbing his throat, he said, "I was right, though, you are different. You're not like us."

"Just get out," I barked, and turned my back on him.

"Are you a vampire?" he whispered, just in case someone might be listening.

"No, I'm not a vampire," I snapped. "Now get out."

"What are you then?" he asked, coming towards me.

I turned to look at him, and flashing my fangs and letting

my wings tremor, I said, "I'm dead, that's what I am."

"So it was you in the newspaper," he gasped. "It was you on the beach that day."

"I wasn't on any beach with you," I spat. "I don't know what you are talking about."

"But that was you in the paper, right?"

"Yes," I told him.

"So how? Why...?" Sam stammered, and I could see that he couldn't take his eyes off me. He didn't look scared, exactly, just curious. "How come you are walking around with wings, fangs and stuff? The newspaper said you were dead."

"I don't have time for this," I said. "I need to get..."

"On with your mission," Sam cut in.

"What are you talking about?" I sighed. "What mission?"

"To save me and the others who are locked up in here, that's why you're here, isn't it?" he asked, his eyes wide and full of hope.

Looking at him with pity, I said, "Sam, I'm not here to save you or anyone else. Despite what you believe, I've never seen you before. I wasn't there on the beach that day with you, the first time I ever spoke to you was by the Poor Box and my parents didn't drown."

"So why are you here then?" he asked me.

"To find out who murdered Miss Clarke," I told him. "I have friends waiting for me on the outside. That's why I wanted to search Miss Clarke's room. I was looking for that camera. I left it in the woods today to be collected by my friends."

"I don't believe you," Sam said softly, sounding let down. "I have seen you before. You're like an angel who's been sent to rescue us. You even have wings like an angel."

"I've had these wings all my life, Sam," I said. "Way before I was murdered and died. It's who I am. That's why I used to get bullied, because I was different from the other girls I went to school with."

"But you were made different for a reason, Kayla," Sam said. "Can't you see that?"

"Whatever the reason may be, Sam," I said gently, "it isn't to come here and rescue you. I'm sorry."

"Me too," he said, slumping down onto my bed.

"I wish I could help, but me and my friends can't risk bringing attention to ourselves," I tried to explain.

"Are your friends like you then?"

"Yes. And they'll be waiting for me to contact them," I said. "If the stuff on that camera shows what happened to Miss Clarke, I can get out of here."

"Take me with you," Sam said, getting up from the bed and coming towards me.

"I can't," I whispered. "You're not one of us – it would be dangerous for you."

"Any more dangerous than being matched with a wolf?" he said.

"I'm sorry, Sam," I started, checking my pockets for my iPod. I wanted to speak with Kiera; I was desperate to find out what was on the camera so I could get out of Ravenwood School. But as I fumbled in my pockets, I realised that it was gone.

"What are you looking for?" Sam asked me.

"My iPod," I snapped, now searching the pockets of my blazer.

"You're not allowed to have iPods, mobile phones, or anything like that at Ravenwood," Sam started to explain.

"I couldn't give a shit," I said, not really listening to him now. Then, looking at him I added, "Have you taken it?"

"Why would I have taken it? When would I have taken it?" he asked.

"When I was on the bed," I said. "You could've taken it then."

"Why would I have done that?" he asked, sounding confused. "I want your help – not to piss you off. Maybe it fell out of your pocket as we climbed the tree?"

"Maybe…" I said thoughtfully. "I'm going to have to go and find it. It's the only way I have of contacting my friends." With my fangs, claws, and wings disappearing, I went to the door.

"Where are you going?" Sam asked.

"To find my iPod, of course."

"But you can't," Sam said. "It's almost dark out. The Greys

will be up in those search towers with the lights, they'll see you."

"That's a chance I'm gonna have to take," I told him. "I need to find that iPod."

"I'll come with you," he suggested, as I swung open the door to my room.

"Leaving us so soon?" someone asked, and I looked around to find McCain standing outside my bedroom door.

"I'm going to the bathroom," I lied.

"And what's Brooke doing in your room after dark?" McCain asked, peering over my shoulder. "You know the school rules."

"I wanted to borrow a book," Sam said.

"That's what we have a school library for," McCain barked at him, his bulbous nose glowing red. Then, sniffing, he looked at the both of us and said, "I guess it doesn't really matter, after all, you'll both be leaving here tonight."

"Leaving?" Sam gasped. "What, going home you mean?"

"Yes," McCain said, and his yellow eyes twinkled. "I haven't been able to find a suitable match for either of you."

"But I thought you said..." I started recalling the conversation I'd had with McCain earlier that day.

"I was wrong about that," McCain said, yanking the bottle of nasal spray from his pocket and ramming it up his right nostril. "My sense of smell isn't what it used to be. I can't find a suitable match for you, Hunt."

"So we can go right now?" Sam asked, shoving past me and into the corridor, eager to set off - and I couldn't blame him.

"Not right at once," McCain smiled, putting the nasal spray back in his pocket. "There is some paperwork that has to be completed. But you don't have to worry about that. We are throwing a leaving party in the old chapel – it's our way of saying goodbye. I know it hasn't always been easy for you children, but no harm was ever meant to you. We want you to leave Ravenwood with some fond memories and tell your families that it wasn't so bad here."

I looked at McCain, and I couldn't believe that he was just going to let us walk away from Ravenwood. He stared down at me and smiled.

"So if you would like to make your way to the chapel with the others, I'll finish the paperwork," he smiled again. "I hope you enjoy the party."

I wanted to tell Sam not to go. But, before I'd had a chance to say anything, two of the Greys stepped from the shadows and ushered Sam and me down the stairwell.

Chapter Thirty-Eight

Kayla

The Greys led us out of the school building where the other students, who had been chosen to be set free, were waiting for us. Amongst them I could see Pryor, the Addison twins, and Dorsey. He stood away from the rest of us as usual, alone. I felt sorry for him. I'd never actually spoken to Dorsey. I figured that one way or another, I would be leaving the school very soon, and I would like to have said something to him.

We followed the Greys out across the courtyard and onto the surrounding lawns. The air was crisp and fresh, but not cold. The moon was full and hung low in the sky like a silver disc. As we followed the Greys in single file away from the school building, Dorsey sauntered up beside me. He looked at me as if he wanted to say something.

"You all right, Dorsey?" I asked.

"I just wanted to say, you didn't have to do that for me the other day," he said angrily.

I was taken aback by the anger in his voice and said, "It's okay – it wasn't your fault – it was that idiot, Pry -"

"What I meant to say is, I can fight my own battles, you know. I don't need you sticking up for me."

I frowned and said, "I only did it to help you."

Hearing how Dorsey had spoken to me, Sam cut in and said, "Listen here, you ungrateful little…"

"No, that's okay," I interrupted.

"Okay?" Sam said, then turned on Dorsey. "Kayla could've got herself in the shit by sticking up for you."

"I didn't ask her to stick her nose in," Dorsey spat.

"From where I was standing, Pryor was getting ready to…" Sam started.

"Don't worry about it, Sam." I looked at Dorsey, and trying to hide my disappointment, I said to him, "Look, Dorsey, I'm sorry for butting in, but I was trying to be a mate – that was all. I just wanted to help..."

"Like I said, thanks but no thanks," he hissed, then sped off up the line.

"Can you believe that?" Sam sighed. "What an ungrateful little turd!"

"Maybe he's right. Perhaps I shouldn't have stepped in for him. I probably embarrassed him," I said.

"You saved him from a good beating, that's what you did!" Sam insisted.

"Let's just forget about it. I'm not bothered, really."

"Like I've already said, Kayla, I've never met anyone like you before," Sam half-smiled at me.

I watched Dorsey walk away, and although I could understand the point he was trying to make, I did feel a little hurt. Then, looking at Sam, I smiled back, and said, "Let's get this over and done with and get out of here."

The Greys led us around the outside of the school and away from the back of the building. We reached a clump of trees, and thinking this was where we would stop, they continued, until we stepped out into a large open area. In the middle was a stone-built chapel. It had a spire that stretched up into the night. It wasn't as small as I had imagined it to be. There were a set of steps leading up to a white wooden door which was open. From inside I could hear the sound of music seeping out into the night. It wasn't choir music, it was rock music. It was like a party was in full swing inside. I could feel an excitement running through the group of kids around me as they whispered to one another about being freed and getting to see their families again.

Leaning towards Sam, I whispered, "Are you sure you want to go in?"

Sam nodded his head. "Hell yeah."

"Why?" I whispered over the *boom-boom* of the music coming from the chapel.

"Because I just want to get out of here."

"But do you really think that McCain is just gonna let you go?" I asked him.

216

"You heard what he said," Sam smiled at me, and I could see the hope in his eyes. Then, he was gone, heading along with the others towards the open chapel doorway.

Half of me wanted to go after him and drag him back, but what was I dragging him back to? Maybe McCain had been telling the truth? Perhaps we were all going home. Then, I was prodded in the back. I turned around to find a Grey standing behind me. Without saying anything, it pointed in the direction of the chapel. Not intending to stay for too long, I made my way towards the doorway. Even if I only stayed long enough to say goodbye to Sam, what was the worst that could happen?

No sooner had I stepped inside the chapel, the door was closed behind me. The sound of music was very loud now. There was a small foyer which led into the main part of the chapel. Unlike any other chapel I'd been into, there weren't any pews, font and instead of an altar, there were turntables and a D.J., who looked like a reject from a Tim Burton movie. He was thin, gaunt-looking, and wore a tall hat which any undertaker would have been proud of.

Around the edges of the walls, there were tables which had been covered with the most delicious-looking food I had ever seen. There were plates of sandwiches, pizza, hot dogs, bowls of popcorn, marshmallows, and every other kind of cake and dessert that I could imagine. Maybe this really was a leaving party, I thought. I had no idea what strange customs and rituals this weird new world had.

I headed across the chapel to where some of the other students had started to dance with each other. Not since arriving at Ravenwood had I seen such looks of happiness on their faces, and I couldn't help but feel my own spirits rising.

"Hey!" I heard someone shout and I looked around to see Pryor and the Addison twins standing in a nearby alcove. He waved his hand at me, and beckoned me over. Ignoring him, I turned away.

"Hey, Hunt!" he shouted again.

I looked back and could see that he had my iPod in his hand. Without hesitating, I headed across the dance floor towards him. He grinned at me from the shadows.

"Look what I found by that big old chestnut tree," he smiled.

I reached for my iPod and he snatched it away. "Give it back to me," I said.

Then, swiping his thumb across the screen he opened the messages. "Say, look at this," he smiled, then he read aloud the message I had sent earlier to Kiera. "Kiera, camera hidden on south side of school near to stream and huge pile of bushes. If Isidor can't track my scent then he should be able to smell the dead body! Will have to explain later. Got to go! Kayla."

"Give it back," I said, holding out my hand, and the Addison twins sniggered like a couple of hyenas.

"So you've been over the wall?" Pryor asked with his annoying grin, but his eyes looked crazy – almost wild. "What's with the dead body and who the fuck is Isidor? What sort of fag name is that?"

I couldn't bear the thought of him being nasty about Isidor, so shooting my hand forward, I grabbed him around the throat and brought my forehead smashing down onto his nose. I heard a sickening crunching sound and felt his nose spread across his face. Pryor fell to the floor screaming, blood pumping through his fingers.

"She's broken my freaking nose!" he screamed like a baby. "She head-butted me!"

I reached down and snatched my iPod from his blood-stained hand, fighting hard not to tear his head clean off. Then, whispering in his ear, I said, "Don't you ever say another bad word about my brother, because if you do, you won't fucking believe what happens next!"

"You can't do that," one of the Addison twins mumbled from beside me, as they looked down in horror at their bleeding friend.

Then, flashing my fangs at him, I hissed, "Shut your fucking face before I start sucking on your brains!"

Both twins looked at me, their faces white as snow, eyes wide. Smiling to myself, I walked away, needing to find somewhere alone so I could contact Kiera. Before I'd had a chance to find anywhere, Sam came running towards me, a smile spread across his good-looking face.

"I really think we're going home," he shouted over the music.

"Do you really believe that?"

"Don't you?" he asked me, the grin still plastered across his face.

"I'm not sure," I said back. I wanted to believe it but it sounded too good to be true. "What about you?"

"What about me?" he said, pulling me close so he could hear me over the music.

"What are you gonna do when you get out of here?" I asked him, knowing that he didn't have parents to go back to.

"I was still hoping that I might get you to change your mind," he smiled, slipping one arm around my waist.

"About what?"

"Letting me tag along with you and your friends," he asked again.

"You can't, Sam," I said, shaking my head.

"It's meant to be," he said. "I know you don't believe me, but I did see you on the beach that day, and you did know my name."

"It wasn't me," I told him.

Then, the music changed and *Candyman* by Christina Agulera started to play. Not wanting to go over the whole beach thing again, I smiled and said, "I love this song."

"Let's dance then," he grinned, and before I knew what was happening, he was spinning me around and around in his arms. Sam wasn't a bad dancer and he swirled me this way and that as he held my hands. His smile was infectious, and within moments, he had me smiling and laughing too. I couldn't remember the last time I felt so happy. *Candyman* finished and *Watching The Moon* by Bruno Mars started.

The lights in the chapel were dimmed and before I could walk away, Sam pulled me into his arms and started to dance slowly with me.

"I'm sorry I stabbed you," he said.

"I seem to have that effect on guys," I said back.

"I bet there aren't too many guys who have to say sorry for

doing something like that on their first date," he said, trying to make a joke, but I could tell that he was sorry.

"So you think this is a date then?"

"The closest I think me and you will ever get to one," he said.

"I guess," I smiled.

"Even though you say that it wasn't you on the beach that day," he whispered, resting his cheek next to mine, "I'm glad that I got to meet you here, Kayla."

"Why?" I whispered, always feeling uncomfortable when I was being paid a compliment.

"I wanted to tell you something the other day, but I chickened out," he said, pulling me close as I slipped my arms around his neck. "I guess it doesn't matter if I make a complete jerk of myself, as we'll never see each other again after tonight."

"So what was it that you wanted to say to me?" I asked, swaying against one another.

Leaning back from me so he could see into my eyes, he said, "You shouldn't let the memories of those girls who bullied you haunt you forever." Then, swallowing hard, he quickly added, "I think you're hot, Kayla."

With my hand placed gently on the back of his neck, I wanted to pull him forward and kiss him. But before I'd had the chance, the music stopped, the lights went out, and everyone started screaming.

Chapter Thirty-Nine

Kiera

Banner led us into his office and slumped behind his cluttered desk. He eyed Potter and Isidor with suspicion and said, "So, who are your friends, Hudson?"

"Just friends," I said. Then, taking the camera from my coat pocket, I placed it on the table in front of him and said, "I've been trying to solve a puzzle, and here is a big piece of it."

"Puzzle?" Banner said, looking down at the camera.

"Emily Clarke?" I reminded him.

"Clarke?" he replied, scratching his thick, white hair. "Oh yeah, I remember now. The girl that went missing."

"That's right," I said. "She worked as a teacher at Ravenwood."

"Look, I don't really have time for this right now," he groaned. "I'm kinda busy. Got a couple of guys down in the cells for burglary."

"I'm pleased for you," I said dryly. "But what about Emily?"

"Look, Hudson," Banner said, "I'm really busy. Neither of the scum downstairs is talking. I got some of the boys to take 'em both round the back of the station and give 'em both a slap - but they still didn't talk. So I went and paid 'em a little visit in their cells. Even when I had their nuts squeezed tight in my hand and I thought their eyes were gonna pop straight outter their heads – they still wouldn't talk about those burglaries."

"Screw the burglaries," I spat. "Emily Clarke has been murdered..."

"Murdered?" Banner smiled nervously. "Don't talk such rubbish."

"Watch the tape," Potter said from the corner of the room.

"Why?" Banner asked, picking it up in one of his huge hands.

"Because it shows Morris McCain butchering Emily Clarke," I said, trying to stay calm.

"Bollocks!" Banner cried and rubbed his thick white moustache, nervously. "McCain wouldn't dare."

"Why wouldn't he dare?" Isidor asked him.

"Because it would all be over!" Banner shouted. "The treaty and everything would be finished. The treaty says that any wolf to be caught murdering a human would be put to death. McCain might be a bit of a bully, but he ain't dumb enough to go murdering your friend, Emily Clarke."

"Look, I haven't got time to stand here and argue with you," I told him. "If you don't believe me, watch the footage on the camera." Then, realising that Potter was right, and I was being made to feel about as welcome as a fart in an elevator, I went to the door.

"Where are you going?" Banner called out.

"To get my friend back before she becomes another one of McCain's victims," I said.

Chapter Forty

Kayla

I could hear the sound of paws padding across the dance floor. The claws attached to them made clicking sounds. The wolves crept into the chapel, the sound of their breathing deep and rasping. There was panic amongst the students, and Sam gripped my hand and pulled me close.

"We haven't come here to be set free, have we?" Sam whispered. "This is a matching ceremony, isn't it?"

"I guess," I whispered, letting go of Sam's hand and releasing my claws. I felt something big and covered in fur brush past me and it made a snarling noise. I flinched backwards.

"Kayla, where are you?" Sam called out, losing me in the dark.

"I'm right here," I whispered. "Keep still."

I could hear the sound of feet rushing past me – not wolves – the other students trying to find a way out of the chapel in the dark.

"Put the lights on!" someone screamed.

There was a scuffling noise and I spun around. Then, the song *Candyman* started again, as if whoever had gone in search of the light switch had hit the wrong button. They must have tried again, as the strobe lights suddenly came on and I wished they hadn't. In those sudden flashes of bright white light, I saw the wolves that had crept into the chapel. They had positioned themselves near to the students who they were planning on matching with. I wasn't the only one who had seen the giant-sized wolves with their bristling fur and gaping jaws, as the chapel burst into chaos. In the glimpses of light, I saw the wolves leap through the air and smother the children standing before them. I looked to my right. Sam was standing there, his eyes wide as he stared ahead. I followed his gaze and saw a wolf rear up onto his back legs as it lunged at Sam. With the song *Candyman* blasting around the chapel, I leapt forward, plunging my claws into the throat of the werewolf.

The lights pulsated on and off and everything seemed to slow down. I felt my fist enter the wolf's throat. It howled so loud that for a moment the music was completely drowned out. Its cries of agony must have alerted the other wolves, as each of them turned to face me. And in the flashing lights, I caught just glimpses of their razor-sharp teeth and flaming yellow eyes as they came towards me.

I pulled my fist from the wolf's throat and a stream of black blood jetted up and splashed Sam. "Get behind me," I screamed over the throbbing music. Never in my wildest dreams did I ever imagine I would be slaying werewolves while listening to *Candyman* by Christina Agulera.

The wolves came towards me, circling slowly, while those they had come to be matched with fled to the furthest corners of the chapel. Then, I saw one of the wolves come forward. He was jet black and sleek-looking. His bright yellow eyes stared into mine.

"Oh, Kayla," he woofed. "I've got someone real special for you to match with."

"I'm not going to be matched," I whispered, unable to stop myself from looking into his eyes.

"But you haven't seen who I've brought for you," he barked over the roar of the music.

Then from behind him slinked the most beautiful wolf that I'd ever seen. Its fur was white and shimmered like glass in the strobe lighting. "Who is she?" I asked the wolf.

"The Wolf Man's intended bride," the wolf started, and over the blast of the music, I finally recognised his voice. It was McCain. "You are beautiful, Kayla Hunt. And you'll be even more beautiful once you have been matched with Lola. She will complete you."

"You don't understand, McCain," I said, staring into his eyes. "I can't be matched like the others. I'm different."

"And that's why you will be such a perfect match for Lola," he woofed, then licked his nose with his tongue. "She is brave and courageous, just like you. She has a spirit that can't be tamed. Matched together, you will make the perfect bride."

Then, as if I'd lost control of my own body, I started to walk towards Lola who stood on all fours in front me.

"Kayla, what are you doing?" Sam screamed over the music. "Don't go to her."

Although I could hear him, it was like I just couldn't stop myself. It was as if McCain had control over me somehow. I felt Sam grab for me, and I brushed him aside. I moved slowly closer towards Lola, and it was her burning eyes that I was staring into as she reared up on her back legs and lunged for me.

There was a crashing sound from somewhere in the darkness and more screaming, but it was faint, drowned out by the music and the sound of Lola's panting as she placed her giant paws onto my shoulders and stared into my eyes. In the flashing lights, I saw her giant pink tongue roll from her jaws and she ran it down the side of my face. It felt warm and rough. And as I looked into her eyes, it was like I could hear her howling inside my head – it was as if she were brainwashing me, taking over my mind.

Suddenly, her howling changed. It was like she was in pain. Lola let go of my shoulders and flew backwards across the chapel. The spell she had cast over me was broken. I looked through the pulsating lights and could see her lying on the floor, a wooden stake sticking out from her side. Then, all hell broke loose.

Chapter Forty-One

Kiera

We had been drawn to the chapel by the sound of the beating music – the screams told us we were heading in the right direction. The gates to the school were locked, and peering through them, I could see several cloaked figures racing back and forth across the lawn. The school with its high walls, search towers, and wide gravel path were just how I had seen it in my nightmare. And as I watched the figures racing around, I knew these were the Greys that Kayla had spoken about. I had seen them in my nightmare too – they had come from the school and had dragged that man back inside. But what or who were they?

There was a grinding sound. I looked right to see Potter breaking the chains that were fastened around the black iron gates. They came away in his claws and clattered to the ground. The music continued to beat in the distance and so did the terrified screams of children. I looked left and Isidor threw open his coat, and with lightning speed, his crossbow was in his hands.

"Ready?" I asked, looking at the both of them.

"I'm always ready, tiger," Potter winked back at me. Then, he was gone, racing away up the gravel path in the direction of the music and the screaming. His claws glinted in the moonlight and a small part of me pitied anyone who got in his way tonight. I knew that Potter had been frustrated hanging out at the farmhouse, and now that he had the chance to hunt some werewolves, I don't think anyone or anything could stop him.

I glanced at Isidor, who still stood beside me, his crossbow at the ready. "Let's get Kayla and then get out of here."

"Sounds good to me," he said, racing up the winding path after Potter.

I hung back for just a moment, and when they were both some way ahead of me, I reached into my pocket and took out the bottle of Lot 13 that I'd sneaked from Isidor's supply which he had brought with him to the farmhouse. I unscrewed the cap and brought the little glass tube to my lips. I didn't want it. I really didn't – but I couldn't risk cracking-up if I needed to change into my half-breed form while trying to rescue Kayla. And by the sound of the chaos unfolding in the distance – I guessed that the chances of that were pretty high. So, tilting my head back, I poured the gloopy pink liquid into my mouth. I screwed up my nose at once. It tasted disgusting. *How had the others managed to drink this shit?* I wondered. It was so bitter in taste, my eyes began to water. Closing my eyes, I gulped the rest down. I placed the empty tube back into my coat pocket and headed after Potter and Isidor.

My feet whispered over the gravel path as I raced forward. I looked down and my feet were just a blur beneath me. This was the first time since returning from The Hollows that I had tapped into those inner abilities that being a half-breed gave me. As I raced forward, it felt incredible to feel the wind against my flesh and my long, flowing hair. Deep inside of me, I understood Potter's desire to be his true self for as much of the time as possible. Being a half-breed was a rush. Maybe I was finally beginning to accept what I truly was.

In the distance I could see Potter standing over several of the Greys who were now lying on the ground at his feet. Isidor caught up with him just before I did. I looked down at them, their grey robes so tattered and torn, they looked as if they had been put through a paper shredder. The grass looked black and sticky, and I could see that it was blood. Some of the Greys had been decapitated, and their hooded faces lay some way off from the rest of the bodies.

"What happened here?" I said, looking down at the carnage.

"He did," Isidor said, gesturing towards Potter with his crossbow.

"Why?" I asked Potter.

"They got in my way," he said.

227

"But..." I started.

"But nothing," Potter said, staring at me. "I did them a favour."

"How do you figure that out?" Isidor asked him, looking at the Greys spread across the grass before us.

Potter reached down with one blood-soaked claw and lifted up one of the Greys' heads by the top of its hood. Swinging it before him like a lantern, Potter yanked back the hood and I stumbled backwards. The face beneath the hood was hideous. It was grey and wrinkled like a rotten prune. The mouth hung open to reveal a set of yellow-stained teeth. But it was the eyes. It looked like they had been burnt out with hot pokers. There were scorch marks around them, and the eye sockets were deep and surrounded by flaky black skin.

"What's happened to their eyes?" I gasped.

"Werewolves have been staring into them," Potter said, tossing the head aside.

"Who or what are they?" Isidor asked. "They look human."

"I'm guessing that they were the former teachers of this school," Potter said. "McCain and his merry bunch of wolves would have needed to control them somehow – to get them to go along with his cruelty. If they went against him, then they used their good old-fashioned mind control by staring into their eyes. Some of these Greys might have even been the parents who we've heard tried to break their children out. Who knows and who really cares? They're dead now. Let's leave them in peace."

"But why do this to them?" I asked him.

"He's not allowed to kill them, remember – goes against the Treaty," Potter said.

"So why kill Emily Clarke?" Isidor asked him.

"How should I know?" Potter shrugged, heading off towards the music and the screaming, which was coming from the other side of a tall line of trees.

We followed him, but Isidor's question wouldn't leave me. So why had McCain murdered Emily Clarke if he could have silenced her another way?

Potter burst through the tree line. There was a chapel with a white wooden roof and a spire that stretched up into the night. The screaming was coming from within the chapel. But now that we were closer, I could hear another sound, one that I had last heard in The Hollows. It was the sound of wolves snarling, barking, and howling.

"Game on," Potter said, his black eyes almost seeming to sparkle with excitement.

"Let's just try and get Kayla, then go," I told him. "No more killing if we don't have to."

"Sure," Potter said, wiping the Grey's blood from his claws, as if cleaning them before going into battle.

"I'm being serious, Potter," I told him.

"I'm deadly serious," he said back, and before I'd the chance to say anything else, he was running towards the chapel, shredding his shirt free as he went. Isidor and I ran after him, but Potter was already raking apart the locked chapel doors with his claws by the time we had caught up with him.

The door fell away in splinters, and once there was a hole large enough to squeeze through, Potter leapt inside. There was a small foyer, and now that we were inside, the music was deafening. The chapel was illuminated in random flashes of bright white light. I peered through the darkness and froze. Kayla was standing in the middle of the chapel, with a giant wolf standing before her. She looked as if she had been hypnotised. Kayla's face was blank-looking, her mouth open, as the wolf stared into her eyes. Then, the wolf was flying backwards across the chapel. I looked right and I could see Isidor reloading his crossbow.

Chapter Forty-Two

Kiera

With the chapel door lying in splinters at our feet, a flood of shrieking and terrified children shoved past us and out into the night. A timid-looking girl with tears streaming down her face spotted Potter's huge claws and came to a standstill before him. She looked up into his face, her bottom lip wobbling and her body trembling. She was so fixated on Potter that she failed to see the giant paw that lunged from the darkness of the chapel and grabbed for her. Potter saw it though, and in a blaze of movement, he had seized hold of the attacking werewolf and dragged it into the foyer.

With his claws and fangs flashing in the strobe lighting, he pulled apart the wolf's giant jaws. The *cracking* sound that came from the wolf as its face was torn apart was so loud that it could be heard over the *boom-boom* of the music which was still playing.

The young girl stood rooted to the spot and watched as Potter sunk his fangs into what was left of the wolf's giant head. Then, as if in the early stages of throwing a fit, the girl began to shake all over in fright. Her mouth dropped open and she began to scream. Potter snapped his head up and looked at the girl. With blood smeared around his mouth and stringy pieces of flesh hanging from his fangs, he said to the girl, "If I were you, sweetheart, I'd get out of here before this turns nasty."

How much nastier Potter intended this rescue to become, I dared not imagine, but heeding his warning, the girl turned on her heels, and screaming, she fled the chapel. With her cries fading into the distance, Potter stood and wiped the blood from his mouth with his forearm.

Catching me staring at him, he looked at me and said, "What?"

"Nothing," I said back and turned to look at Isidor, who was now firing wave after wave of stakes into the flashing darkness. The sound of howling nearly drowned out the song *The Time* by The Black Eyed Peas, which was now thundering throughout the chapel. Then, from within the darkness, I saw a series of bright yellow lights begin to flash. It took me a moment to realise that it wasn't part of the strobe lighting that I could see, but the burning eyes of the wolves as they came towards us.

"I'm going to get Kayla," Isidor shouted over the pumping music and the snarling that was now coming from the approaching wolves.

Before I had a chance to say anything, Isidor was leaping and spinning over the heads of the wolves and releasing a volley of stakes into them. The wolves raised their colossal heads and gnashed their foaming jaws at him. But Isidor was too quick for them, and their jaws crunched down on nothing more than air. Some turned to go after him, but the main pack fixed their crazy yellow eyes on Potter and me and charged us.

"Ready, sweetcheeks?" Potter grinned at me, and just like the words in The Black Eyed Peas song that was playing, he looked as if he was having the time of his life. Then he was gone, launching himself through the air at the wolves. His arms moved so fast that they were nothing more than a blur of movement. Fur and chunks of wolf flesh spattered the walls, ceiling, and floor of the chapel.

I watched several of the wolves bound towards Potter, knocking him off his feet and sending him skidding on his back across the dance floor. And in the strobe lights that continued to pulse and flash all around us, everything seemed to move in slow motion. I watched as Potter disappeared beneath a mountain of fur and muscle, and I shot through the air, fangs and claws gleaming.

My razor-sharp fingernails sliced in the flanks of a wolf, and as I felt it spasm beneath me, it snapped its giant head around to see who or what was on it. With its teeth just inches from my face, it gnashed at me. Jerking my head backwards, I buried my free claw into one of its massive eyeballs. Something close to puss burst from its eye socket and splashed me. It felt warm and sticky against my face. I ripped my other claw from its belly, dragging my nails in a zigzag motion so the wound could never be closed. The wolf shrieked and convulsed as its entrails spilled from the ragged hole that I had cut in it. Within seconds the wolf lay motionless, its giant pink tongue lolling from between its jaws. I stood up, then was swiped sideways across the chapel. I crashed into the far wall, splinters of wood showering through the air. I rolled onto my back as a huge black wolf leapt on me. Pinning me down with his giant paws, it looked into my face with its seething eyes.

"Who are you?" the wolf roared over the music, the sounds of ripping, tearing, and howling now seemed louder than the music. "What sort of creature are you?"

I tried wriggling free of him, but he was so heavy that I found it difficult to breathe, let alone move.

"How dare you interrupt my ceremony!" he howled into my face, his breath so hot, that it felt as if I were staring into a furnace.

"You call stealing the souls of children a ceremony?" I spat.

"Do you not know who I am?" he roared. "I'm McCain, the Match Maker."

Realising who it was beneath the fur and remembering how he had ripped Emily Clarke to pieces, I knew that I was in trouble. I could fight back, but I didn't want to kill him. I wanted McCain alive, but I doubted he felt the same way about me.

"You're nothing but a murderer, McCain, and I'm gonna prove it," I screamed at him. "I'm gonna bring your whole world down around you. I'm going to make sure that you never hurt another child again!"

"And how are you going to do that when you're dead?" he woofed, then licked the length of my face.

With his whiskered snout so close to my face, I lifted my head off the dance floor and whispered in his ear. "I'm dead already."

Then, I sunk my fangs into him.

"Potter's v
Kiera?"

"Under tha
floor.

"Go and he
him into my ar

"You can't

"He's human."

"I'm not lea

"Potter isn
me.

"That shou
as I carried San

Chapter Forty-Three

Kayla

It was like I was coming awake after an operation. The wolf had been staring into my eyes one minute, then she was gone, howling and flying back across the chapel. The wolf, Lola, seemed to be in my head as she had stared into my eyes. I could hear her breathing and a sound that I hadn't heard inside me for a long time – the sound of a beating heart. Lola had been matching with me. But something had stopped her before the process had been complete. I looked up, and through the flashing lights I could see someone or something spinning through the air towards me. At first I thought it was a wolf, but the figure coming towards me was too agile. They moved with lighting speed as they fired...fired their crossbow.

"Isidor!" I screamed, feeling as if I was going to explode with happiness. I watched him spin through the air like some freaky trapeze artist as he rained down stakes on the wolves that leapt into the air after him. The wolves he hit flew backwards, their claws scraping against the wooden dance floor.

"Kayla!" someone shouted, and I spun round to see Sam being pinned to the floor by a silver-haired wolf. Its face was just inches from Sam's, and a glistening line of drool swung from its foaming jaws and spattered against his face. "Kayla!" Sam screamed again, and then fell silent.

I raced across the dance floor, my claws out. But as I made my way towards Sam, I watched as the wolf's eyes began to light up like two burning pits. Sam's face glowed yellow beneath their stare. My friend stared back into the eyes of the wolf and then something strange started to happen. I had seen a lot of things in my young life, but nothing so freaking weird as what I was now witnessing. Sam's face seemed to be stretching upwards, like it was made of putty. It was like the wolf was pulling his face off with his eyes. I watched as Sam's face almost seemed to wrap around the wolf's head like a

Chapter Forty-Four

Kiera

McCain roared in pain as I sunk my fangs into his shoulder like a set of knives. He twisted above me as he tried to shake me off, but I clamped my jaws down hard. He swiped at me with his paws and missed. This seemed to heighten his anger and he bellowed in rage. I didn't know for how much longer I could keep hold of him. I knew that as soon as I released him, he would rip my head off and that would really kill me. I doubted that the Elders would give me another chance – and if I were honest with myself – I wouldn't have wanted one. The next time I died, I wanted to stay dead – just not yet.

With the muscles in my jaw beginning to ache, I knew that it would only be moments before I lost my hold on him. Then, from the corner of my eye I saw Isidor sweeping across the hall, his crossbow trained on McCain. If he fired, I knew that McCain would be dead and I didn't want that. So, removing my fangs from McCain's shoulder, I screamed, "No, Isidor. Don't kill him!"

McCain seized his chance and lunged at my face, his teeth like spikes. I shut my eyes and waited for the pain, but it never came. Suddenly, I felt weightless as I was dragged out from beneath the wolf and thrown backwards through the air. Without having to even think about it, my wings sprung open, those little black claws opening and closing, as if glad to be free again. Hovering in the air, I looked down to see that it was Potter who had yanked me from beneath McCain. In the flashes of light, Potter seemed to flit to and fro around McCain. I could see that his chest looked like it had been almost ripped to pieces. He was soaked in blood and his wings looked as if Edward Scissorhands had been at him. But still he didn't stop fighting with the last remaining wolves. His arms worked like pistons as he punched, swiped, and stabbed at the wolves that lunged for him.

From above, I watched as one of the wolves, that just moments ago looked as if it was dead, scrambled back to its feet and raced across the chapel towards Potter. With my wings pointed behind me, I dropped through the air like a stone. When I was within reaching distance, I raked my claws down the length of the wolf's back, removing a ragged flap of fur-covered flesh. I spun away, and glancing back over my shoulder, I could see the wolf's spine and ribcage glistening wetly up at me. Then, the wolf collapsed, as if its legs had just been kicked from beneath it.

Spinning around amongst the wood beams that held the ceiling together, I looked down to see McCain roll over onto his paws. He spotted Isidor and bounded towards him. Isidor instinctively raised his crossbow. Then, as if remembering that I'd told him not to kill McCain, he lowered it again. In that moment of hesitation, McCain was on him. With one mighty swipe, McCain knocked him from his feet and sent Isidor smashing into the chapel wall. The whole building shook, sending dirt and dust showering down from the beams above me. Stunned, Isidor slid down the wall and onto the floor as McCain smothered him. I shot down and arrived on the floor just as Potter saw the trouble Isidor was in. Within an instant, he was on McCain, who had opened a hole in Isidor's chest with one of his giant claws. Isidor cried out and dropped to the floor, blood pumping from him.

Potter looked down at Isidor as he lay bleeding. Looking at McCain, Potter shook his head, and said, "Big mistake. The kid's my friend." Then, he went berserk.

As a wolf, McCain was a giant, as big as a bear. His head sat between two colossal shoulders that rippled with muscle. His eyes seared like two burning moons in his skull. His gaping jaws hung open, revealing his blood-stained teeth. Potter launched himself at McCain with such ferocity that the wolf flew backwards through the air. Before McCain had even landed, Potter was racing towards him with his tattered wings. He grabbed hold of McCain in mid-air and spun around. The wolf's long, bushy tail whisked upwards as if trying to knock Potter free of him. He rolled his head back, his ferocious teeth gnashing just inches from Potter's face.

Isidor groaned beside me, a claw pressed to his chest. "Help Potter," he said.

"Are you okay?" I asked, watching the blood begin to congeal around the claw covering his chest.

"Just help him," he said, closing his eyes.

With my wings spread, and their little claws grabbing at the air, I shot towards Potter as he continued to struggle with McCain.

"What kept you?" Potter growled, as he tried to drag McCain back towards the dance floor.

"You looked like you were having such fun!" I shot back, gripping McCain's tail and dragging him down. The wolf kicked wildly with its powerful back legs. I dodged left and right to avoid them striking me.

The three of us smashed into the floor, the sound of wooden boards splintering beneath us. Taking McCain's skull in his claws, Potter smashed it repeatedly into the dance floor. Dust and splinters of wood shot up like there were a series of timed explosions going off beneath us. I looked into the wolf's eyes and could see that the light in them was fading. McCain's tongue lolled from the corner of his mouth as he howled in pain.

Once Potter had McCain subdued, he coiled his arms around his neck and held him in a headlock. McCain's tongue twitched like a rattlesnake as Potter applied pressure to the wolf's throat.

"Don't kill him," I shouted. "We need him alive."

Potter glared up at me, his teeth locked together as he tightened his grip.

"Potter!" I hissed. "Don't you dare."

"He's a murderer!" Potter roared. "He steals the souls of children!"

"Killing him won't stop that," I shouted. "We have to get Banner to show the world that video. Show them what the wolves, like McCain, have been doing – what they are capable of."

Potter locked eyes with me, then slowly he loosened his hold on McCain and as he did, the wolf began to change. I watched as its face twisted and contorted. Its legs shrunk in size and took on human form. McCain cried out as if in pain and his eyes rolled in their sockets. His claws looked like they were being sucked back into his fingers. Potter released him. We both looked down at McCain as he lay panting, his hands to his throat.

"I haven't murdered anyone," he snarled.

"Well I've got evidence that says different," I spat.

"What now?" Potter asked me.

"We take him to Banner," I said.

Holding out his hand, Potter looked at me and said, "Handcuffs?"

"You know I don't have any handcuffs," I said, flashing him a false smile.

Then, without warning, Potter stamped down on McCain's leg. The sound of his ankle snapping was sickening. "What did you do that for?" I gasped.

"It's a long way back into town. We don't want him running away from us." Then reaching down, he dragged McCain to his feet.

McCain screamed out in pain, the tendons in his neck standing out through his white skin.

I stood and watched Potter drag McCain across the dance floor and out towards the splintered doorway. McCain's screams were deafening, and the thumping music did nothing to mask them. I turned and ran back across the chapel to Isidor, who had managed to pull himself up into a sitting position.

"How are you doing?" I asked, wrapping my arm around his shoulder.

"Okay, I guess," Isidor winced. "I think the wound is healing.

"Let me have a look," I said, opening his coat. Where there was once a gaping hole, was now a purple and black knotted lump of dead flesh. But there was something else. The skin around the wound looked as if it were cracking, like a shattered piece of stone.

Covering it with his coat, I hoisted Isidor to his feet and helped him from the chapel. We stepped out into the night, to find Potter holding onto the groaning McCain, and Kayla who was holding an unconscious looking boy in her arms.

"I haven't murdered anyone," McCain continued to protest.

"Shut the fuck up or I'll break your other leg," Potter snapped. "Christ, I need a cigarette," he added.

I headed towards Kayla who held the boy. His face was hideously disfigured. "This is Sam, the boy you told us about, isn't it?" I asked her.

She nodded her head, and looked down at him. "Can we take him with us?"

Before I'd had a chance to say anything, Potter shouted, "No way. No more hanger-ons."

Ignoring him, Kayla looked up into my eyes and said, "Please, Kiera, we can't just leave him."

"We'll take him to the nearest hospital, but that's as far as we take him," I told her softly. "Potter is right, we can't..."

"But he knows about me," Kayla cut in. "He knows what I am."

"And so do I," McCain groaned, as if somehow trying to bargain his release with us.

"And who is going to believe a freaking murderer?" Potter said. "No one will believe a word you say after that video has been shown..."

"What video...?" McCain started, but stopped when Potter's fist broke his nose.

"Sorry," Potter shrugged, looking at me. "He was getting on my tits."

Over the sound of McCain's groaning, I looked back at Kayla and said, "What do you mean, he knows what you are? Did you tell him?"

"I didn't have to," Kayla started to explain. "He said that he had seen me before – on a beach, and that I'd known his name.

But he doesn't understand how, because he knows that I was murdered."

"How did he know that?" Isidor cut in.

"He read it in a newspaper," Kayla said. "He showed it to me. It said that my dead, naked body was discovered on the side of a mountain, and Sam thinks I then showed up on some beach, then at this school."

I couldn't make sense of what Kayla was telling me. In the distance I could hear the *whoop-whoop* sound of approaching police vehicles. I looked up and could see the night sky was alight with strobes of blue and white. Knowing that the official police were on their way, I looked down at the boy in Kayla's arms, then at her.

"Okay, we take him back to the manor, but only until we find out what he knows, then we cut him loose," I said.

"Thanks, Kiera," Kayla whispered.

"Oh great," Potter snapped. "Just another one to add to the already overcrowded Mystery Machine."

"Give Isidor your lighter," I said to Potter, ignoring his remark.

"Why?" Potter asked, fishing it from his trouser pocket.

Isidor took it from Potter. "Now set light to that chapel," I ordered.

"Why?" Isidor asked.

"To destroy any trace that we've ever been here," I said. "When they find a room full of disembowelled wolves, they're gonna know that no human did that."

Without saying another word, Isidor set the chapel ablaze. The sound of the approaching sirens grew louder and with the chapel burning behind us, we made our way back down the gravel path towards the school gates.

Looking like humans again, we stood and watched Banner bring his unmarked police car to a screeching halt. The door flew open and he climbed out.

"I watched the tape," he shouted as he came running towards me. Several other police cars pulled up behind his vehicle. "You were right, Hudson, McCain is a piece of

241

murdering scum." Then, spotting the raging fire behind us, McCain limping and crying out in pain as Potter held onto him, Banner looked at me and said, "What in the name of sweet Jesus has gone on here?"

I looked into Banner's eyes and said, "You told me once that I had a police badge, and that I should use it. Well I just have."

Then, Potter shoved McCain into Banner's arms, and we left the grounds of Ravenwood School and made our way back to Hallowed Manor.

Chapter Forty-Five

Kiera

The next few days were spent locked away at the manor, giving our bodies the chance to heal and recover from what had happened at Ravenwood School. On the very next morning after handing McCain over to Banner, I telephoned Elizabeth Clarke and told her what I had discovered. She wept over the phone, as she had been unable to come straight down to see me. I didn't want Elizabeth to find out what had happened to her sister by watching the news or reading it in a newspaper.

Elizabeth said that she needed just a couple of days, then she would come to Hallowed Manor to find out everything that I had discovered. Over those few days, Kayla spent most of her time looking after Sam, who we had placed in one of the many spare rooms. Potter seemed less agitated than before. Isidor seemed quiet and content as he sat quietly in the study and passed his time by reading. If he had noticed the cracks around his healing wound, he didn't say anything. I considered talking to him about it, but I felt the time wasn't quite right. I didn't understand it myself.

Several times I went back to the summerhouse, but the statue had gone. I went to the tiny graveyard hidden beneath the willow trees, and to my surprise, I found Murphy's crucifix hanging from the cross that Potter had made for his friend. Taking the crucifix in my hands, I listened to the wind rustling through the willows, then hung the cross back around my neck.

I was glad I had told Elizabeth about her sister when I had, because the news of McCain's arrest and what had happened at Ravenwood was front page news, and occupied hours of airtime on the TV. The Council of Wolves and the United Nations Commission of Wolves held emergency meetings. The video was undeniable proof, that a werewolf – Skin-walker – had breached the Treaty of Wasp Water by murdering a human. The punishment for McCain, for the breach, was to be sentenced to death. The Council of Wolves was enraged by this, and threatened to walk away from the Treaty if McCain was executed. But the United Nations held firm and said that all parts of the Treaty had to be adhered to, and that McCain would be sentenced to death for his crime. McCain continued to protest his innocence. But beneath the grounds of Ravenwood, forensic teams had found a chamber where the teachers and some parents had been held. A shack was found on the grounds of the school, where children claimed they had been held prisoner for days, fighting off giant rats that came to feed on them. The children had given this shack a name – they had called it the Rat-House. McCain didn't deny this, but he continued to protest that he was innocent of the murder of Emily Clarke. His lawyers persisted that a body had never been found, but the prosecution said that the video evidence and the amount of blood found at the scene was enough to prove beyond a reasonable doubt that Emily Clarke was indeed dead.

But what really sealed his fate was how he rambled on and on about a group of winged creatures who had killed thirteen wolves at the chapel during the matching ceremony. His talk was brushed aside as nothing more than the insane ramblings of a killer. Justice proved swift in this new world that had been *pushed*, and McCain's execution was going to be televised live across the world. It was to be shown on the night that Elizabeth Clarke was coming to visit.

I didn't want to watch McCain be beheaded live on TV, but Potter did and he brought a portable television into the study, which I had prepared for Elizabeth's visit.

"You are kidding me?" I breathed as he placed it on the table.

"No, why?" he asked, a cigarette dangling from the corner of his mouth.

"Do you really think Elizabeth is going to want to watch McCain being beheaded on TV?"

"She might," Potter said, positioning the television. "It's all part of the healing process, sweetcheeks."

Before I'd had the chance to object further, the door was opened as Isidor and Kayla led Elizabeth Clarke into the study. Again, I could see that Isidor was struck by her beauty.

I wasn't the only one who noticed this, as Potter looked at him and said, "For crying out loud, kid, put your tongue away as you're gonna trip over it."

Isidor flushed red and took a seat at the table, next to Kayla. Elizabeth sat down, her thick long blond hair resting on her shoulders, lips painted bright red. She didn't look like someone who was in mourning.

"Thank you for coming down to see us," I said.

"No, thank you, Miss Hudson, for uncovering the truth about what happened to my sister," she smiled, her eyes almost seeming to sparkle. "He was right about you; you don't leave any stone unturned in your search for the truth."

"Sorry?" I asked, starting to feel confused.

"The person who recommended you to me," she smiled back.

"But I thought you said you saw Kiera's advert in that shop window?" Kayla asked.

"Yes, yes," Elizabeth said. "But it was a friend of mine who actually recommended you."

"Who's your friend?" Potter asked her, his voice flat. Like me, he sensed that something wasn't quite right.

"I can introduce him to you, if you'd like," she smiled again, taking a mobile phone from her pocket.

I looked at Potter and he glanced back at me. Where was this going? I wondered.

With the phone to her ear, Elizabeth said into it, "Come in, they'd love to see you."

Then, whoever it was she had brought with her must have been waiting on the other side of the door the whole time, as it slowly opened.

"Hey, that's the Oompa Loompa we saw help McCain carry Emily's body from her room," Potter snapped, as the burnt little boy from the video stepped into the study.

"Dorsey, what are doing here?" Kayla gasped.

"This is my son," Emily said.

"He's that burnt kid?" Potter sniped, looking at me in disbelief.

"They are not burns," Elizabeth said, standing and placing a hand on the boy's shoulder. "They are the result of a bad matching."

"Apart from seeing your son on that video helping to carry your murdered sister from her room, I've never seen him before," I frowned, realising that there was now more to this murder than I had first seen. "How could he have recommended me?"

"Oh no, it wasn't my son who gave you such a glowing report," she smiled down at me.

"No, it was me, Kiera Hudson," someone said, and I looked up to see Jack Seth stroll into the room.

Chapter Forty-Six

Kiera

Jack Seth towered over us. His rake-thin figure was covered by a loose-fitting denim shirt and jeans. Around his scrawny neck was tied his red bandana. His face was as emaciated as ever, and on his head he wore a baseball cap. The beak was pulled down low over his brow, and his crazy yellow eyes burned in their deep, sunken sockets. The lines around his mouth looked like valleys and his teeth were nothing more than brown rotting stumps.

Potter pushed his chair back and jumped up, his claws out.

"Sit down, Potter," Seth grinned, flapping a long fingered hand at him. "I haven't come here to scrap with you."

"So why are you here?" I breathed, getting up and standing next to Potter. "I thought you were dead – I thought you died in The Hollows."

"Sorry, but no," Seth sneered, taking a seat and putting his feet up the table. "It seems that the Elders had other plans for me."

"Like what?" I asked, still reeling with shock at the sight of him.

"For nearly two hundred years, I've waited for this moment, Hudson," he smiled at me, but I knew it was false, I could see rage seething in his eyes.

"What are you yapping on about?" Potter snapped.

"The Elders brought me back, just like they did you," he sighed, leaning back in his chair and crossing his legs at the ankles. "But my punishment was far greater than any of yours."

"Punishment?" I asked him, his burning eyes never leaving mine.

"I'd resisted you, Hudson," he said, and rubbed his bony temples with his fingers. "I'd *resisted* a lot. All I wanted was my curse to be lifted. I didn't want to be a Lycanthrope anymore. I hadn't killed in lust for years. I'd paid my dues for what I'd done, and all I wanted was to reach the Dust Palace and have my curse lifted by the Elders."

"And you really thought they were going to do that..." Potter started.

But before he'd finished, Seth had sprang from his chair. Smashing one of his skeletal-like fists down onto the table, he screeched, "I helped you!" Then, looking around the room, he seethed, "I helped all of you." Spittle swung from his mouth and dribbled down his chin. "All you had to do, Kiera Hudson, was make one simple decision, and I could have been free of my curse."

"The decision I had to make wasn't simple," I tried to remind him.

"You used me!" he roared, his eyes blazing. "You threw yourself at me – you made it impossible for me not to kill you."

"Once a killer always a killer," Potter barked at him.

"Not true!" Seth shrieked, punching the table so hard with his fist again that the TV Potter had placed on it actually bounced up and down. Then, coming around the table, Seth looked into my eyes. I saw Isidor and Kayla jump up, fearing that Seth might strike me, but he brushed them aside. Standing before me, he looked into my eyes and I stared into his. "I resisted you right up to the last," he whispered, and it was like there was only us in the room – in the world. "How I fought my desires to take you, Kiera. It drove me half insane to be near you and not be able to take you then kill you." And in his eyes, I could see myself as he hurt me. And although I was in pain and just wanted to scream over and over again until my throat was raw, I let him do those unspeakable things to me. It was like I was unable to resist him. His naked form was disgusting, like a skeleton that crows had picked the flesh from. In his eyes, I could see myself groaning with desire as I pulled him on top of me. He had me locked in his stare and I would have done anything for him, I would have let him do anything to me – kill me. My desire for him was unimaginable and I wanted him more than I had ever wanted...

...Potter dragged me backwards and spun me around. "Don't look into his eyes, Kiera!" he barked. "Don't look into his eyes."

Seth began to chuckle, then took his seat back at the table next to Elizabeth and the burnt-looking boy that Kayla had called Dorsey. "But you weren't looking into my eyes in The Hollows, were you, Kiera?" Seth grinned and I caught a glimpse of those rotting stumps that protruded from his black gums.

"I didn't have to," I whispered.

"You didn't have to because you used me," he said, and I could hear his anger again boiling beneath the surface. "You knew that if you threw yourself at me, told me that you wanted me, I'd be unable to resist you."

"I couldn't make the choice that the Elders said I had to," I said. "It was impossible. The only way out was for me to die. All of my friends had died and I didn't want to be alone..."

"So you got me to make the decision for you!" Seth roared. "You coward – you silly little bitch."

"Get out of here!" Potter barked at him, heading around the table. Seth seemed unmoved by Potter's display of anger and he remained seated.

"Have you any idea what you put me through?" Seth screeched, spittle flying from his lips again. "The Elders punished me all over again for killing you, Hudson. But this time their curse was so much worse than the original curse of the Lycanthrope. They sent me back to that night – nearly two hundred fucking years ago, made me re-live it all over again. Only this time, as a Shape-Shifter."

"A Skin-walker?" Kayla cut in.

"More than a Skin-walker," Seth hissed. "I don't need to steal skins like them. I can change into any living creature."

"Cool," Isidor breathed.

"Cool!" Seth bellowed, his wrinkled lips curling back. "It's a fucking curse, I tell you! I don't want to live under this spell anymore. I want to be a man again – just man."

"You were never a man," Potter spat. "You were a filthy murdering killer."

"I know I was," Seth hissed. "And maybe I deserved the curse of the Lycanthrope. But I had tried to change. I was so close to having the curse lifted, until *she* set me up in the Dust Palace."

"So the last two hundred years hasn't mellowed you then?" Potter asked him.

"I've had two hundred years of waiting until we met again," Seth said. "I didn't know when you would all put in an appearance, but I've bided my time. It gave me years to make plans, get myself ready for your return."

"What plans?" I asked him.

"How I would finally get the great Kiera Hudson to make a choice," he grinned at me, and his eyes spun in their sockets. "But first I had to flush you out. I got myself in with the wolves, as I can look like one of them at will – and I don't need no children's soul to look like a human, either. I took it upon myself to name a certain school after a certain Doctor Ravenwood. An unusual name that I knew you would be drawn to. But still you didn't come. I thought and thought of how I could flush you out, and knowing how much you hate injustice, it was me who suggested the matching between humans and wolves when the Treaty was drawn up."

"So you're this Wolf Man that we've heard so much about?" Potter sneered at him.

"No," Seth grinned back at him. "I am not he. So, the Treaty was signed and I waited and waited. Then, I read a very interesting news article about a young woman who had sat bolt upright during an autopsy and fled into the night with three strange-looking friends. One of which carried a crossbow," he explained, eyeing Isidor. "I tracked down that pathologist, and very wild she was too. She enjoyed me so much, that she would have told me anything. And she did."

"What did she tell you?" I asked him, feeling sickened at the thought of him tricking that pretty young pathologist into bed with him.

"What she told me, although it was hard for me to understand her as there was a lot of moaning and groaning going on at the time," he winked at me, "is that as you fled the mortuary, she asked you your name, and you told her."

I remembered that.

"I had you at last," Seth said, rubbing his long hands together. "Knowing that it wouldn't be too long before you started sticking your nose into why, and how the world had been changed, my good friend here got herself employed at Ravenwood School, as I guessed the name would arouse your interest."

"But it was your sister, Emily, who was employed at Ravenwood school," I said, looking at Elizabeth.

"I have no sister," Elizabeth smiled. "I have no twin. There is only me. I'm Emily."

"But we saw you being murdered on that video footage," Isidor said.

"It was all just an act," Seth chuckled. "Skin-walkers – wolves - can heal very quickly."

"You're a wolf?" Kayla gasped, staring at Emily.

"I prefer Skin-walker," Emily smiled quite sweetly back at Kayla. "But, yes under this human skin I am a wolf. I was matched some years ago..."

"Look, this is all very interesting," Potter snapped. "So McCain didn't actually murder anyone?"

Sighing, Seth looked at Potter and said, "Coming back from the dead hasn't sharpened your brain at all, has it? McCain didn't know anything about anything. As far as he was concerned, Emily Clarke was just another teacher who decided to leave, albeit leaving her room in a rather bloody mess."

"That's why he was in her room that night, sniffing the walls," Kayla breathed. "He was trying to figure out what had happened to her."

"But we saw McCain on the video..." Isidor started.

"He's slow to catch on, isn't he?" Seth smiled. Then, looking at Potter, he added. "You two aren't related by any chance, are you?"

"That was you on that video," I said, fitting all the pieces of the jigsaw together. "You said that you were a Shape-Shifter. You could look just like him at will."

251

"Not totally at will," Seth smiled. "It's a little bit more complex than that. I needed some of McCain's blood. Not much, just a drop and that's where Dorsey fit in so nicely. McCain had no idea that he was Emily's son, he thought he was just another student."

I glanced at the burnt-looking boy.

"It wasn't very hard for me to find myself in trouble with McCain." Dorsey said. "That prick Pryor was always ragging on me, so I spent a lot of time in McCain's office being punished. But I didn't care that Pryor beat me, teased me, it didn't hurt none. In fact, the more that he beat up on me, the more chance I had of stealing what Mr. Seth needed from McCain."

"And what was that?" Kayla asked curiously.

"That freak was always suffering from nosebleeds," Dorsey said. "He couldn't breathe properly half of the time. McCain was always ramming one of those little bottles of medicine up his nose. So, one day as he punished me, I took my chance and stole one of those medicine bottles from his pocket. And just like I knew it would be, the tip of the bottle was covered in blood from one of his nosebleeds."

"A drop was all I needed," Seth smiled. "I licked the end of the bottle clean and I became him. Not for long, just for a few days. Long enough to make it look like McCain had murdered Emily Clarke in front of the camera, which we set up." Then, reaching inside his shirt, he produced a packet of Cadbury's chocolate fingers and threw them onto the table. "Sorry, I couldn't think of what else to buy."

"So it was you who used the credit card?" I gasped.

"Yes," Seth smiled. "Emily lent it to me. I knew you would check that out. I wanted you to see McCain using her card – it just made the whole thing more believable and stacked the evidence nicely against him. And the rest you know."

"But why frame McCain?" I asked him. "It doesn't make any sense."

"It makes perfect sense," Seth hissed at me. "I knew that if I sent my friend Emily to you with some mystery murder, you wouldn't be able to help yourself from investigating. I knew that if Emily mentioned the camera, you would go snooping for it. Although I must say, I was surprised you used the girl. I thought you liked taking all the glory."

"I couldn't very well disguise myself as a school teacher," I snapped at him.

"I was hoping that you were going to dress up as a school girl," Seth smiled back at me. "That would've been worth catching on camera. I could have watched it over and over again. I would have gotten a kick out of that."

"Shut your filthy mouth, child killer!" Potter shouted.

"Not anymore," Seth grinned. "I haven't killed anyone for years. I wish the same could be said for your lover over there," and he looked at me.

"What's that supposed to mean?" I asked him.

"You're just about to let McCain die, aren't you?" he grinned back at me, and I had to fight the urge to knock his crumbling teeth down his throat. "I think the execution is just about to start." Seth, then lent forward and switched on the TV.

The screen flickered into life and revealed an aerial shot of Wembley Stadium, where the execution was to take place. A news reporter was chatting excitedly about how people, most of them parents, had queued through the night to get tickets to watch McCain's beheading.

"But he hasn't actually murdered anyone," I breathed, and looked at the so-called victim, sitting across the table from me.

"I know," Seth chuckled. "What a dilemma you face."

"Dilemma?" I quizzed him.

"So, what is the great Kiera Hudson to do?" Seth hissed, his anger simmering again. "Sit back and watch an innocent man die or..."

"I can't do that," I said, looking at the TV which now showed a close-up of McCain. He was stripped to the waist, hands tied behind his back, his right foot sticking out at an odd angle. They hadn't even bothered to fix his broken foot, I realised. Behind him stood his hooded executioner, sword in hand.

"So what are you going to do, Hudson?" Seth gloated. "Only you can stop this from happening. You could call your friend Banner right now and tell him that you've made a mistake, and get McCain a stay of execution. But if you do that, everything goes back to the way it was before. McCain goes back to being in control of the matching, and we all know what will happen to those poor little children. On one hand, you could sit back and let him die. I mean the guy isn't entirely innocent of child cruelty and playing mind tricks with all of those parents. On the other hand, you could let the execution take place and the wolves will react with violence. The Treaty that has kept an uneasy peace over the last two hundred years will fall apart, and the wolves will go back to killing indiscriminately, and this time around, there are no Vampyrus to stop them. The humans will fight back and there will be war between the wolves and the humans again."

Realising the decision that he was forcing me to make, I looked at him and said, "You bastard, Seth."

"What will it be, Kiera?" he screeched at me. "Time is running out!"

I looked at the TV screen at the eighty thousand people crammed into Wembley Stadium, as the billions of people and wolves around the world watching the TV waited with drawn breath for the sword to fall against McCain's neck.

"Choose!" Seth screamed at me. "Make your choice, like the choice you should have made in The Hollows!"

I looked at the TV again and with gooseflesh crawling all over me, I watched in horror as I realised I was too late to make my choice; McCain's head was sliced from his neck. It spun away, and the crowds in the stadium went into a frenzy. They roared with delight but others roared in anger. These were the Skin-walkers who, hidden beneath their human skins, had snuck into the stadium. McCain's head hadn't even stopped spinning across the ground when the Skin-walkers changed back into wolves and started to devour the humans cheering all around them.

Wembley Stadium erupted into something that looked close to a bloody slaughterhouse. The screen then flickered and changed shot, as other news reports started to come in from across the country, as wolves took to the streets and ripped the first human they came across to pieces.

Seth stood and snapped off the TV. Then, turning to look at me, he began to slowly applaud. "Kiera Hudson, you really are something else."

I just looked back at him, the consequences of what was now unfolding, barely comprehendible.

"I've got to give it to you and your merry team of misfits," Seth sighed, heading for the door. "You've been back such a short time, and already you've destroyed a Treaty that had been working to keep peace for the last two hundred years, and reignited the war between humans and the wolves. And for every human woman, man, and child that dies, their blood will be forever on your hands."

I watched speechless, as Emily and Dorsey stepped out into the hall, leaving Seth alone with us.

"I should rip your fucking head off," Potter roared at him.

"I wouldn't do that if I were you," Seth smiled at him.

"Give me once good reason why not," I spat.

"Because only I know the secrets of how to put this whole mess right again. You were right, Kiera, the world has been *pushed*, but you've just gone and knocked it over!" Seth laughed, staring into my eyes again. "And besides, Kiera, I know you don't want me dead just yet."

"How do you figure that?" I asked, using every ounce of willpower to not leap across the room and rip his crazy-looking eyes from his skull.

Looking at me, Seth said, "You don't remember how I killed you back in The Hollows, do you?"

"No," I said, shaking my head.

"But you do want to know," he said, running his grey tongue over his cracked lips. "And one day I will tell you. But for now, let's just say that you loved every moment of it."

"Get out of here!" I screamed at him.

Smiling one last time at me, Seth said, "I'll be in touch."

Then, he was gone, and all I could hear was the sound of him laughing as he made his way down the hall. I turned to face Potter and whispered, "Oh my God, what have I done?"

'Dead Night'

(Kiera Hudson Series Two)
Book 1.5
Now available!

More books by Tim O'Rourke

Vampire Shift (Kiera Hudson Series 1) Book 1
Vampire Wake (Kiera Hudson Series 1) Book 2
Vampire Hunt (Kiera Hudson Series 1) Book 3
Vampire Breed (Kiera Hudson Series 1) Book 4
Wolf House (Kiera Hudson Series 1) Book 4.5
Vampire Hollows (Kiera Hudson Series 1) Book 5
Dead Flesh (Kiera Hudson Series 2) Book 1
Dead Night (Kiera Hudson Series 2) Book 1.5
Dead Angels (Kiera Hudson Series 2) Book 2
Dead Statues (Kiera Hudson Series 2) Book 3
Dead Seth (Kiera Hudson Series 2) Book 4
Dead Wolf (Kiera Hudson Series 2) Book 5
Dead Water (Kiera Hudson Series 2) Book 6
Witch (A Sydney Hart Novel)
Black Hill Farm (Book 1)
Black Hill Farm: Andy's Diary (Book 2)
Doorways (Doorways Trilogy Book 1)
The League of Doorways (Doorways Trilogy Book 2)
Moonlight (Moon Trilogy) Book 1
Moonbeam (Moon Trilogy) Book 2
Vampire Seeker (Samantha Carter Series) Book 1

Printed in Great Britain
by Amazon

10532348R00149